PRAISE FOR THE JONATHAN QUINN SERIES

"Brilliant and heart pounding"—**Jeffery Deaver**, *New York Times* bestselling author

"Addictive."—**James Rollins**, *New York Times* bestselling author

"Unputdownable."—**Tess Gerritsen**, *New York Times* bestselling author

"The best elements of Lee Child, John le Carré, and Robert Ludlum."—**Sheldon Siegel**, *New York Times* bestselling author

"Quinn is one part James Bond, one part Jason Bourne."—**Nashville Book Worm**

"Welcome addition to the political thriller game."—***Publishers Weekly***

ALSO BY BRETT BATTLES

THE JONATHAN QUINN THRILLERS

THE CLEANER
THE DECEIVED
SHADOW OF BETRAYAL (U.S.)/THE UNWANTED (U.K.)
THE SILENCED
BECOMING QUINN
THE DESTROYED
THE COLLECTED

THE LOGAN HARPER THRILLERS

LITTLE GIRL GONE
EVERY PRECIOUS THING

THE PROJECT EDEN THRILLERS

SICK
EXIT NINE
PALE HORSE
ASHES

THE ALEXANDRA POE THRILLERS
(with Robert Gregory Browne)

POE

STANDALONES

THE PULL OF GRAVITY
NO RETURN

For Younger Readers

THE TROUBLE FAMILY CHRONICLES

HERE COMES MR. TROUBLE

THE ENRAGED

Brett Battles

A Jonathan Quinn Novel

For more information about the author, please visit www.brettbattles.com.

This one's dedicated to my amazing fans,
for all the support you've given me over the years.
I can't thank you enough,
but I'll say it anyway:
Thank you!

CHAPTER
ONE

"HOW MANY OTHERS know?"

Jonathan Quinn made no response, his eyes focused across the room as if he were the only one there.

"Answer me! How many?"

Not a blink. Not a flinch.

"Your silence won't save anyone. I'll find them like I found you."

The corner of Quinn's mouth drifted up as he finally looked back at the man.

"What makes you think *you* found *me*?"

The man's stare turned into a sneer, and his mouth opened to reply.

"Now," Quinn whispered.

In an instant, darkness filled the room.

CHAPTER TWO

EIGHT DAYS EARLIER
AUGUST 26th
SAN FRANCISCO, CALIFORNIA

THE E-MAIL SAT unopened in Helen Cho's inbox for nearly thirty minutes.

It wasn't that she was in a meeting or otherwise occupied and hadn't seen it. She had been sitting at her desk when her computer softly dinged, announcing the e-mail's arrival.

There were times when she would ignore incoming messages for hours or even days. But this wasn't one of those. This one she'd been expecting, had even called to make sure she would receive it as scheduled.

She knew much of what was written in the attached report, and had already seen most of the accompanying photos. So why was it so hard to open?

There was only one answer, of course. Acceptance, for reading the report meant she would finally have to acknowledge Peter was dead.

Ironic, she knew. It wasn't like death was something she never had to deal with. In her line of work, it was a common occurrence. As head of a growing network of government security and intelligence agencies, she had long ago hardened herself to the reality that people in the business died. Information gathering, targeted terminations, asset acquisitions—these were some of the elements that made up her day. So another death should have been just that.

No emotional attachment. Accept and move on.

And yet here she was, her personal feelings affecting her job.

When the e-mail first arrived, she told herself she had more important things to attend to. Which was true, but they were dealt with in a matter of minutes. Everything after that was just busywork.

Except the unopened e-mail.

She stared at her monitor, the cursor positioned over the message. "Damn you, Peter," she said, and clicked.

The e-mail itself was brief. The subject line: REPORT: LKR-2867c91. The message: SEE ATTACHED.

She downloaded the report, ran it through her decryption software, and opened the resulting file. The report concerned events that had taken place on Duran Island in the Caribbean Sea, forty-eight hours earlier. Most of the information had come from sources within the Isla de Cervantes government. Their security forces had responded to the call that something had happened on the smaller island. When they arrived, they had found over a dozen bodies laid out side by side in the old fort that dominated the strip of land. The only people found alive were locked together in a different room upstairs, all of them uninjured.

Among the dead was Duran Island's owner, the former Isla de Cervantes presidential candidate Javier Romero. According to preliminary interviews with the survivors—all of whom appeared to have been in service positions for Romero, such as nurses, maids, and cooks—Romero had built up a small army, and then forcibly brought in several men, all hooded and bound, and locked them in cells inside the fort. There was some discrepancy about how many men had been held captive—some said five, others said as many as ten—but all agreed that the detainees had been tortured multiple times.

Apparently these same men had somehow escaped, and turned the tables on Romero and his forces, killing most of them before leaving the island. Isla de Cervantes officials also believed that it was someone connected to the escapees who had called in the tip about Duran, and provided information about a boatload of Romero's men who'd fled the fight and were sailing for Isla de Cervantes.

In addition to the dead at the fort, the security forces had discovered two more bodies along an empty runway on the other side of the island. Though officials had no idea who they were, Helen's people had been able to identify them after running photographs of the dead men through a facial recognition system.

The big man was named Janus. According to the file in the archives, he worked mainly as hired muscle for whoever was willing to pay.

The older man, though, was Peter, former head of a defunct agency known as the Office.

The Office was the organization Helen's own core agency had been created to replace. She had been apprehensive about taking the job at the time. Peter had always been a friend, and, in many ways, a mentor. Though she knew it was an excellent opportunity, without Peter's blessing she would have declined the assignment. He had given it without hesitation.

The two of them hadn't always seen eye to eye, but Peter had never refused to take her calls, and had often been the only person she could turn to for advice.

The few additional details contained within the report that weren't part of her original briefing were minor at best, and unimportant. She ignored the photos of the dead, and clicked through to the back of the report to read a short analysis prepared by her people.

It was her team's belief that the deaths had been a result of an act of revenge gone wrong, its roots stretching back several years to when Javier Romero had made his run for president of Isla de Cervantes.

> At the time, it was the opinion of nearly every nation in the western hemisphere that a Romero presidency would have been a

catastrophe that could have created a ripple effect, not just through the Caribbean, but also through Latin America.

A plan was put in place, and a termination team was dispatched to remove any chance of Romero winning the election. While the mission failed in its surface goal of eliminating Romero, the long-term goal of keeping him out of office was achieved, due to the severe injuries he incurred during the attempt on his life.

The Office supervised the project. Given the presence of that organization's former director, and the obvious abilities of the men who had been held with him and subsequently escaped, it is believed that Romero had rounded up the team sent to kill him years before so he could avenge what they had done.

We have not at this time been able to locate records of the operatives assigned to that mission, nor did Romero have any record of whom he'd locked up. It is possible the information was on the memory card that had been in a plastic bag attached to Romero's shirt when he was found, but it was destroyed by one of the bullets he'd taken to the chest. Some of Romero's surviving staff did claim to have heard several names used when those abducted were being led around. Because of the discrepancies between what each recalled, the accuracy of the list that follows is not guaranteed, nor is it known if it's complete.

Layer
Berkeley
Cousin
Cohen

Helen sat back. As much as she would have liked to deny it, revenge was an emotion that helped drive her industry, taking so many unnecessary lives over the years.

You do this to me. I'll do this to you.

And so on, and so on, and so on.

Now the cycle had taken Peter.

At least Romero was dead, too. If he weren't, it would've been Helen's turn to jump in, as she would not have hesitated to order him killed immediately.

She'd arranged through back channels for his body to be brought to the US, where it would be cremated, and she could then scatter his ashes somewhere serene. But that bit of info was not in the document in front of her.

What *was* left on the report was a place for her digital signature. She stared at the empty box for a moment before finally hitting the keys that would affix her name, and not only approve the report but officially confirm Peter's death.

That's it, she thought as she closed the document. *Finished.*

She ran the now signed report through the encryption program, scrambling what she had earlier unscrambled, attached it to a new e-mail, and sent it off for final distribution.

She then stared at her computer screen, feeling like she should say something, anything, to mark the event and honor her dead friend. But when no words came, she did the only thing she could, and focused on the next item that needed her attention.

THE REPORT'S DISTRIBUTION was not handled by a person. The address Director Cho had sent it to was an automated system that forwarded the report to three locations. The first was to the active archives where the report could be quickly accessed by those with clearance; the second was to Antarctica, the name for the remote backup system used by Helen's burgeoning network of agencies; while the third was another automated distribution system, the one that handled human recipients. There, the report number would be run through a database looking for requests to receive the information. If there were no matches, the e-mail would be irretrievably erased.

In the case of report number LKR-2867c91, there was one request.

The automated software created a new e-mail, attached the report, and forwarded it. It didn't matter that the receiver was someone on the outside, and not a member of Helen's team. The software was following its programming.

Just before the original was about to be securely removed from the system, a subroutine kicked in, staying the command. The bit of code was not part of the official program. It had been added in the last two months, and was unknown to anyone within the organization. It had been created for a single purpose. As reports passed through the secondary distribution node, it would perform a rapid keyword search, something it was able to do whether the document was encrypted or not. In the sixty-odd days since it had been attached to the software, the sought-after keywords had not shown up.

This time, however, all relevant terms appeared in the appropriate order. Per design, the subroutine sent a message to a privately owned P.O. box store in Raleigh, North Carolina, telling the manager that a letter the store had been holding should now be mailed. Once this was accomplished, the original e-mail was erased, as had been the main program's intent.

The subroutine's final act was to destroy itself and any evidence of its existence. This, like its other task, was executed perfectly.

WASHINGTON, DC

"YOU'RE SURE?"

Kyle Morten grabbed the side of his laptop as if he were going to turn it around. "I could show you the photo."

Like he knew would happen, his client quickly turned

her head away. “Absolutely not! I just want to know that you’re sure.”

Morten glanced at the picture of the body splayed across a patch of bloodstained ground. “Peter will no longer be a problem.”

“Finally,” she said, allowing herself the slightest of smiles.

Morten held back his displeasure at her implication. This had *not* been a protracted operation. As soon as he’d found out the problem existed, he’d moved into action, identified a creative solution, and—with Griffin’s assistance—implemented a plan to keep the truth from ever getting out. So in light of the careful steps needed to ensure the termination of the Office’s former leader, the operation had been quick and efficient.

The client rose from her chair and straightened her jacket. “And we’re positive no one else knows what he was looking into?”

“Positive.”

“His personal files? I assume those have been taken care of.”

“Do you want the details? Or…” Apparently the woman needed to be reminded that creating a wall of plausible deniability was part of the services Morten’s company, Darvot Consulting, provided.

She gave him a look he’d seen on clients’ faces a thousand times before, a blend of arrogance, annoyance, and reluctant admittance he was right.

“You’ll update me if there is anything else I need to know,” she said.

“There won’t be.”

“I’m counting on that.”

She picked up the leather portfolio she’d walked in with and headed for the exit. Griffin, who had been standing quietly at the back of the office, stepped over to the door and opened it. As she had when she entered, the client left without even acknowledging the man’s presence.

When they were alone, Morten said, “Are the teams in

place?"

"Ready and waiting."

"Give them the go."

Griffin pulled out his phone and fired off a text that would activate the two teams of housebreakers, one positioned at the Georgetown apartment building where Peter had lived, and the other outside the nearby townhouse Peter had sometimes used as a satellite office. Both locations would be searched for anything that might pertain to the private investigation Peter had been conducting. So, the real answer to the client's question would have been, No, the files hadn't been secured yet, but they soon would be.

"When is O & O scheduled to begin?" Morten asked.

"This evening," Griffin said. "Needed to give our people enough time to look around first."

O & O was a for-hire, quasi-government security agency that had proved extremely useful to Darvot over the years. Because it had a poorly defined management structure, Morten had been able to use O & O to obtain sensitive, top-secret information without the organization even realizing what they'd handed over.

O & O was also useful when it came to assignments Morten and Griffin would rather not use their own men for. In this case, Griffin had engaged the agency to watch the apartment and townhouse once the search was complete, and deal with anyone who might show up in the next few weeks. To support the latter point, a thick file of false documentation had been provided to O & O, indicating anyone who entered either place during that specified time frame was likely connected to a particularly violent Islamic terrorist organization, and should be considered an imminent threat to the country.

The reason for the stakeout was that, contrary to what Morten had told his client, he was far from positive no one else knew what Peter had learned. While he felt confident that prior to being kidnapped, Peter had kept his investigation to himself—especially given the personal nature of what he was looking into—the concern was about *after* the old intelligence officer had been taken to Duran Island. Morten thought there was at least an even chance Peter had guessed how Romero had come to possess his and the other men's names, and had shared his suspicions with his fellow prisoners. This wouldn't have been a problem if that jackass Romero had pulled off his plan to kill them all. Unfortunately, it appeared that everyone but Peter had escaped. Which meant there were four men out there somewhere who might be a problem.

That's why the apartment and townhouse needed to be watched. It was also why Griffin had hired some freelance trackers to hunt down the four men. To this point, none of the fugitives had resurfaced.

As Morten mentally went through everything again to make sure he hadn't missed any angles, the desk phone rang. Griffin walked over and picked it up.

"Yes?" He listened for a moment. "Okay, thank you." He hung up and looked over at Morten. "Your car's here."

Morten pulled himself from his thoughts, satisfied they'd covered their bases, and walked over to where his shoulder bag was waiting. The rest of his luggage for his flight to Europe was with the doorman downstairs, and undoubtedly being loaded into the car at that very moment. "Anything comes up, *anything*," he said, "contact me immediately."

"Of course," Griffin said, opening the door.

"I'll be back the evening of the third. Let's have it wrapped up by then, shall we?"

"Yes, sir."

CHAPTER THREE

FIFTY-ONE HOURS EARLIER
AUGUST 24th
DURAN ISLAND

"NO, NO, NO, no, no!" Jonathan Quinn dropped to the ground beside Orlando.

Blood covered most of her shirt. More saturated her left pant leg, the wounds courtesy of the now-dead Janus. She wasn't the only victim. Before Quinn and Daeng had taken Janus out, the man had also shot Peter, who was dead before he hit the ground.

"Orlando. Orlando, can you hear me?"

A flicker in her eyes.

"Orlando? Come on, baby, stay with me!"

Quinn grabbed her hand, hoping she would grip back, but her fingers lay motionless across his.

"Do you hear me? Baby, please stay with me!"

A slow, long blink.

"You're going to be okay. You're going to be fine. Just stay with me. Please. Orlando, come on. Stay with me!"

When her lids slid closed again, they stayed that way.

"Orlando!"

Someone grabbed his shoulders and pulled him back.

"No!" he yelled.

"You need to move out of the way," Daeng said calmly.

Quinn snapped his head around, ready to shove his friend away, but stopped when he saw Liz and Nate running up with the first-aid gear from the plane that had come to take them off the island. Nate skidded to a halt and fell to his knees, then ripped open the Velcro seam of the bag he was carrying.

Quinn's sister, on the other hand, froze when she caught sight of Orlando. "Oh, Jesus."

"Give me that," Daeng said to Liz, grabbing her bag. He motioned at Quinn. "Get him out of the way."

Liz tore her eyes away from Orlando and put an arm around her brother. "We need to give them some room."

"I'm not going anywhere," Quinn said, twisting away from her.

"Don't be stupid. You'll only make things harder."

He glared at her, then looked down at Orlando.

"Come on. Please," Liz said.

He closed his eyes and took a deep breath. "Okay," he whispered.

Liz guided him off to the side.

Working at skill levels equal to that of seasoned EMTs, Nate and Daeng ripped away the clothes covering Orlando's wounds, and set to work stopping the bleeding. Once they'd done what they could, Daeng pulled a transfusion kit out of the bag.

"What's her blood type?" he asked.

Before Quinn could think of the answer, Nate said, "B positive."

"I'm B negative," Daeng said. "She can take from me."

As he set up the transfusion line, two of the men they had just rescued—Lanier and Berkeley—jogged up with a stretcher from the plane. Once blood was flowing out of Daeng's veins and into hers, they moved Orlando onto the stretcher, lifted her, and, with Daeng jogging alongside, headed quickly toward the aircraft.

Quinn started to follow, but caught sight of Peter's crumpled form and slowed, unsure what to do.

Nate came up behind him, carrying the first-aid kit. "I know," he said. "But we don't have time."

Leaving Peter's body seemed wrong. He deserved more than just being part of the carnage they were leaving behind on the island, but Nate was right. Orlando was in critical shape, and if she didn't get medical attention soon, she would also die.

Liz put a hand on Quinn's arm and pulled. "Let's go."

He took one last look at Peter before running with Nate and his sister toward the small jet.

The moment the last person had climbed aboard, Nate yelled toward the cockpit, "Go!"

In the back of the plane, Quinn knelt beside Orlando, took her hand in his, and gently squeezed it.

"I'm right here," he whispered. "I'm not going anywhere."

He searched her face for some sign that she'd heard him, but saw nothing.

Moments after the plane's wheels left the runway, Nate tapped him on the shoulder.

"Sorry," Quinn's former apprentice said. "I don't want to disturb you, but, well, it's just that I'm not sure where to tell the pilot to go."

Nate had been held captive for several days on Duran Island, arriving there with a black bag over his head, while Quinn had come open-eyed, intent on rescuing Nate and the other men who'd been taken by Javier Romero.

There was only one choice.

"Isla de Cervantes," Quinn said. The island was a short flight from Duran.

"Okay." Nate headed toward the cockpit, fighting against the incline of their assent.

Under any other circumstances, Isla de Cervantes would have been out of the question. The events at Duran Island were deeply interwoven with Isla de Cervantes's political history. Who knew how the authorities were going to react when they discovered what had happened on Duran? If they somehow learned Quinn and the others had been involved, and were still around, there would undoubtedly be questions.

Hard, difficult questions.

What Quinn and the others really needed was assistance from someone in the area, someone who could help cover their tracks. Quinn's closest contact was Veronique Lucas, based an hour away in Puerto Rico. She had already proved incredibly useful by arranging for the plane they were now using. Maybe she had resources on Isla de Cervantes, too.

The plane was equipped with several satellite phones. The nearest was in a small cabinet next to the bathroom. Quinn retrieved it and made the call.

"Yes?" Veronique answered cautiously.

"It's Quinn."

"Quinn?" she said, happily surprised. "Is it martini time al—"

"Veronique, I need your help."

"More?"

"Orlando's been shot."

The playful tone in her voice vanished. "What?"

"We're flying to Isla de Cervantes now. We need help. Fast."

"Can you bring her here?"

"Too far. She's...she's not doing well."

"You're flying into St. Renard's?" The island's main airport.

"Unless there's another place that would be better," he said.

"No, that'll be fine. How soon?"

"Fifteen minutes or so, I think. Not much more than that."

"I'll have an ambulance waiting."

Quinn's gaze flicked to Nate and the three other freed prisoners. "We have others who need medical attention, too."

"How many?"

"Four, but none are as bad off as Orlando."

"Understood. So they could wait a little if they had to."

"Yes."

"Okay. Let me—"

"One other thing," he said. "No one can know we're there. It could get...problematic."

"You might want to tell me why."

Quinn hesitated for a moment, but knew if he really wanted her help, she needed to know. "Do you remember a man named Javier Romero?"

"Hell, yeah. Kind of hard to forget."

He gave her the CliffsNotes version of what had happened on Duran.

"*Virgen Santa*," she said when he was done.

"You could also do us a favor and have their navy pick up the boat of Romero's soldiers that got away. Someone should go to the island pretty soon, too. We left Romero alive, but who knows what Janus did before he came after us."

"Okay. I need to get working."

"Thanks, Vee."

AS VERONIQUE PROMISED, an ambulance was waiting for them when they taxied to a stop.

A doctor, nurse, and two EMTs rushed on board the moment the stairs were in place. Quinn tried to stay nearby as they examined Orlando, but one of the EMTs motioned for him and the others to get off the plane. The only one who was allowed to stay was Lanier. He had O-negative blood, which made him a universal donor, and had taken over transfusion duty from Daeng mid-flight.

As the EMTs carried Orlando off the plane, Quinn caught Lanier's eye, silently asking how the examination had gone. Grim-faced, Lanier tried to smile, but couldn't pull it off. Once he and Orlando were in the ambulance, Quinn moved to climb on board with them.

"No room," the doctor said, motioning for Quinn to stop.

"Make some," Quinn growled.

After the nurse and doctor exchanged a glance, the nurse scooted over so Quinn could squeeze in next to her.

The ambulance raced from the airport, sirens blaring. Quinn figured they would probably head to Cristo de los Milagros Hospital. It was the largest on the island, and the same hospital he and Orlando had been in less than twenty-four hours before as they'd tried to track down information on

Nate's abductor. But instead of driving into the city where the hospital was, they turned onto a highway that circled around the edge.

The neighborhood they ended up in was a quieter one just south of the capital, composed mainly of what appeared to be industrial businesses and warehouses. A few streets in, they passed through the gate of a walled compound, and stopped in front of a three-story, windowless structure near a double door entrance. Within seconds, the doors swung open and several people ran out, pushing a gurney.

Since Quinn was jammed in at the very back, he opened the ambulance door and hopped out first. Lanier exited next. The EMTs had removed him from the transfusion tube during the ride.

"*Háganse a un lado*," a woman next to the gurney said.

Quinn pulled Lanier to the side so they wouldn't impede the others. Working in concert, the EMTs in the ambulance and the personnel outside carefully transferred Orlando from the vehicle onto the rolling bed. Once straps were secured across her torso, she was pushed into the building.

Quinn grabbed one of the orderlies. "He needs help, too," he said, motioning to Lanier before taking off after Orlando.

He followed the gurney all the way to the surgical room door, but the staff would let him go no farther. Knowing it was useless to fight, he allowed himself to be escorted to a waiting room, where he pulled out his phone and called Veronique again.

"How is she?" she asked.

"They've just taken her into surgery."

"Did they give you any indication on her chances?"

"No one's saying anything." He paused. "Who owns this place?"

"No one you would know."

"Government run?" he asked.

"No."

"They must know about it."

"They probably do," she said. "But it's a money

generator. Most of the clients are from off island. You know, they come to get procedures done they'd rather their friends back home didn't know about. So as long as the government receives its cut, it keeps its hands off."

"You're sure we're safe here?"

"You're safe. Trust me," she said. "But I've gotta say, even if the authorities do find out who you are and what you did, they're more likely to pin a medal on your chest than throw you in jail."

NATE, LANIER, BERKELEY, and Curson were all admitted to the nameless hospital and taken to individual rooms. They'd been whipped, electroshocked, and beaten while held prisoner by Romero. Though their wounds were not life threatening, the men were in serious need of treatment and rest. So only Daeng and Liz were able to keep Quinn company while he waited for word on Orlando's condition.

Two hours passed.

Then three.

Then four.

Every scenario that ran through Quinn's mind ended with "I'm sorry. We did all we could." Not knowing what was happening was driving him crazy. More than once, Daeng and Liz had to stop him from leaving the room in search of answers.

"They'll let us know as soon as they can," Liz told him. "You'll only get in the way otherwise."

When Orlando's surgeon finally did walk into the waiting room, Quinn braced himself.

"I'm Dr. Montero," the man said, speaking in nearly unaccented English. "Your friend is very lucky. There is no question she would have died without the transfusion you gave her."

Quinn stared at him. "She's alive?" he finally managed to whisper.

The doctor nodded. "At the moment."

"What do you mean? Are you saying she's not going to make it?"

The doctor held up a hand, palm out. "It is far too early to know. Your friend was shot three times. One of her kidneys is destroyed, and her left lung was punctured. The third bullet hit her knee. There's a lot of damage there, but we haven't had time to fully assess it. We concentrated more on the life-threatening injuries. And even with the transfusions, her blood loss was significant." He paused. "We believe we've removed all the bullet fragments, and she's stable for now. If she stays that way and is strong enough, she'll have to go back into surgery in a few days. The next twenty-four hours are critical."

She's alive. She's alive. Quinn grabbed on to that thought and held it tight. "I want to see her."

The doctor looked as if he was about to say no.

"Please," Quinn pleaded.

The man hesitated for several seconds, and finally said, "Follow me."

"We're coming with you," Liz said.

The doctor held up his hand again. "Better only one."

"It's not open for discussion," Liz told him.

Apparently realizing it would be useless to argue, the doctor led them to a room on the second floor. Quinn was allowed to enter first. The hospital bed was all but hidden from view by four nurses, some monitoring equipment, and a couple IV stands.

One of the nurses turned as he approached. "*No deberia estar aqui*," she said.

"It's all right," the doctor told her, also speaking Spanish. "Let him see her."

The nurse's eyes narrowed in disapproval as if some sacred law had been broken, but she stepped to the side.

Quinn moved all the way to the bed and looked down at Orlando.

She looks so small, he thought.

She wasn't big to begin with—five feet tall and barely a hundred pounds on her heaviest days, but now she looked…diminished, like she would float away if a breeze blew through the room.

"Hey," he whispered as he touched the hair above her ear. "You're going to make it, but you need to fight, and be strong like you always are." He skimmed her cheek with the back of his finger, her skin so pale and soft, and then leaned down and kissed her on the lips. "I love you. You better damn well come back to me. Understand?"

CHAPTER FOUR

EIGHT DAYS LATER
SEPTEMBER 1st
WASHINGTON, DC

MISTY BLAKE STARED out the window of her apartment. She'd been there since a little before five a.m., when she'd given up trying to sleep. In front of her sat yet another untouched cup of coffee, cold and forgotten. She was dressed in the same T-shirt and gym shorts she'd gone to bed in, the same clothes she'd worn the day before. The same clothes she'd worn since the day Quinn had called her and told her Peter was dead.

Misty had been Peter's last assistant at the Office, working with him right up to the end of the organization as they'd closed everything down and were then transferred in different directions. Their relationship had continued even after she started her mindless job at the Labor Board. To Misty he was still her boss, and anytime he needed help, she was there.

When she'd gone to Peter's house at Quinn's request almost two weeks earlier and discovered the signs of Peter's kidnapping, she had been terrified she might never see him again. But Quinn was one of the few other people in the world Peter fully trusted, and Quinn had said he would do all he could to bring Peter back. She had taken hope in that.

But days had passed without any news, and the terror had returned, eating her up and turning her into a nervous wreck. When she finally heard Quinn's voice, for a second—just a second—she allowed herself to hope again.

"Misty, I'm sorry. He…he…"

Silence.

"He's dead," she said.

"Yes."

In that instant, her terror was replaced by a deep dark hole that seemed to go on forever. She remembered asking a few questions, remembered hearing answers, too, but what she didn't remember were the words. All that stuck in her head was that Peter was gone.

The fact that there was no funeral made it worse. There was no closure to her grief, no outlet to pay tribute to the man who had not only been her boss, but often a second father. So she'd taken bereavement leave from her work for an unspecified relative's death, locked herself in her apartment, and mourned in solitude.

Now, when the doorbell rang, she didn't move.

It rang again, this time followed by a knock.

She looked up at the kitchen clock—9:18 a.m. *Go away*, she thought.

There was no knock after the third ring, only the quick sound of whoever it was rubbing something against wood below her peephole.

She almost let it go, but pulling off what had been left there—an advertisement, most likely—and dumping it in the trash would at least get her out of the chair.

She forced herself up, and shuffled through her apartment to the door. When she opened it, she found no one there. Not a surprise. She'd assumed the person had moved on. Was glad, in fact. The surprise came when she looked at what had been left behind. It wasn't an advertisement at all, but a notification from the post office.

She pulled it off and took a closer look. It was for a certified letter that she had to sign for. She stuck her head into the corridor and looked both ways. The postal worker who'd left the note was nowhere in sight.

Couldn't be far, though. If she could catch him, it would save her a trip to the post office, something she hated doing even when she wasn't mourning a friend's death.

She slipped on her gym shoes, grabbed her keys off the little table by the door, and went in search of her letter. She found the postman on the first floor, filling the mailboxes.

"You left this on my door." She held out the notification.

The postman kept stuffing the boxes. "Let me finish this first, then I can help you."

She watched him move slowly from box to box—two letters here, four there, mailers from the neighborhood grocery store, catalogs—and had to stifle the urge to take his bag from him. When he finally finished, he shut the main door, locked it in place, and turned to her.

"Let me see that, please."

She handed him the notice.

He read it, and said, "Right. This is you? Misty Blake?"

"Yes, it's me."

He handed it back. "You're going to have to sign it."

"Oh, um, I don't have a pen."

He rolled his eyes and pulled a pen out of his pocket. "Don't you walk off with that when you're done."

"I won't."

She signed the slip, and held it and the pen out to the postman.

"Just hold on to it for a second." He pulled an envelope out of his bag. "Gotta sign this, too."

There was a green card attached to the front. As she signed it, she glanced at the return address. It was typed—address only, no sender's name.

Raleigh, North Carolina. She'd never been there, and, as far as she could remember, knew no one who lived there.

The postman took the card, snagged his pen back, and said, "All yours."

"Thank you."

As she neared her apartment, the weight of Peter's death once more descended on her. She let herself in, and retuned to the kitchen table where she'd spent the morning. Her letter opener was all the way back on her desk in the bedroom, so she rustled up a kitchen knife and cut open the top of the envelope.

She wasn't sure what she expected to find, but a second envelope was not it. She pulled the enclosed envelope out and began turning it around so she could look at the front. But when she caught sight of the handwriting scrawled in the center, she dropped the letter on the table.

The envelope spun as it fell, so that the front, while remaining visible, was upside down. Still, there was no mistaking what she'd seen. In blue ink was written:

Misty

She knew the handwriting as well as her own.

Peter's handwriting.

She had no idea how long she stared at it. It could have been minutes. It could have been hours. At some point she sat down, and used the tips of her fingers to turn the envelope so that it was facing the right way.

What could be inside? Why did it come now? *How* did it come now?

She double-checked the exterior envelope. No way Peter could have sent it. It was postmarked after he died.

A part of her didn't want to open it, telling her by keeping it closed, in some small way, Peter was still alive. And while she knew she couldn't listen to that voice, she was having a hard time convincing herself to pick up the knife and slice open the flap.

Peter sent this. Peter wanted you to open it. If you don't open it, you're dishonoring him.

That thought finally did it. Careful, so that she didn't damage anything inside, she slit the top open. There was no additional envelope this time, just a white, three-by-five-inch index card. She pulled it out and set it gently on the table.

There were three lines of text written on it. The first was the oddest:

Y7(29g)85KL/24

Her mind was too muddy at the moment to even guess what it could mean.

The second and third lines, though, she could actually understand:

I need your help.

Call Quinn. A last assignment. For both of you.

She stared at the words, reading the message over and over.

I need your help.

She guessed the fourteen characters in the first line had something to do with the assignment, but she didn't know what that connection might be.

Quinn must know what they mean.

She reached for her phone.

CHAPTER
FIVE

ISLA DE CERVANTES

OVER THE OBJECTIONS of the medical staff, Quinn moved into Orlando's room within hours of her initial surgery, sleeping in the chair pulled up next to her bed when he could no longer keep his eyes open. The rest of the time he held her hand, wiped her skin with a damp cloth, and read to her from a copy of *The Man in the Iron Mask* the hospital had in its small, mostly Spanish-language library.

Not once did she open her eyes or indicate she knew he was there, but at least there had been no setbacks.

The doctors waited eight days before performing the second surgery, this one focused primarily on her leg. When she was wheeled out of the room at five a.m., Quinn moved downstairs to the waiting room so he could be that much closer to the surgical suite.

It wasn't long before Liz and Daeng joined him, and tried to distract him with conversation. But all Quinn could do was pace back and forth, as the helpless anger he felt continued to boil inside.

Dr. Montero finally walked into the room right before nine thirty a.m. Quinn stopped moving the moment he saw him. He tried to get a read on the doctor's face, but Montero was as stoic as always.

"Well?" Liz asked. "How did it go?"

To Quinn, the brief pause that followed felt like it lasted a million years.

"As planned," Montero said. "She's being taken back to her room now."

"And?" Quinn asked.

"I'm not going to lie to you. She will need a knee replacement when she's up for it. But we've cleaned up what we could, and we're confident her leg is otherwise going to be fine."

"What about her overall condition?" Quinn asked, worried that the surgery would put too much strain on her system.

"Still serious, but she's stable, and her vital signs are stronger."

"So she's going to make it," Liz said.

Montero turned to her. "There are no guarantees."

"Is she going to pull through or not?" Quinn asked.

"Time is the important factor now. If her condition continues to improve, her chances are considerably better."

"How much better?" Quinn asked.

"That's hard to say. I will make an evaluation—"

"Forty percent? Fifty? Sixty? Seventy? What?"

Montero looked uncomfortable. "Sixty is a good number, I would think."

The knot in Quinn's stomach loosened a little.

Sixty-percent chance she would survive. That was considerably better than the number the doctor had given the first day.

"How long until she wakes up? Until I can talk to her?"

"Not for a few days."

"A few days?" Quinn said.

"The thing that will help her recover most right now is rest. I think it's best if we keep her sedated for a while." Before Quinn could say anything, Montero added, "She will be constantly monitored. When everything looks good, we'll bring her out of it."

"How *long* until I can talk to her?"

Montero pressed his lips together, clearly not wanting to

be backed into a corner. "Three days. Could be four or five."

"Five days?"

Liz put her arm around her brother's back. "They're doing all they can. If Dr. Montero says this is for the best, then it must be."

Even if his sister was right, Quinn didn't know if he could last five more days not hearing Orlando's voice, not seeing her smiling eyes, not knowing if she could hear him when he said, "I love you." The frustration and anger building up inside his chest was almost too much to bear.

"I should get back," Montero told them.

Quinn's phone vibrated in his pocket.

"Unless you have more questions," the doctor said.

Questions were all Quinn had, but he wasn't about to keep the doctor from taking care of Orlando, so he shook his head and watched Montero leave.

In his pocket his phone rang for a fourth and final time. Twenty seconds later there was a long buzz indicating he'd received a voice mail. He didn't bother checking.

"How about some breakfast," Liz suggested. "We don't want to go back to the room until they've got her all set up again, anyway. We'd only be in the way."

"I'm not hungry," he said.

His phone vibrated again, a double buzz for the receipt of a text message. Someone really wanted his attention, but he headed for the door, ignoring whoever it was.

"I'll be upstairs if you're—"

Once more, the vibration in his pocket. Another phone call.

What the hell? he thought. He pulled out his phone, ready to take out all his anger on the caller, but then he read the display: MISTY.

He closed his eyes and tried to calm down. While he was still annoyed that she was calling him right now, there was no way he could be mad at her. She had to be hurting just as much as he was, maybe even more.

He held the phone out to Daeng. "It's Misty. Can you talk to her?"

The Thai man looked uncomfortable. "I don't actually know her."

"Tell her I'll call her later."

Daeng took the phone and pressed ACCEPT. "Hello?" He listened for a moment. "No, it's Daeng. His friend. He's a little…preoccupied." Another pause. "She's hanging in there. Just came out of another surgery…Yes, yes, that's why…I'm sorry?" Confusion clouded Daeng's face as he turned and looked at Quinn. "Hold on, okay?" He put a hand over the phone.

"What is it?" Quinn asked.

"I think you'll have to talk to her."

"I just…I can't talk to her right now."

"She received a letter this morning."

"So what?"

"It's…from Peter."

Quinn furrowed his brow, and took the phone. "Misty? It's Quinn. What's this about a—"

"Thank God. I'm, um, I'm a little freaked out." Misty's words spilled out rapid fire.

"Relax. Just take a breath, okay?"

He could hear Misty force the air out of her lungs in a jagged torrent. She breathed again, not perfect, but better this time.

"Daeng said you got a letter from Peter," Quinn said.

"It's actually more of a note."

"He told me you received it today."

"The mailman knocked on my door about twenty minutes ago."

"Misty, think about it. It can't be from Peter. The timing is off. It must be some—"

"It's from Peter." She told him how the note had been contained in a separate envelope sent by someone else.

"Have you looked up the address?"

"No, I've been too busy trying to get ahold of you."

He could tell she was on the verge of losing it again, so he said, "No problem. We can do that here. Give me the address." Putting his hand over his phone, he repeated it for

Daeng. "Find out what's located there."

"On it," Daeng said.

To Misty, Quinn said, "Do you mind reading me the note?"

"That's why I called you. It's for both of us."

"Both of us?"

"You'll see." She read off a string of letters, numbers, and symbols, then, "'I need your help. Call Quinn. A last assignment. For both of you.'"

As she finished, Daeng held out his phone so Quinn could see the screen. The address belonged to a private P.O. box place in Raleigh, North Carolina.

"Misty, hold on." Quinn covered the phone again. "Call them," he said to Daeng. "No. Wait." He looked at his sister. "*You* call them." He quickly explained about Peter's message and how it was delivered. "Tell them you're Misty Blake, and you received the letter they sent. Ask them what their instructions were, where it came from, how long they had it. Can you do that?"

"Yeah, sure," Liz said.

While Liz and Daeng moved to the other side of the room, Quinn brought his phone back up to his ear. "What does the message mean?"

"I was hoping you would know," Misty said.

"You don't?"

"No."

"Any ideas?"

"I was thinking it might be code, but the more I looked at it, the more it reminds me of the kind of passwords Peter liked to use."

"If it's a password, what's it to?"

"Who knows?"

"You must have some ideas."

"Off the top of my head...well, could be to one of the computers he stashed at his apartment or at the townhouse that we used as the Office's backup headquarters." When she spoke again, a hint of reluctance entered her voice. "I could go check, I guess."

"Not alone," Quinn said. "Let me see if I can get Steve to go with you." Steve Howard was the DC-area operative who'd accompanied Misty the last time she went to Peter's apartment.

"Okay," she said, sounding relieved. "Thank you."

"I'll call you right back."

After he hung up, he glanced at the other two, but Liz was still on the phone, so he located Howard's number and gave him a call.

"It's Quinn," he said.

"Hey, can I call you back?" Howard said. "I'm a little tied up right now."

"Are you on a job?"

"Yeah."

"So you're not home."

"No. Boston. I'll be back late tonight, though."

"That might work. Call me when you get home. I might have something for you."

"Will do."

When Quinn hung up this time, Daeng and Liz were waiting for him.

"Well?" he said.

"I talked to the manager," Liz said. "Didn't take much to convince him I was Misty, which, I've got to tell you, convinced me never to rent a box from him."

"Did he tell you anything?"

"Oh, he was more than happy to share. Said he never met the sender in person. All their communications were by e-mail, except when he received the envelope he was supposed to forward. A messenger brought that in. The envelope was already addressed to Misty, with the mailbox place's return address typed. His instructions were to send the letter if he received an e-mail telling him to do so within the next six months. If he didn't, the envelope was to be burned. The only other instruction was that it needed to be signed for."

The skin on Quinn's arms started tingling. A dead-man switch, only in this case not one designed to stop a machine from working if the operator died, but to trigger the e-mail that was sent to the P.O. box business in Raleigh upon news of Peter's death.

How? Quinn didn't know, nor, for the moment, did it matter. What did was the fact Peter knew he might die, and had a message he wanted to make sure was sent in the event of that happening.

Peter's words echoed in Quinn's head.

I have a pretty good idea where the leak came from.

That had been nearly the last thing he ever said to Quinn. He'd been talking about the list naming the members of the team who'd worked in the ill-fated Romero assassination, the list that had been *leaked* to Romero so that the madman could exact his revenge.

Ignoring the connection was impossible. Peter had apparently known his life was in danger just months before someone had handed him over to Romero. Could the message he had sent to Misty point to the identity of the leaker? The person may not have physically been on Duran Island torturing the men, but he or she was as responsible for what had happened as Romero and his people. No, *more* responsible. For Peter's death. For the injuries suffered by Nate and Lanier and Berkeley and Curson.

And for nearly ending Orlando's life.

Whoever it was had set the events in motion.

Quinn could feel an abrupt change to the anger coursing through him. No longer was it unfocused and debilitating. It was now directed at someone out there who needed to pay. Someone who needed to feel Quinn's wrath.

The first step would be finding out what Peter's message meant.

He looked at Liz and Daeng. "Dr. Montero said three days until Orlando wakes, right?"

Daeng nodded.

The only thing Quinn wanted more than tracking down those responsible was to be by Orlando's side when she opened her eyes again, but sitting through days waiting for that to happen would be wasting time that could be spent hunting.

"Can you watch her for me?" he said to Liz. "Sit with her so she's not alone?"

"You're going to go see Misty?" she asked.

"I'll be back tomorrow. Next day, latest." He looked at Daeng. "I want you to come with me. I could use another set of eyes."

"Of course," Daeng said.

"Wait," Liz said. "I don't understand. What are you expecting to find?"

He explained about the list, and what it would mean to find out who had given it to Romero.

When he was through, she locked eyes with him. "Go. I'll keep an eye on Orlando. But you have to promise me one thing."

"What?" Quinn asked.

"That you'll find whoever this bastard is."

THE FLIGHT NORTH left Isla de Cervantes right before noon, landing at Dulles International Airport outside Washington, DC less than three hours later.

Quinn sent off the same text twice as they taxied to the arrival gate.

We're here

The first went to Liz. She responded almost immediately with a two-word text of her own.

No change

The second reply came from Misty thirty seconds later.

Meet at curb. Dark gray Camry.

When they exited the terminal, Misty was waiting as promised behind the wheel of her nearly twenty-year-old Camry. Daeng crawled into the backseat, while Quinn climbed in beside Misty.

"It's good to see you," he said.

Misty's lower lip trembled. "I'm so glad you're here."

Quinn motioned into the back. "You haven't met Daeng yet."

Leaning forward and holding out his hand, Daeng said, "We talked on the phone earlier."

"Right," she said, shaking. "Good to, um, meet you."

Quinn eyed her for a second. "Do you want me to drive?"

Instead of answering, she half leaned, half fell toward him, burying her face in his shoulder, and started to cry. He put an arm around her, knowing the intensity of her grief was his fault. She'd been alone for a week, unable to talk to anyone about Peter. Quinn should have arranged for someone he trusted to come by.

"Sorry," she said, between gulps of air. "I told…myself…I wouldn't…do this. Dammit."

"It's all right," Quinn said. "You don't have to keep it in. It's fine."

"I didn't think he'd—" She stopped herself. "It just doesn't seem possible."

"I know."

After several more sobs, her breath caught in her throat. "My God. Orlando. How is she?"

"Things are…progressing, so I'm hopeful."

"That's good. Do they think—"

Someone knocked on the window.

"Hey, get this thing moving."

An airport cop stood beside Misty's door, motioning for them to drive off. Quinn was about to tell the guy where he could stick his hand when Misty turned and looked at the officer.

"Sorry," she said, rubbing her eyes.

The cop looked suddenly ill at ease. He took a couple of steps back. "Uh, just, uh, get moving as soon as you can."

Misty reached down and turned the key. "We're leaving now."

"You sure you don't want me to drive?" Quinn said.

"I'm fine," she told him, wiping the last tears from her face. She set her jaw and shifted the car into Drive. "I think we should start with Peter's place."

"Okay."

They made it out of the airport without incident, and hopped on the interstate.

"Can I see the note?" Quinn asked.

Without looking, she pointed over her shoulder. "It's in my purse. Should be on the floor back there."

"Got it," Daeng said.

A moment later, he handed an envelope forward with Misty's name written on it. Quinn opened the top and pulled out the card. The message was exactly as Misty had read. He checked both sides in case there was any indication of a hidden message, but saw none, so he slipped the card back in the envelope.

"May I look?" Daeng asked.

Quinn passed it back to him.

Misty glanced at Quinn, then back at the road. "Do you know if he felt it? I mean, was it painful?"

"No," Quinn said. "It wasn't painful." The bullet had killed Peter instantly. Of course, the torture he'd undergone in the weeks before that had not been so merciful, but Misty was only asking about the end.

"That's something, I guess," she said.

The tremor in her voice made him think she might start crying again, but while a few tears did slide down her cheeks, she held her emotions in check.

Once they crossed the Potomac River into DC, they headed into Georgetown, eventually parking on a quiet, residential street.

Misty pointed ahead. "Hard to see from here, but Peter's building is right behind those trees."

Without another word, they exited the car and walked down the block. The building was an old, stately structure with a white stone façade and matching steps leading up to a surprisingly modern, windowed entrance.

There, Misty used a key she pulled from her pocket to let

them in, and led them across the lobby to the elevators. Once they arrived on Peter's floor, she headed down the hallway until she came to a door marked 17A. She flipped open a small, numbered keypad in the wall next to the jamb, and raised her finger to punch in the code. Before she could, Quinn put a hand over hers.

"Hold a moment," he said.

"Is something wrong?" she asked.

"I assume there's some sort of alarm."

"It deactivates once the code's entered."

He scanned the door, looking for signs of a break-in, but saw no scratches or other damage that would imply forced entry.

"How many people know the code?" he asked.

"Just Peter and I as far as I know."

"The security company?" Daeng suggested.

Misty shook her head. "No security company. The alarm used to go straight to Office headquarters. After we were shut down, it would alert Peter wherever he was so he could decide what to do. He always said he had better resources than any alarm company did."

And yet the people who kidnapped him must have had the code, too, Quinn thought, but he kept that to himself.

"Okay, go ahead," he said.

Misty entered an eight-digit code on the pad and opened the door.

Before she could step inside, Quinn said, "Let us check first."

Quickly, he and Daeng moved through the apartment, making sure no one else was there. While the flat was empty, it was clear someone had been inside recently.

"You can come in now," Quinn said as he and Daeng reentered the living room.

Misty made it only two feet past the doorway before she stopped and stared. "Who…how…?"

The living room, like the rest of the apartment, had been tossed. Tables upended, couches and chairs sliced open, bookcases and cabinets emptied. Even the paintings and photographs that had been on the walls had been pulled down.

This wasn't a normal search. There was an eeriness to the mess left behind. Peter's possessions had not been haphazardly dumped on the floor. Everything was in neat piles, as if each item had been individually inspected first. A quiet, methodical exploration that would not have been noticed by the neighbors.

Quinn knew this was not the way the apartment had looked on Misty's last visit. He'd seen it himself on the video call Misty and Howard had made to him at the time.

"Shut the door," he told Misty.

She blinked, pulling herself out of her spell, and did as he asked.

"What happened?" she said, moving farther into the room.

"It seems someone was looking for something," Daeng said. "I guess the questions are: What was it? And did they find it?"

"Most importantly," Quinn added, "does it even matter to us?"

"It matters to me," Misty said, anger beginning to replace her shock.

"Of course it does," Quinn said. "But we need to stay focused on why we're here."

She stared at him before finally nodding.

"So, where do we start?" she asked.

THE SIGNAL WAS routed through the existing SG Security fiber-optic line that had been installed in the Georgetown building two years earlier to service customers in apartments on the third, fourth, and fifth floors. The line's purpose was to alert the security company to potential break-ins, fires, carbon monoxide leaks, and—in the case of a client on the third floor—heart failure registered by sensors placed throughout her apartment.

If this particular signal had originated from a flat owned by one of SG's clients, it would have appeared on the monitor of one of the company's emergency operators, and the appropriate authorities would have been dispatched. This signal was not, however, from a registered SG Security user. Instead, it bypassed the company's system completely and traveled across DC to a nondescript industrial building on the edge of Hyattsville, Maryland, housing the administration of the organization known as O & O. Nothing fancy about the initials. They stood for Observe and Operate.

For the first few days of the assignment, the apartment had physically been watched by rotating, two-man O & O teams. Since nothing had happened, the director of O & O determined that electronic surveillance would suffice, and the teams were reassigned to other projects—a side benefit of this being that the money saved found its way, after passing through appropriate filters, into the director's personal account.

"Central? Terminal Eight." The voice came out of the computer speaker on the duty supervisor's desk. Though different individuals manned the station, they were always referred to as Central.

Central tapped the Talk key on his keyboard. "Go ahead, Terminal Eight."

"Sir, I have a door-open signal for RZ-47."

Central entered the identifier into the database and saw that RZ-47 referred to an apartment in Georgetown. A quick scan of the notes revealed that protocol on this particular case required interception of any transgressors, followed by isolated detention, and, if the client deemed it necessary, termination. The identity of the client on this job was, as always, omitted from Central's file. The whos and whys were left to those with higher pay grades at O & O.

"Terminal Eight, who's up next?"

"Sir, we have a team that just wrapped up at RY-23. Fifteen minutes out."

Central frowned. Fifteen minutes might be too long. "No one closer?"

"They're the closest, sir."

If they were closest, they would have to do. "Send them."

"Yes, sir," Terminal Eight said.

Central barely had time to wrap his fingers around the can of Sprite sitting by his keyboard when the speaker came back to life.

"Central? Terminal Three."

"Go ahead, Terminal Three," Central said, RZ-47 already forgotten.

CHAPTER
SIX

"IT'S GONE," MISTY said.

They were in Peter's bedroom. The hidey-hole along the base of the wall, behind where the nightstand had been, was wide open and empty. According to Misty, they should have found a laptop inside, but whoever had searched the place must've gotten to it first.

"Are there any other computers here?" Quinn asked.

"I don't know. This is the only one he told me about."

"How about other secret compartments?"

"Three that I'm aware of."

"Show us."

As Quinn moved out of her way, he felt a crunch of glass under his foot. He looked down and saw he'd stepped on a picture frame that had probably been on Peter's nightstand. When he lifted his shoe, he remembered something Misty had said to him over the phone that night she had checked the apartment with Howard.

... the picture of his wife...

Until she had said that, Quinn had never known Peter was married.

He leaned down, dumped the glass onto the floor, and picked up the picture.

Misty had said Peter's wife had been dead ten years. Quinn had already begun doing jobs for Peter at that time. Was it possible he'd been working for Peter when she'd passed away? He couldn't recall any changes in Peter's demeanor that year or, for that matter, in the years that surrounded it. On the surface, that could have been interpreted to mean Peter hadn't cared about what happened to her. And yet, a decade on, he still had her picture by his bed.

The shot was a candid, the woman no more than thirty-five years old. Her face was three-quarter profile to the lens, her gaze focused on something in the distance. She had brown, curly hair that drooped down onto her shoulders, and was wearing a mischievous grin that hinted she was aware her picture was being taken.

"Miranda," Misty said from behind him.

"How long were they married?" Quinn asked.

"Six years."

"Children?"

She shook her head. "No children."

"How did she die?"

Misty took a few seconds before answering. "Car crash."

Quinn could see the promise in Miranda's face, the possibilities of the future that Peter surely saw, too. But the promise and possibilities went unfulfilled, leaving only an empty reality Peter had had to live with after she was gone.

"We should…" Daeng said, letting the thought hang in the air.

"Right." Quinn set the picture on the bed. They didn't have time to waste. He thought it unlikely those who had searched the place would come back, but there was always a chance.

Misty took them to two more hidey-holes, one in the bathroom, and one in the second bedroom. Both were empty.

"There's one more," she said. "His safe."

"Where's that?" Quinn asked.

"Down here."

THE O & O TEAM arrived in two cars, and parked in the first available spots they could find. The two men in the second car—each, like their colleagues, outfitted in black business suits—exited their vehicle and climbed into the backseat of the first.

Roberts, the team leader, gave them each a nod before grabbing the mic for the encrypted radio. "Terminal Eight, this is Team Three."

"Go, Team Three," Terminal Eight replied.

"We've just arrived on scene. Any further update?"

"Hold, Team Three." The pause lasted several seconds, after which Terminal Eight said, "We've accessed a security feed from an adjacent building, and have identified three individuals entering the target structure four minutes prior to the alarm. Two men and a woman. Both men are between five-ten and six feet. One black hair, shoulder length. Darker skin. The other, shorter hair, brown. Caucasian. Woman is approximately five foot three. Long hair, light brown or dark blonde. Unfortunately the distance and angle were wrong for getting facial shots. We put the probability that these are the intruders at ninety-two percent."

"Copy that, Terminal Eight. How do you want us to proceed?"

"The order is to apprehend, but if they pose a danger to you and your team, you are cleared for takedown."

"Copy that, Terminal Eight. Team Three out."

"Team three out. Copy."

Roberts returned the radio to its slot under the dash and looked at the others. "You heard her. Grab 'em or drop 'em. Whatever's easiest."

THE SAFE TURNED out to be in the linen closet at the end of the hall. Piled along the wall nearby were the sheets, towels, and other supplies that had apparently been inside. As Misty pulled the door toward her, Quinn prepared himself for the fact that they'd find the safe as empty as the hidey-holes. What he saw first, though, were empty white shelves.

"Where it is?" he asked.

Misty reached around the doorway, and ran her fingers up the inside molding that covered the jamb until a distinct click echoed through the frame. She pulled her hand back, and removed the middle shelf. Reaching into the closet, she pushed on the wall right where the shelf had been.

Another click, followed by the wall swinging open, revealing the safe.

"It's still closed," she said, surprised.

"I assume you know the combination," Quinn said.

She nodded.

The safe had a double lock—part old-fashioned dial, part digital keypad. Misty navigated through the combination and turned the handle. Inside was a stack of file folders about two inches thick, a Beretta 9mm, and a box of ammo. There was no computer.

Leaving the gun where it was, Misty pulled the files out and opened the first one.

"We don't have time for that right now," Quinn said, trying to contain his frustration at not finding anything useful.

"What?" Misty looked at him, confused, before realizing what he was talking about. "Oh, right."

She moved the files under one arm and reached in to close the safe.

"Wait a second," Quinn said.

"I'm not leaving these here," she told him, pulling the files close. "Peter wouldn't have wanted anyone to find them."

"That's not what I meant. May I?"

After she took a step back, Quinn reached in and retrieved the Beretta and ammo. Since they couldn't bring weapons with them on the flight north, they had arrived in DC unarmed. Up until the moment they'd entered Peter's apartment, Quinn hadn't thought it was necessary. But the fact that someone had searched the place changed things.

He shut the safe, closed the wall over it, and put the shelf back into place. When he was done, he looked at Misty and said, "Anything else we should check?"

"Not here," she said.

"Okay, then let's head over to the townhouse. How far away is it?" He tried to sound positive, but he knew whoever had searched the apartment had likely done the same there.

"Close," Misty told him. "Under a mile."

They locked up the apartment and made their way to the

elevator.

As they were heading down, Misty said, "Do you think it was there before? Whatever it is Peter wanted us to find?"

"Let's not worry about that until we've checked everywhere," Quinn said.

A ding signaled the approach of the ground floor. As soon as the doors parted, Quinn started to lead the others out, but abruptly stopped.

While the building's lobby was empty, standing right outside the glass front door were four hard-looking men in dark suits. That alone would have been enough to register on Quinn's internal radar. The visible lumps of concealed weapons under their arms amplified the alarm.

He backpedaled into the car, nearly knocking Misty over in the process.

"What are you doing?" she asked.

Instead of answering, he jabbed the button for the top floor and peeked back into the lobby. When he'd first seen the men outside, they'd been conferring with each other, and hadn't appeared to notice that the elevator had arrived. But now, as the doors began to shut, one of them was peering through the window.

"What is it?" Daeng asked.

Quinn looked at Misty. "You're sure Peter didn't have any kind of arrangement with a security firm to watch his place?"

"Positive," she said.

A gentle jolt rocked them as the car began its slow ascent.

"I'm not talking about your standard rent-a-cop place," Quinn said, thinking about what the men outside had looked like. "Top tier."

"Not unless something changed he didn't tell me about. What's going on?"

"We've got company."

"How many?" Daeng asked.

"I saw four," Quinn said. "There might be more."

Misty stared at Quinn. "What do they want?"

"My guess would be us."

"I THINK THAT'S them," Moss said, pointing through the window of the building.

Roberts turned and looked, but all he caught was the elevator door closing.

"What did you see?" he asked.

"Three people. Two men and a woman. I think they were starting to get off, but I swear they stopped when they saw us."

"They match the description?" Girardi, one of the other team members, asked.

"I only had a really good look of the man in front. He did have short brown hair. The other guy looked like he might have been darker, but he was in the shadows."

That was more than enough for Roberts. "Open the door," he ordered.

AS THEY NEARED the top floor, Quinn said to Misty, "I want you to press up against the front corner. When the door opens, I'll do a check. If it's clear, I'll let you know and you can get off."

She nodded.

To Daeng he said, "Emergency stop button. I don't want this going back down."

Daeng's nod was followed by the sound of the elevator's bell heralding their imminent arrival.

While his two friends jammed against the side of the car, Quinn positioned himself in the middle, the Beretta pointed at the doors, ready to fire at the first sign of trouble.

The car crept to a stop and the doors started to part. The hallway appeared empty, but he remained tense and ready, knowing that someone could easily be hiding off to one side or the other. As soon as the doors were open all the way, he launched himself into the corridor, and twisted around so he could catch anyone who might be hiding.

No one was there.

"Let's go," he said.

Misty came first. Daeng delayed his departure only long enough to pull the emergency stop button before joining the other two in the hallway. The elevator panel buzzed annoyingly, but not so loudly as to attract the attention of the residents on the floor.

Quinn touched Misty on the back. "Do you know this building at all?"

"I've only been to Peter's apartment."

"All right. No problem."

He scanned the hallway, looking for the entrance to the stairwell he knew had to be nearby, and finally spotted it off to the left, where the corridor they were in T-boned with another.

"This way."

He ran over, carefully opened the door a few inches, and listened. Footsteps, more than one set, pounding up the stairs toward them. That option was off the table.

He spun around, scanning the hallway. There was really only one thing they could do.

"Stay close," he said.

He sprinted to the left and began pressing doorbells. After pushing the final one, he moved into the middle of the hallway so he could react to whichever door opened.

"Yes?" A tired male voice came from behind the very last door.

Quinn hurried over. The door's peephole was black, so he donned a friendly smile, knowing the man inside was probably looking at him. "There's a water leak in the apartment below yours," he said. "We need to check the plumbing in your bathroom and kitchen."

"You're not with the building," the man said.

"Plumber."

"You don't look like a plumber."

"Thanks, I think. Look, this will only take a minute."

"I should call down and check."

"All right. Call. I'll wait."

As he heard the man walking away, Quinn pulled out his wallet and removed a credit card-sized, carbon-fiber, lock-pick set. Within seconds, he had the door open.

They found the man in the kitchen, picking up a cell phone from the counter. He was probably in his fifties, and was wearing a robe over a faded green Yoda T-shirt. He also had the runny nose and watery eyes of someone with a cold.

"I'll take that," Quinn said.

The man jumped in surprise. "How did you…what are you…You can't be in here! This is my home!"

Quinn lifted his gun, not exactly pointing it at the man, but close enough. "Give me your phone."

Shaking and wide-eyed, the man held out the cell.

Once Quinn took possession of it, he said, "Why don't you have a seat in the living room. The couch will be perfect."

"Okay. Sure. Please, don't hurt me."

"No one's going to hurt you."

Despite his apparent illness, the man moved quickly to the bright white couch and dropped in the middle.

Quinn followed and squatted down so that he was at the man's eye level. "I appreciate someone who knows how to cooperate. Thank you. Now, a simple question. Fire escape?"

"What?"

"I assume you have one."

Quinn had seen a metal fire escape on the outside near the front of the building, but didn't know where it would be for this back apartment.

"Oh, um, through the bedroom," the man said. "Uh, first door down the hall."

Daeng left the room and returned a few seconds later. "It's there," he said.

"Outside?" Quinn asked.

"All clear for the moment."

"Okay. You two get going."

Daeng put a hand on Misty's back and led her out of the room.

The fear gripping the man on the couch seemed to grow tenfold. "What are you going to do? You're going to kill me, aren't you? I won't say anything to anyone! I promise I won't!"

"What's your name?"

The man hesitated. "Philip."

"Well, Philip, I think you watch way too much TV. No one's going to kill you. What I am going to do is tie you up."

"Sure, sure. No problem."

"Do you live here alone, Philip?"

"No. My wife—" He stopped as if realizing he'd said more than he should have.

"Good. Then you'll only have to stay tied up until she gets home."

Philip looked relieved. "Right. Only until she gets home."

Using some extension cords that Philip kindly directed him to, Quinn secured the guy to a dining room chair he repositioned next to the couch.

"If anyone rings your doorbell, don't yell," Quinn told him. "Those guys out there are a hell of a lot nastier than I am. Trust me."

"I won't say a word. I promise."

Quinn rose to his feet. "I'm just telling you for your own sake."

As if to underscore his words, a doorbell belonging to one of Philip's neighbors chimed. Philip tensed again.

"It'll be all right," Quinn whispered. "Just remember, stay quiet."

Not waiting for a response, Quinn entered the room with the fire escape and climbed outside.

ROBERTS LEFT GIRARDI in the lobby to both cut it off as a potential escape route, and to monitor the elevator's progress so he could report what floor it stopped on. Roberts, Moss, and Cruz, the fourth member of the team, then bolted up the stairs.

They were passing the second floor when Girardi radioed that the car had gone all the way to the top.

As far from the lobby as possible, Roberts thought. If this wasn't the trio he and his men were after, he'd be surprised. When they passed the floor where the broken-into apartment was located, he ordered Cruz to check it out while he and Moss continued up.

Reaching the top floor, they paused at the stairwell exit and listened for anyone who might have been in the hallway beyond. All was quiet, so Roberts signaled for Moss to open the door.

The stairway exited into a junction between two hallways. Both were empty.

Moss looked at Roberts, silently asking for orders.

Roberts scanned one way, then the other. He hadn't heard them on the stairs, and they hadn't gone back down in the elevator—the car was still at the top—so they had to be on this floor somewhere.

"Did you hear that?" Moss whispered.

Roberts nodded. It was a male voice shouting in one of the apartments down the hallway they'd been facing. He motioned for Moss to follow, and moved toward the sound. It didn't take long before he pinpointed it as coming from the last apartment. A few more steps along the hall and he could make out the words.

"Help! Help me! Please, someone, help me!"

Roberts nodded at the door and mouthed, "Lock."

Moss knelt down and quietly picked it open.

Taking turns covering each other, they moved into the apartment and worked their way up to the edge of the foyer to get a look further inside. To the right was a large living room, and smack dab in the center was the shouting man. He was tied to a chair, his back to the door. To the left of the foyer was a hallway. Roberts signaled Moss to check it out.

"Help me, please! For God's sake! I need help!"

Moss returned and shook his head.

Roberts frowned. He'd been hoping the suspects were hiding in back. Now he was beginning to wonder if he and Moss had just stumbled onto some weird sex thing. He took a loud step into the room.

The man whipped his head around. "Oh, thank God! Please untie me!"

Roberts didn't move. "What's going on here?"

"These people, they burst into my apartment. They had a gun and—"

"How many?"

"Uh, uh, three."

"Two men and a woman?"

"Yes. The white guy tied me up, and—"

"They weren't all white?"

"The girl was. The other guy, I think he was maybe Asian? I don't know. Please, can you let me loose?"

"Where'd they go?"

The man grunted in frustration. "I don't *know*. Come on. Come on. Untie me!"

Still not moving, Roberts said, "They didn't go back out the front door, so where are they?"

"The fire escape, I think. What does it matter? Help me out!"

"Where is it?"

"Where's what?"

"The fire escape. Where is it?"

Looking exasperated, the man said, "Bedroom."

As Moss moved back into the hall to check, Roberts touched his radio. "Suspects are out of the building, probably around the back. Girardi, go check. Cruz, reposition to the lobby."

"Yes, sir," Girardi replied.

"Heading down now," Cruz said.

A few seconds later, Moss reappeared and said, "The fire escape's there, but nobody's on it."

Roberts nodded to a window at the far end of the living room. "Check there."

When Moss ran past the guy in the chair, the man said, "Hey, this isn't funny. Untie me. I gotta cold. My nose is running!"

Roberts walked over and leaned in front of the man. "I don't care. Now shut up."

The man turned away, unable to hold Roberts's gaze. Under his breath, he mumbled, "He was right."

"Who was right?" Roberts said.

"What? Nothing. Just do whatever you want to do. I won't say another word."

Roberts brought up his pistol and pointed it at the man's chest. "*Who* was right?"

"The guy from before," the man sputtered. "The one who tied me up. He…he said you guys would be a lot worse than them."

Roberts leaned back. Whoever these people were, they knew Roberts's team would be looking for them. No question at all now. These were the people who'd broken into the apartment.

"I see one of them," Moss said. "He's crossing the alley."

"Take him out."

CHAPTER SEVEN

QUINN JUMPED THE final few feet from the fire escape to the ground and whipped around, looking for Daeng and Misty, but they were nowhere in sight. Since they could have gone only one of two ways, and the first—heading to the main road—was out of the question, Quinn turned toward the back of the building, and weaved his way around several trash bins before reaching a narrow alley.

A little darkness would have been nice, but the summer sun was still a few hours from setting. Quinn checked both directions, looking for his friends, but the alley was deserted.

Directly across from him was a twelve-foot-high brick wall that extended for a dozen yards in either direction. To the left, it butted up against another building, but on the right there seemed to be an opening to a passageway.

Quinn eased down the alley, keeping as tight to the structures on his side as possible. Reaching the point opposite the end of the wall, he confirmed there was indeed a path that went clear through to the next street over.

He checked both ways again, saw that the alley was still empty, and raced across. Just as he entered the passageway, one of the bricks at the corner exploded from the impact of a bullet. He turned on the speed.

Ahead at the next street, he could see a sidewalk and cars parked along a curb, but between him and them was a tall, wrought-iron gate—chained closed.

Knowing the path behind him would not remain empty

for long, he could neither turn and go back nor stop and pick the lock.

Without slowing his pace, he assessed the gate. At the top, the vertical bars ended in pointed spears that could not be ignored. Other than that, all Quinn had to worry about was the cracked, uneven cement on the other side, waiting to twist his ankle or break his leg.

He was fifteen feet from the gate when he heard a bullet whiz by his head and strike the side of the building to his right. What he hadn't heard was the gunshot itself.

Suppressors. Not surprising, but it did confirm that the men shooting at him weren't part of some average, everyday security team.

He angled toward where the fence met the wall, and leaped, grabbing the gate as he planted his right foot against it. Using his momentum, he scrambled up the V-shaped junction.

A second bullet hit the fence where his foot had been seconds before, then a third smacked into the wall, sending shards of brick onto his back.

He reached the top and flung his legs over, barely clearing the tips of the deadly spears. He dropped onto the broken pathway, and rolled as he hit the ground to avoid injury.

A double *clang* as more bullets hit the gate.

Getting to his feet, he could see one of the suited men preparing to take another shot. Quinn raced down the remaining few steps of the pathway and turned down the main sidewalk. Thankfully, there was more traffic on this street than there had been on Peter's. He moved onto the road and shot through a gap between the cars to the other side, and then sprinted down the block.

As he turned onto the new street, he glanced over his shoulder. The suits were nowhere in sight. He knew it would be a mistake to stop, so he ran for two more blocks before allowing himself to slow down.

Not much farther on, the residential area gave way to businesses fronting sidewalks peppered with pedestrians. Just ahead, he spotted a bar and grill with a substantial happy-hour crowd both inside and around tables out front. He took a spot behind a group of twentysomethings, and used them to shield his presence as he watched the street.

"What can I get you?"

The waitress was a tall brunette dressed in jeans and a red T-shirt that was too small for her.

He donned an easy smile. "What do you have on tap?"

As she went through the list, he returned his gaze to the street.

"...also, um, Speakeasy Big Daddy, Blue Moon, uh, Rolling—"

"Speakeasy? That's a West Coast beer."

"Is it?" She didn't really seem to care.

"I'll take that," he said.

"You got it."

Quinn watched the road for another few minutes before finally pulling out his phone and sending Daeng a text.

Think I'm clear. You?

Ten seconds later, Daeng called.

"We're okay," Daeng said.

"Where are you?"

"In the basement of a building a few blocks from Peter's place. You?"

"I'm in a bar." Quinn looked around. "I didn't catch the name. They chased me down an alley, but I seemed to have lost them."

"A bar? I should have thought of that. Has to be a lot more comfortable than here." Daeng paused. "So what would you like us to do? Stay put? Go to the townhouse?"

"No," Quinn said quickly. "The townhouse is out. If Peter's apartment was being monitored, then I'm sure the townhouse is, too. Just stay there for now and let me know if you have any problems. I'll call you in a little while."

"What are you going to do?"

"Find out who our new friends are."

"SON OF A bitch," Roberts mumbled to himself.

His team had searched the area around the apartment building, but the brown-haired man and his two companions had eluded them.

He walked back over to where his men were waiting for him by the team's vehicles, and said, "Moss, Cruz, you're with me. We'll take one of the cars and widen the search area. Girardi, we'll leave you the other. Stay here and keep an eye on the building in case any of them shows back up. Questions?"

There were none.

IT TOOK QUINN ten minutes to discreetly work his way back to Peter's street. The encroaching evening was finally playing in his favor. Though the sun was still above the horizon, the shadows had grown dark and wide.

Somehow the men in the suits had found out Quinn, Daeng, and Misty were there. A watcher perhaps, but unlikely, given the time lag in their response. What seemed more realistic was an alarm somewhere in Peter's place had been tripped.

Whatever the case, he knew it was highly probable that most of the men were long gone now, and he hoped at least one had been left behind to keep an eye on the building in case Quinn and the others returned. It's how he would have handled it.

Where, was the question. A watcher could be almost anywhere—in a car, a building across the street, one of a half dozen rooftops. He could be in Peter's building, maybe even in Peter's apartment, looking down on the street. If Quinn had to bet, he'd have put his money on either a car or a roof. Those were the quickest to set up.

The shadows were deeper on the opposite side of the street from Peter's place, so Quinn entered the block there, and stepped into the recessed doorway of the first building he passed. From the slightly elevated position, he could see almost the entire street without fear of being spotted.

One by one, he examined each parked car he could see into, first on his side, then the other. His gaze stopped on an Audi A4 parked along the opposite curb, approximately halfway between his position and Peter's building. A man was sitting in the driver's seat. Given the deteriorating light, he wasn't much more than a shadow.

It could have just been someone listening to the radio, or maybe a guy who'd arrived early for a date and was waiting for time to pass.

Or it could have been one of the suits.

Quinn mentally marked the car before scanning the rest of the vehicles. As far as he could tell, the others were all empty. Next he searched the rooflines of the buildings on Peter's side. The sky was still bright enough that any silhouette would stand out, but he didn't spot so much as a suspicious bump rising above a retaining wall.

The only things left were the rooflines on his side. He'd have to cross the street to check them.

He looked back at the Audi. The driver's arm was up, his hand either on the side of his head, or in front of his face. It was impossible to tell from Quinn's angle. A few seconds passed, then the hand lowered. Quinn could see it was holding a box or…

…binoculars.

There was no way to know for sure, but his instincts told him he was right.

He slipped back down the short set of steps, and snuck along the sidewalk in a crouch so that the watcher couldn't spot him over the other parked cars. When he was across the street from Peter's building, he cut between a sedan and SUV, and walked deliberately out into the road. Keeping his pace slow, he looked up and down the street as if checking to make sure he was alone. After several seconds, he jogged the rest of the way to Peter's building. Misty still had the key, but his picks worked quickly enough.

Once inside, he raced down the hallway that ran along the side of the elevators. As he'd hoped, it went all the way to a rear exit on the alley side. He slammed through the metal security door, and ran back up the same passageway where the fire escape had deposited him earlier, not stopping until he was only a few feet from the front corner. Pressing himself against the stone wall, he ease forward until he could peek around the edge.

What he saw didn't surprise him in the least. The driver's seat of the Audi was now empty, because the man—the *suited* man—who'd been sitting in it was walking cautiously down the sidewalk toward Peter's place. His eyes were trained on the entrance, and while he wasn't holding a gun, he did have a hand hovering near the buttons of his coat.

You radioed your friends the second you saw me, didn't you? Quinn thought. *What did they tell you to do? Can't imagine it was to try to take me yourself. Keep an eye on me? Wait for them to get here?*

The man's pace continued to slow as he neared the steps up to the building. When he reached them, he stopped and craned his neck, attempting to get a look through the glass door into the lobby.

One step up. Another look. But it still wasn't enough, and he kept going until he was standing right in front of the door. He leaned in, moving his eyes as close to the window as possible, his attention fully focused on the lobby.

Quinn crept quietly over to the nearest parked car, crouched behind it on the street side, and peered through the sedan's window. He had a perfect view of the watcher as the man leaned back from the glass door. A few seconds later, the watcher walked back down the stairs and started retracing his steps to his car.

Keeping in a crouch on the other side of the vehicles, Quinn followed him nearly all the way back to the Audi, stopping one car shy and slipping around the front end so he'd stay out of view. The man stepped around the front of his car and walked to the driver's door, his back now to Quinn.

That was the moment Quinn had been waiting for. He closed in quietly, and as the watcher reached for the door handle, Quinn stuck the muzzle of the Beretta into the small of the man's back.

"If I pull the trigger, your spine will be gone," Quinn whispered. "You'll die, but you'll bleed out first, and I guarantee it won't be pleasant. Do you understand?"

"You don't have a chance," the man told him. "Put it down and maybe—"

Quinn shoved the gun forward, knocking the man against the car. "One-word answer. Yes or no. Do you *understand*?"

"Yes."

With his free hand, Quinn took possession of the man's gun, a Smith & Wesson complete with suppressor. Since it would make less noise, he switched it with the Beretta, putting his own gun in his pocket. "Who do you work for?"

The man kept his mouth shut.

"I said, who do you work for?"

No answer.

Quinn searched the man for ID, but the only thing the guy was carrying was a hundred and fifteen dollars in cash.

"We're going for a walk," he said.

"Like hell we are."

The words were barely out of the watcher's mouth when Quinn smacked the suppressor against the side of the man's head. The watcher groaned in pain, and started to reach a hand up to where he'd been hit, but Quinn used the gun again to slap the arm down.

"We're going for a walk."

"Fine," the man said, his teeth clenched, blood trickling down the side of his head.

Quinn grabbed the back of the man's jacket and pulled him away from the car. Keeping the gun pressed against the watcher's back, Quinn guided him to the sidewalk, and over into the passageway beside Peter's building.

When they reached the back end, Quinn said, "Left."

Two buildings down, he found an enclosed area built to house a couple Dumpsters. A solid metal door was pulled across most of the opening. It wasn't the greatest solution, but it was better than standing out in the alley. After Quinn pushed the watcher inside, he shoved him against the grimy back wall.

"Sit," Quinn said.

The man took a moment before doing as ordered. Once he was on the ground, Quinn closed the metal door the rest of the way.

"Now," Quinn said, "who the hell are you?"

The man scoffed. "I didn't tell you before. You think I'm going to tell you now?"

"I know you are."

A mocking grin. "You don't scare me."

"Then apparently you don't know who I am."

"I'm not paid to know who you are. I'm just paid to deal with you, and I will. Don't worry."

Quinn pointed the gun directly at the man's head. "Who are you?"

"You're not going to shoot me. I know your kind. All talk and luck and no real—"

Quinn repositioned the gun and pulled the trigger.

The suppressor kept the noise to a muffled *thup*, but there was no masking the scream of pain that exploded out of the watcher's mouth when the ring finger and pinkie on his left hand were blown off.

"God*dammit*! Shit, man!"

The watcher squeezed his palm, trying to stanch the flow of blood, his face scrunched in agony.

"Who are you working for?" Quinn asked.

"Fuck you!"

"Your foot's next, and I won't just be going for your toes."

The man rocked against the wall, blood soaking his shirt and jacket.

Out in the alley a voice called out, "Hey, what's going on? Is someone hurt?"

"Don't answer," Quinn whispered.

"I heard a yell," the voice said, getting nearer. "Is someone in there?"

Quinn leaned down near the watcher. "If you want help, tell me who you are and who sent you."

Panting, the man glared at him, his eyes a mix of pain

and anger. "Go to hell."

Someone grabbed the outside handle of the metal door and started to pull it open. Quinn knew he wouldn't get anything from the watcher, so he rose to his feet, and reached the door just as a bald guy with a protruding gut opened it wide enough to see inside.

Pushing past him, Quinn said, "Excuse me."

"Hey, was that you?" the man asked. "Were you the one who yelled? Are you okay?"

Quinn silently walked on for another few feet.

Behind him, the man must have looked back into the garbage area, because it was only a few seconds before he said, "Oh, my God. What happened? Did that guy do this to you?"

Quinn picked up his pace.

CHAPTER EIGHT

QUINN REACHED M Street moments before the eastbound number-thirty-two bus pulled up to the stop. He hopped on board and paid the fare. The bus was about a third full, most of the passengers concentrated in the front few rows, while a huddle of teenagers claimed the back. Quinn grabbed a seat in a relatively empty section near the middle, pulled out his phone, and called Steve Howard.

"Hello?" Howard said.

"Steve, it's Quinn. I know you're still on your job, but do you have a moment?"

"Sure. Just sitting around, waiting. You know how it is. What's up?"

"I have a location problem."

"How can I help?"

Howard made his home in Virginia right outside DC, so if anyone had an intimate knowledge of the area, he would.

Once Quinn had filled him in on what had happened and what he was looking for, Howard said, "I'm sure I can come up with something. Let me check and call you back."

"Thanks, Steve."

After he hung up, Quinn checked in with Daeng.

"Everything's okay?"

"We've repositioned," Daeng said.

Quinn leaned forward. "Was there a problem?"

"Hold on." Something moved over the phone, a hand probably. Quinn could hear Daeng's muffled voice, indistinct as he talked to Misty. Some movement, and finally Daeng again, now in a whisper. "Misty was getting a little anxious being so close to Peter's place. We were careful. Nobody saw us."

"Where are you now?"

"Outside the Dupont Circle Metro station."

"Don't go in," Quinn said. There would be security cameras everywhere. Whoever sent the watchers might've also had access to the video feeds.

"Wasn't planning on it."

"Just melt into the background for a little bit. I'm arranging for someplace we can meet up. Once it's set I'll call you back."

"Will do."

The bus was on H Street, passing the White House, when Quinn's phone rang again.

"I have an address for you," Howard said.

"I TAKE IT you read the e-mail," Griffin said.

"I would have rather not," Morten replied. From the sound of his voice, Griffin knew his boss was using his speakerphone. "This is bullshit."

Griffin had sent Morten the message five minutes earlier. Attached to it was a preliminary report from O & O concerning a break-in that afternoon at Peter's apartment. Most disturbing was that the trio who'd been there had escaped.

"How did this get screwed up?" Morten went on. "It should have been simple. Or am I not reading this right?"

"You're reading this right," Griffin said. It *should* have been simple. If he had been there with Darvot's team, the intruders would either be in a detention cell or dead.

"So they've just disappeared?" Morten said. "That's it? That is unacceptable."

"I haven't lost faith that they'll be found."

Morten snorted. "You think O & O is going to find them?"

"I'm also putting some other feelers out."

"Not our people," Morten said quickly. "The less this can be tied to us, the better."

"No, not our people," Griffin said, though if the results of the search continued to be unsatisfactory, that would have to change.

The line went quiet for a moment.

"Okay. Good," Morten said. "Find out who these intruders are."

"We will."

"Keep me updated," his boss said, then clicked off.

THE HOUSE HOWARD arranged for Quinn and the others to use was on the Virginia side of the Potomac, in an area known as Arlington Ridge. It was one of over a hundred single-family, brick homes in the area. Being an old neighborhood, the trees and bushes were tall and wide, all but obscuring the house.

The home's interior could be best described as spartan. The large living room was furnished with four folding chairs, a table, a single couch, and an undersized TV. The kitchen was stocked with enough dishes, glasses, and silverware for four people to eat one meal, and just enough pots and pans to make it. Food-wise, there were some dry stores in the pantry, but that was about it.

The second-floor bedrooms were equally underwhelming, each of the three smaller bedrooms boasting dual sets of adult-sized bunk beds, while the master was outfitted with a fourth pair. Sheets and blankets were in the bedroom closets, while towels were stacked on the bathroom counter.

The place was a way station, a safe house. Who owned it? Quinn didn't know, nor did he want to. Howard had vouched for the place. That's all that mattered.

Quinn arrived twenty minutes before Daeng and Misty. From an upstairs window, he saw their taxi drop them off half a block away and across the street. He headed back to the first floor, and waited until they reached the front steps before he opened the door.

Misty looked shell-shocked and exhausted, her nervous eyes rimmed with red, while Daeng looked like he always did, relaxed and slightly amused.

They let Misty have a few minutes to freshen up as best she could, and then gathered around the living-room table. It was story time first—Quinn recounting his escape and subsequent attempt to question one of the watchers, followed by Daeng describing his and Misty's efforts to avoid detection.

"So if the townhouse is out, what now?" Daeng asked.

"Maybe we've been looking at this wrong," Quinn said. "Perhaps Peter's message isn't a password at all."

"Then what?" Misty asked. "If it's some kind of secret message, how do we decode it?"

"Do you have it with you?"

"It's in the bag with the files." She looked around, apparently not remembering where she left it.

"I'll get it," Daeng said, standing.

He made a quick trip to the couch, and returned with a cloth shopping bag that he and Misty must have picked up somewhere.

"Thanks," she said as he handed it to her.

She rooted around inside, then started pulling the files out and setting them on the table until she finally found the envelope. Removing the card, she placed it between her and Quinn.

He read the first line again.

Y7(29g)85KL/24

"It doesn't look like any code I'm familiar with," Misty said after studying the note for a moment.

Most codes were not easy to identify, but there were ones that employed unique character usages or patterns that could tip off someone in the know. Unfortunately, nothing was clicking for Quinn, either. Who he really needed to give this to was Orlando. She'd know how to figure it out. But she was not an option, so he pushed the idea out of his mind before thoughts of her could consume him again.

As he looked away from the note, his gaze fell on the stack of folders. He picked one up and asked, "Any chance there might be something useful in these that he might have wanted us to find?"

Misty took the folder from him. "These numbers on the side." She turned it so both Quinn and Daeng could see what she was talking about. There was a nine-digit, alpha-numeric sequence running vertically up the edge. "It's a project number. It's how we tracked everything." She ran a finger quickly down the other files. "They all have them, which means these are all old mission files."

She opened the file she was holding and scanned the top document. Looking like she'd read something unexpected, she put the file down, and grabbed the next one off the stack. Another quick scan, and another new file. She kept up the routine and worked her way through the entire group.

"I know these files," she said as she laid the last one down.

"You put them together, didn't you?" Quinn said.

"Three of them, yes. The others are before my time, but that's not what I mean."

"Okay. Then what?"

"Peter always kept these files close. They're all jobs where something went wrong. Someone died or was severely injured, compromising the mission. He said they were to remind him of his failures so that he wouldn't repeat them."

"How far back do they go?"

"Seventeen years."

"Seventeen? That's a long time. I know the Office had a pretty good track record, but there must've been more than just seven failures."

"A lot more. But these were the ones he said stuck with him the most." She looked at the files. "There used to be eight, though."

"One's missing?"

"Yeah."

"Do you know what it is?"

Misty hesitated, obviously not wanting to answer.

"Misty. If it's important, we need to know."

"It's not important. It was...personal. Not a job like these." She fell silent for a second. "It was letters from his wife, and a few pictures. That's all." Each word seemed to cause her pain, like she was divulging a secret she had no right to share. "I'm sure after he brought everything home from the Office, he just kept it someplace else. There would have been no reason to store it with the job files at that point. I was used to seeing them all together, that's all."

Quinn felt embarrassed for forcing her to share a glimpse into Peter's personal life, but he had to ask, "Why would that be among his failure files?"

She seemed lost in a memory for a moment. "He always thought Miranda deserved more than he gave her, and after she died, he never had the chance to do better." She closed her eyes and rubbed her forehead, looking more tired than ever.

Quinn put a hand on her back and gently rubbed her shoulder. "It's been a full day. Maybe it's time to get some rest."

She nodded and opened her eyes. "Yeah. That's probably a good idea." Rising out of the chair, she started to put the files back in the bag. "I'm sorry I haven't been more help."

Quinn barely heard the last part. There was something about the files that caught in his mind, pulling at a memory, a thought.

Once Misty stuffed the last one in, she turned for the stairs. "Good night."

She was nearly across the room when Quinn said, "Hold on."

The files. It had been one of the Office's job files that helped Quinn figure out what had happened to Peter, Nate, and the others Romero kidnapped. Misty had found the information for him. Only it hadn't been a physical file, but a digital one. She had found it in...

"The Office archive," he said. "You accessed it from Peter's place?"

She shook her head. "It's not located there."

"Where is it?"

Again, she looked uncomfortable, the secrets she'd promised to keep fighting against desire to help. "It's...it's hidden in—" She stopped and gaped at him. "My God. You're thinking that's it, aren't you? It didn't even dawn on me."

"I'm not saying that's it. I'm just saying that we should at least see if Peter's message works on it." He stood up. "Maybe there's a computer here. We can check right—"

"We can't," she said. "Peter was the only one who could log on remotely."

"So we have to go where it's stored?"

"Yes. But they won't be open until the morning."

Quinn's brows furrowed. "Open? Where did Peter store it?"

"Library of Congress."

CHAPTER NINE

ISLA DE CERVANTES

NATE WOKE IN a sweat. It wasn't the first time. In fact, since getting off Duran Island, he seemed to always wake up drenched.

It was his dream, the same one every night. He was back on the island, racing through the jungle, looking for a way out of the tangled mess. But the vines and bushes and trees seemed to go on forever, trapping him more times than not, and twisting around his arms and legs to keep him from moving onward.

He would yank and rip at the plants holding him in place. Sometimes he would get an arm free or even a leg, but invariably he would wake up with a start, not having been able to break away.

In the real world, the world of the hospital room where he slept, his sheets would be soiled from his imaginary flight, the top one often pushed to the foot of the bed, or wrapped around his waist or legs.

Usually, he'd find Liz sleeping in the chair a few feet away, unaware of his ordeal due to her own exhaustion, but even in the semi-darkness he could see tonight the chair was empty.

Careful not to pull too much at the welts across his back, he turned so he could check the clock on the nightstand.

Eleven seventeen p.m.

Liz should have been there. She was always in the room by ten at the latest.

He glanced at the bathroom, thinking maybe she was using the toilet, but the door was open and the room beyond was even darker than the one he was in.

Where was she?

His condition was not one that required being hooked up to an IV or a pulse monitor or an oxygen tube, which was good, given how active he'd become in his sleep. Surely he would have ripped any needle right out of his arm the very first night. He swung out of bed and hopped over to the closet. As he'd hoped, his prosthetic leg was inside. Once it was fitted in place, he went over to the door and pulled it open.

Light from the hallway rushed in. He blinked until his eyes adjusted to the brightness, and then looked both ways, wondering where Liz might have gone. The only person he saw was one of the night nurses, sitting at a station down the hall, her gaze focused on her desk.

He headed over. Though he wasn't trying to be quiet, she didn't hear him until he was only a few feet away. She jerked up, one hand clutching her chest, as the other accidentally brushed the book she'd been reading onto her lap.

"I'm sorry," Nate said. "I didn't mean to startle you."

"You shouldn't be up," she said. Like all the medical staff he'd come in contact with, she spoke to him in English.

"I'm looking for my friend. The woman?"

"Señorita Liz?"

"Uh, yeah."

The nurse smiled. "She is sitting with your other friend."

"Which other friend?"

"Woman."

"Orlando."

The nurse clearly hadn't heard that name before.

"Which room?" he asked.

"ICU."

"Can you take me there?"

She hesitated, but said, "Follow me."

The intensive care unit was on the other side of the

hospital, in a wing that had been divided into six private rooms off a central hallway. At the head of the hallway was a desk manned by another nurse. She looked surprised to see Nate and his escort.

The two women spoke in hushed Spanish for several seconds. When they were done, the one at the desk stood up.

"She will show you to your friend," the first nurse said. "I have to return to my desk."

"*Gracias*," Nate said.

She smiled. "*De nada.*" Then her face turned serious as she pointed at him. "Don't stay long. You need rest."

The new nurse led him down the hallway to the last room on the left, nodded at the closed door, and, without a word, headed back the way they'd come. Nate quietly opened the door, not wanting to wake Orlando if she was sleeping.

Orlando's room was much more elaborate than his. Diagnostic equipment and monitors all but surrounded her bed. The only thing in the room that was the same as in his was the chair Liz was sitting in. She was asleep, a magazine lying against her chest, her head lolled to the side.

Nate eased the door closed and stepped over to the chair. If Liz stayed in her current position, she would have a hell of a sore neck in the morning. Gingerly, he lifted the magazine out of her hands and set it on the nightstand. He then repositioned himself in front of her, and attempted to move her into a more comfortable position.

He was only seconds from success when her eyes eased open. For a brief moment, she looked at him as if she couldn't comprehend who he was or what he was doing, then she sat up with a jolt.

"Nate?" She blinked to push away the sleep and looked around her. "Wait. This isn't your room."

"No. It's Orlando's."

"Right, right." She started to relax, but then her brow furrowed again. "What are you doing out of bed?"

"Looking for you. I woke up and you weren't there."

She put a hand on his arm. "I'm sorry. I was going to tell you, but you slept through most of the day."

"Tell me what?"

"I promised Jake I would watch Orlando while he was gone."

Jake, Quinn's birth name, and one Liz still used.

"Gone? Where?"

"He and Daeng went to DC to see Misty."

"Misty?" He could understand if Misty wanted to talk to Quinn about Peter's death, but they could have done that on the phone. "Why?"

"You should get some sleep," Liz said. "We can talk about it in the morning."

"I've had more than enough sleep, so we can talk about it now." When she didn't respond right away, he said, "Liz, I'm going to find out one way or the other."

She rubbed her eyes and let out a deep breath. "He's trying to figure out who's responsible."

"Responsible for what?"

She looked at him like he should already know. "Killing Peter. What happened to Orlando. To you. And the others. What do you think?"

"We know who's responsible. They're all dead."

"No. Jake wants to find who started it all. Who gave Romero the list of names he was working from," she said.

Nate leaned back.

The list. Of course. The list that mistakenly contained Quinn's name. A mistake that was magnified, at least for Nate, when Romero's snatchers thought Nate was Quinn.

"Has he learned anything?" he asked.

"I have no idea. Haven't heard from him since he checked in earlier today, but it's not like he'd share anything like that with me. You know that."

"What about Orlando? Did he talk to her about any of this?"

"Nate, she hasn't woken up yet."

"What?" He looked over at Orlando. "You told me she was doing okay."

"In the grand scheme, she is," Liz said. "But she has a long way to go. I didn't want to worry you too much. You have to concentrate on your own recovery."

Liz's assurances about Orlando *had* allowed him to relax. Still…

"I know you were only trying to help," he said, "but you can't sugarcoat things like that for me, or hide anything just because you don't want me to worry. It doesn't matter what condition I'm in. I can never afford not to know what's going on. Lives could depend on it. You understand that, don't you?"

She turned her head, not meeting his gaze.

"Liz, please tell me you understand."

"Sure," she said, pushing herself out of her chair. "I understand. I'm sorry."

She headed for the door.

"Where are you going?" he asked.

"Out."

"Liz, I'm not trying to—"

"Please. Not now."

She yanked open the door and left.

Nate stared after her, not knowing what he should do. While one voice in his head yelled at him to go after her, to help her understand, another argued to let her be, that she just needed a little time.

And then there was the third voice, the softest of the three that he feared was the closest to being right. "It doesn't matter what you do. She's not of your world. She never will be. What you have together has been nice, but how could there possibly be a future?"

Paralyzed, he stood where he was, watching the ghost of her at the door, and wishing that he were still back in his dream, fighting the jungle and not the woman he loved.

CHAPTER TEN

SEPTEMBER 2nd WASHINGTON DC

“TERMINAL EIGHT, THIS is Central.”

“Yes, sir.”

“Who’s up next?”

“Team Five, sir.”

“Put them on standby. I’ve been told to expect information on a new location for the subjects who broke into RZ-47.”

“Yes, sir. Consider it done.”

There was no missing the enthusiasm in Terminal Eight’s voice, nor was it surprising. Everyone at O & O knew of the failure the previous afternoon, and the maiming of one of their men. Righting the balance was on all their minds.

“I’ll pass on the exact location as soon as I have it,” Central said. “But you can inform the team that it will likely be in Virginia.”

ARLINGTON RIDGE, VIRGINIA

A BUZZ, AS familiar as it was foreign.

Quinn stirred, but didn’t open his eyes until he heard the sound again. His phone, vibrating against the nightstand. He snatched it up. The name on the display read: STEVE HOWARD. The time, almost one a.m.

"Hello?"

"Quinn, get up. Now."

Quinn immediately threw the covers back and swung his feet onto the carpet. "What is it?"

"You need to get out of there," Howard said. "Fast as you can. There's a very good chance the place has been compromised."

Quinn flipped his phone to speaker and began pulling on his clothes. "What happened?"

"The contact who helped me set it up for you is dead."

"When?"

"Sometime in the last thirty minutes. I talked to his friend, another op. They were out having drinks, and my contact went to the bathroom but didn't come back. They found his body in the alley behind the bar."

"How do you know that's related to us?"

"I don't. But his friend said my contact wasn't working on anything, so the last thing he would have done was arrange for the house. Better if we play it safe, don't you think?"

"Yeah. Definitely."

"I can meet you, but it'll take me over half an hour to get there. And you shouldn't hang around that long."

"You're back?"

"Flew in right before midnight. I'll call when I get close, and we can figure out a meeting point then."

"All right. Thanks, Steve."

"Be safe."

Quinn finished dressing and rushed into the hall. He was about to open the door to the room Misty was using when Daeng appeared at the top of the stairs.

"Steve just called," Quinn said. "He thinks this place might be compromised."

"That would explain the men surrounding the house."

Quinn pulled his hand back from the doorknob. "How many?"

"Four that I could count. I was coming up to get you."

"How long have they been there?"

"Just moved in. Before that it was all quiet. There hasn't

even been a car driving by in the last two hours."

"Isn't that just great?" Quinn growled. "Okay, go back down and keep an eye on things while I get Misty up."

Quinn opened the door to Misty's room and moved over to the bed.

"We've got to go," he said, shaking her shoulder.

She turned on her back and opened her eyes. "What? Go? I don't—"

"We've got company."

She sat straight up. "I thought this place was safe."

"Apparently not."

"Who *are* these people?" she asked.

Quinn grabbed her clothes off the dresser and tossed them to her. "As fast as you can," he said before heading into the hall.

While he waited, he called Howard back. "They're already here."

"Son of a bitch. What do you want me to do?"

"Get here as quick as possible. I'll call you after we find a way out."

As he hung up, Misty stepped out of her room.

"Come on. Downstairs," he said. "Make sure to stay away from the windows."

When they reached the bottom of the stairs, Quinn paused and whispered, "Daeng? Where are you?"

Daeng's voice came from down the hallway to the right. "Kitchen."

Quinn motioned for Misty to copy him as he crouched down and crept into the hall. They found Daeng kneeling next to the cabinets by the sink.

"Where?" Quinn asked.

Daeng nodded up at the window above them. "Straight out there's a hedge and some kind of shed. One guy's there, around the back." He twisted around. "If you look out the window by the front door, you'll see a minivan parked across the street. Last time I checked another guy was peeking around it." He pointed left, then right. "The other two are a little harder to see. No direct view. But there's a window in the living room that if you lean far enough over, you'll see a couple of bushes about twenty feet from the house. A guy's in there. The one on the left, as far as I can tell, is pressed right up against the building."

"So still just the four."

"Yeah."

"Just like earlier."

"Was thinking the same thing."

Whether or not it was the same team as the one at Peter's apartment, Quinn figured the men's abilities would be comparable.

"Okay," he whispered. "This is what we're going to do."

WITTEN DIDN'T LIKE it. The house was too quiet. Sure, it was after midnight, but there was a sense of stillness about it that he only picked up when a place was dangerous or deserted. Either way, it was a problem.

The fugitives—two men and a woman whose identities had yet to be determined—were supposedly holed up inside. How the powers that be at O & O had learned this, he didn't know. It wasn't his job. He was only here to make the problem go away.

"Dead or alive?" he'd asked when he'd been briefed twenty-five minutes earlier.

"I'm told alive, if possible, but we don't need all three," the woman acting as Terminal Eight that evening had said. "One will suffice."

Witten had also been told about what had happened the previous afternoon, and was determined that Team Five would not achieve the same less-than-stellar results. Maybe that was why his senses felt more heightened than usual.

"Check," he whispered.

Each member of his team was outfitted with a tiny comm radio—a receiver that fit snugly in the ear, and extending from it, a one-inch microphone that floated above the cheek.

"South, clear," Suggs said.

Johnson was next. "West, clear."

And finally, Brown. "North, clear."

Deserted? Or dangerous? Witten wondered again as he scanned the front of the house. Unfortunately, there was only one way to find out.

"All positions, move in," he ordered.

QUINN COULD FEEL Misty tense as they heard a floorboard creak. He touched her arm and gave it a quick squeeze.

Another creak, closer to the door this time.

It wouldn't be long now.

THERE HAD BEEN no need to pick the locks to get inside. The home in Arlington Ridge was a safe house known to O & O. Terminal Eight had simply supplied the entry codes to Witten, who had then passed them on to his team.

Suggs used the rear-door code to enter through the kitchen, while Witten utilized the one for the front door. Per earlier instructions, Johnson and Brown remained outside to secure the perimeter.

Witten stepped over the threshold into an unadorned entryway. His night vision goggles firmly in place, he could see he was alone. The short foyer led into the main part of the house, where he found a living room, dining area, kitchen, and Suggs.

Using well-practiced hand signals, he learned that Suggs had also spotted no one. Together they moved over to the carpeted stairway leading up to a second floor. Witten went up first. When he reached the top, he paused and listened. Given the hour, if the house was occupied, chances were the trespassers would be asleep, and Witten and Suggs would be able to contain them without a struggle.

There were five doors in the hallway—four to the left and one to the right. Witten ordered Suggs right, and he went left. The first room he came to was a bedroom with two sets of bunk beds. All the mattresses were bare—no sheets, no blankets. The next door opened into a bathroom that had several unused towels piled on the counter.

Before he could get to door number three, Suggs crept up behind him. With a shake of his head, Suggs let Witten know the room to the right was unoccupied.

Together, they moved to the next doorway. More bunks, only this time, sheets and a blanket rested on the bottom mattress of the bunk against the far wall. The bedding was in a tangle, as if the covers had been pushed away in a hurry.

Witten scanned the room before walking over to the mattress and putting his hand on the sheets. Even though the house was not particularly cool, he could tell right away the sheets were warmer than ambient temperature. Someone had been lying there—what, ten minutes earlier? Fifteen? No more than that.

He and Suggs retreated back to the hallway and approached the final door. Once more there were two sets of bunks, and like the room they'd just left, one of the mattresses had been used in the last half hour.

So where were the targets? And why were only two beds used and not three? Had they split up? Were these even the right people?

Witten didn't like questions. Questions made jobs messy. And messy was never good.

They rechecked each of the rooms, making sure to examine every potential hiding place. In the closet of the master bedroom, they found a narrow trapdoor that opened into an attic.

Witten grimaced. Limited-access attics were a bitch. Push it open, stick your head in, and *bang*, bullet to the face. That was not a risk he was interested in taking.

He examined the trapdoor. There were two sliding locks screwed into the wood at one end. Both were open so he slid them into locked position, and pushed gently up on the hatch. It didn't move. If anyone had gone into the attic, the person was not getting out without making a lot of noise.

Satisfied, he and Suggs headed back downstairs, to the only place left they hadn't checked. The basement.

It was accessed via a rough set of wooden steps leading down from a doorway in the kitchen. From the top of the stairs, Witten could see the room below was unfinished—grimy concrete walls surrounding an even dirtier concrete floor. The partial view also revealed a few boxes piled here and there, but to see the full basement he would have to go down. He didn't need to be stupid about it, though.

Leaving Suggs to keep an eye on things, Witten left the house and hustled down the street to where their car was parked. Digging through the equipment kit in the trunk, he quickly found what he was looking for and hurried back.

When he walked into the kitchen again, Suggs signaled that all was still quiet. Witten set the plastic case he'd brought with him on the counter and opened it. Inside was a mirror mounted on a pivot head, and an expandable rod that could be attached to it. Once he had it assembled, he carried it over to the doorway and knelt down.

Witten twisted the mirror back and forth, scanning the room, and established there were no visible threats. That, of course, was not a guarantee the basement was safe, which was why, before descending, he gave the mirror to Suggs so his partner could monitor as he went down.

He had expected the stairs to groan with each step, but they made little noise as he moved into the belly of the house. As soon as his eyes cleared the ceiling line, he paused and took a look around, the barrel of his gun tracking his gaze. There were a few more boxes, several empty shelving units, and directly across from the stairway, a hall leading away into the dark. If anyone was down here, that's where he or she would be.

He signaled Suggs to remain where he was, and then moved quietly across the room into the hallway.

THE EASY OUT was the only reason they were in the basement. If not for that, descending to the lowest level of the house would have been suicide, with the only escape being through the door in the kitchen at the top of the stairs.

Quinn had discovered the easy out when he'd done a check through the house after he arrived. It was located in the back room down the dark basement hallway. This particular easy out came in the form of a ground-level window located high on the wall, facing the backyard. While it looked like it was fixed in place, the entire thing could be removed in a matter of seconds via a concealed release lever built into the frame.

An escape route. An easy out.

"Maybe they left," Misty said.

The creaking boards above their heads had fallen silent a few minutes earlier.

"No," Quinn said. "They're just checking the bedrooms." He gave her a reassuring squeeze on the arm. "It's going to be fine. Don't worry."

"Right. Don't worry."

His words had at least gotten a smirk out of her.

He stepped over to the window and peeked outside. The dark backyard looked as empty as it had the last time he checked, but he knew two men, if not more, were lurking out there somewhere. All the men needed to be drawn into the house before Quinn pulled the release lever, otherwise he and Daeng and Misty would be picked off as they crossed the yard.

The floor above began creaking again.

Quinn moved in front of Misty and looked her in the eyes. "I need you to do exactly what I tell you, okay?" he whispered.

She nodded.

"Good." Placing a hand on her back, he guided her to the front corner of the room. "Tuck yourself in tight right here. You'll be out of sight if the door opens."

Once she was set, he headed toward the corner he would occupy, but stopped before he could get there and cocked his head. Upstairs, someone was moving quickly through the house. This was followed by the unmistakable sound of the front door opening.

Were they leaving?

Quinn exchanged a cautious look with Daeng, but avoided Misty's gaze so as not to get her hopes up.

Quiet descended for several minutes.

He was just starting to consider that maybe the men *had* left, when he heard the front door open again, and the floor once more groaned under the weight of one of the intruders.

So be it, Quinn thought. Quinn moved into position, his plan to draw everyone inside still in play.

Less than sixty seconds later came the sound he'd been waiting to hear—the subtle whine of the basement door swinging open.

Daeng moved to a spot in direct view of the room's doorway, and arranged himself on the floor as if he had fallen there.

Quinn looked him over, and nodded his approval.

They were ready.

THERE WERE THREE rooms along the hall, each with its door closed. Witten stopped at the nearest, and slowly turned the handle. Once the latch was released, he flung the door open and took a step back, his gun held out in front of him.

Nothing.

Only dirt and cracked concrete.

The second room was much the same.

He turned to the final door. If no one was behind this, the house was empty, and whoever had been sleeping upstairs had left before Team Five arrived.

Like he'd done with the others, he turned the knob and pushed the door open.

Immediately he saw this room was different. Lying on the ground a few feet inside was a body.

He stepped forward, stopping short of the threshold.

Male, by the looks of it, but that was about all he could make out. The body was on its stomach with its face turned away.

Who the hell was this?

He scanned the room, able to see everywhere except the space to either side of the door. No one. Only the body.

He was deciding on whether he should look right or left first as he moved inside, when the man on the ground groaned.

Gun extended, Witten stepped into the room. "Don't move."

DAENG PLAYED HIS part perfectly. A second after he groaned, a man holding a gun moved through the doorway.

As the man said, "Don't move," Quinn leapt toward him, his hand aiming straight for the comm gear mounted in the man's ear. Quinn was three feet away when the guy sensed him and started to whirl around, but their unwanted guest was too late. Quinn snatched the radio away with his right, and landed a hook to the guy's jaw with his left.

The man staggered with the punch, but kept on his feet. He opened his mouth to yell. What he hadn't noticed was that Daeng was no longer lying on the ground, and had moved in behind him. Before the scream even began, Daeng whipped his jacket around the man's head, covering the intruder's mouth, and pulled it tight.

At the same time, Quinn grabbed the gun and wrenched it from the man's grasp, then tore the night vision goggles off the guy's face.

"Down," Quinn whispered to Daeng.

Keeping the jacket tight around the man's face, Daeng shoved him to the floor.

Quinn knelt in front of the intruder. "You cooperate, and we won't have a problem. Nod if you understand."

Nothing for a moment, only rapid blinking as the man adjusted to the darkness. Then a nod.

"Good," Quinn said. He rose, intending to put the radio in his ear, and shout in a garbled voice that he heard someone running through the first floor toward the stairs, followed by a quick order for everyone to converge. That's when they'd make their escape. But the radio was not in his hand anymore.

As he started to look around, the captive spoke through his gag. Not a yell, but a single word.

Daeng looked at Quinn. "Did he say what I think he said?"

The man repeated the word.

"Loosen the jacket," Quinn said. "Just a little."

Once more the man spoke.

"Quinn? You are Quinn, aren't you?"

Quinn knelt back down and studied the man's face. There *was* something familiar about him. Quinn ran through names in his head, trying to match one to the face. Finally, he stopped. "Clyde…Witten."

"Yeah. Right," the man said, his voice still muffled, but clearer.

They had worked at least three jobs together that Quinn could remember. Not on the same team. Witten had been ops, and had never helped Quinn on body disposal. Most of their interaction had been brief, but Quinn had felt that Witten was a through-and-through professional. It had been at least four years since the last time their paths crossed.

"You promise not to yell?" Quinn asked.

"You promise not to kill me?" Witten countered.

Quinn looked at Daeng. "Take it off, but if he reneges, knock him out."

Daeng removed the jacket from Witten's face.

"Thanks," Witten said. "What the hell are you doing here?"

"I could ask you the same question," Quinn replied.

After a brief hesitation, Witten said, "We've never had problems, have we?"

"Not that I can recall."

"No reason why we should start now, right?"

Quinn waited.

"You want to know why we're here?" Witten asked.

Quinn gave him a look like that was the most obvious question ever.

"We were sent to capture or eliminate whoever is staying in this house." There was no anger or threat in the voice, only a statement of fact.

"So, us."

Witten twisted his face, uncomfortable. "Why would you be on a kill list?"

"That's a good question. Why don't you tell me exactly whose kill list we're on?"

"You know I can't do that."

"I guess that puts us a bit at odds, doesn't it?"

"Was that you yesterday afternoon in Georgetown? Shot off a couple fingers?"

"The guy's lucky I didn't kill him," Quinn said. "Friend of yours?"

"I don't know him."

"Same organization?"

Witten didn't answer.

"Quinn?" Misty whispered.

All three men looked over, Witten clearly surprised by Misty's presence.

Misty pointed at the ground a few feet away from her. Sitting there was the comm gear Quinn had stripped from Witten. He must have dropped it in the fight.

"I hear voices," she said.

"Watch him," Quinn said to Daeng. He walked over and picked up the earpiece and mic. Someone was definitely transmitting. He returned to Witten. "I want you to talk to them. Tell them everything's all right. If you deviate at all I will—"

"What? You'll kill me?"

"I only eliminate those in my way. Are you going to be in my way?"

"Give me the radio."

After a brief hesitation, Quinn tossed him the gear.

Witten put the earpiece in. "I'm here, I'm here. Sorry. Radio problem…It's okay now…yeah, I'm sure. It's clear down here. The house is empty. Assemble out front. I'll be there in a minute. There's something here I'm checking…no, I got it. Just meet me out front." He listened for a moment longer before he clicked the button that turned off the mic. Looking up, he said, "Satisfied?"

Quinn stepped outside the room and listened. He could hear footsteps moving away from the basement door toward the front of the house. A moment later, the main door opened and all fell silent.

When he returned to the room, he said, "Who are you working for?"

"Ask as many times as you want," Witten said, "but it's

not going to change the fact that I can't tell you."

"You can, and you—"

Witten held up a hand, stopping him. "It doesn't matter who I work for anyway. We're a clearinghouse. We pick up jobs from all over the place, but we don't generate them ourselves."

Quinn cocked his head. "So whoever wanted to take us out hired your organization?"

"In essence, yes, but you're a little off."

"How so?"

"I can tell you for a fact that your name or—" he took a quick glance at Daeng and Misty— "your associates' names aren't on our lists. We were only told there would be two men and a woman. The accompanying descriptions were very vague."

"Then why did you come after us?" Daeng asked.

"The intervention order applies to anyone entering the apartment you were in earlier today."

"And the order is to terminate?"

"The order is to capture and isolate," Witten said. "But if we encounter any resistance, we have the option to eliminate the target." He paused. "The mission parameters also came with a clear indication of the type of people we would be dealing with."

"And that would be…?"

"Foreign operatives with ties to terrorist organizations. The backstory I was given is that the owner of the Georgetown apartment had information in his possession that these operatives might try to obtain."

"We're the only people who would've *ever* shown up at that apartment," Quinn said. "But the last I checked, I'm not a foreign operative in this country. And I definitely never work with terrorists."

He could see in Witten's eyes that the man knew this, too.

"Your agency is being used," Quinn told him.

"Possibly." There was a trace of anger in Witten's voice. Before he could continue, his gaze became unfocused, and he touched his earpiece. "Yes…still here, but on my way out…will be right there." He tapped on the comm again and looked at Quinn. "I need to go. If I don't, my team will come after me."

"How do we know you're not going to just sit out there and shoot us as we come outside?"

"I give you my word we'll move out immediately. Give it ten minutes to be sure, then leave." He paused. "It's up to you whether you want to believe me or not."

Quinn stared at the man for several seconds. All his instincts told him that Witten was telling the truth. "What are you going to tell your bosses?"

Witten shrugged. "That someone was here, but the house was empty when we arrived. They'll probably send out a few investigators to see if they can pick up any clues as to who'd been here—so you might want to make sure there aren't any—but basically our job will be done unless another alarm is triggered."

"I'm going to choose to trust you," Quinn said. He popped the mag out of Witten's pistol, removed the bullet from the chamber, and handed it back.

"Apparently only so far," Witten said.

"There is one thing you can tell me."

Witten eyed Quinn warily. "What?"

"Who the client is."

Witten shook his head. "Doesn't work that way. I don't have that information."

"But you could find out."

"Not necessarily. There are a lot of layers involved."

"I'll pay you."

"Whoa. I'm not going down that road."

"Then do it as a favor."

Witten looked unsure.

"It's clear someone wants me and my colleagues dead," Quinn said. "I'd really like to know who that is."

Witten frowned, but said, "I'll think about."

"That's all I ask."

After Quinn gave Witten an e-mail address he could use

to contact him, he held out his hand. Witten hesitated, then allowed Quinn to pull him to his feet.

"To be clear, even if I do find out, I'm not saying I *will* let you know," Witten said.

"Fair enough."

"Good luck," the man said, and headed out the door.

After five minutes, Quinn said, "Stay here," then left the room and went all the way up to the second floor. From there he checked through windows on all four sides. The yard surrounding the house appeared to be deserted. He returned to the first floor, and carefully let himself out the back door. Holding his empty hands up beside his head, he moved slowly into the yard. No one charging out of the bushes. No shouts to get on the ground.

After doing the same in the side yards and the front, he went back inside, satisfied that Witten had done as promised. He, Daeng, and Misty then spent the next ten minutes removing as much evidence of their presence in the house as possible—wiping down all surfaces they may have touched, and vacuuming for loose hairs and dead skin. In the bedrooms, they removed the sheets and blankets Misty and Quinn had used, and replaced them with clean sets that they then messed up to look used. It wasn't perfect, but it should be enough to cover their tracks.

They left the house with three trash bags stuffed with the sheets and blankets, the towels they'd wiped things down with, and the bag from the vacuum. These they'd dump later in several different locations.

As they headed down the sidewalk, Quinn pulled out his phone and called Howard.

"Where are you?" he asked.

"Four blocks from the house," Howard said.

"Come and get us."

CHAPTER ELEVEN

VIRGINIA

THEY SPENT THE remainder of the night in a motel next to the interstate near Tyson's Corner. Howard arranged the rooms so the night staff would know only his face in case anyone came looking for the others.

Since Daeng had already put in his time on watch back at the house, Quinn and Howard split the rest of the night, with Quinn taking the final shift. Every minute he was up, he wanted to call Liz to find out what was happening with Orlando, but he forced himself to wait until the sun peeked over the horizon before finally sneaking outside with his phone.

The call was answered after three rings.

"Hey, Quinn." Definitely not Liz's voice.

"Nate?"

"Uh-huh. Hold on a sec." Movement and a few grunts. When the younger cleaner spoke again, his voice no longer sounded quite as sleepy. "Sorry. Liz forgot her phone when she left last night."

Quinn tensed. "Left?"

"Down the hall," Nate said quickly. "I'm assuming you want to talk to her."

"I just want to check on Orlando."

"Oh, well, I can do that." A pause. "She looks fine."

"You're in her room?"

"Uh-huh."

"What does Dr. Montero say?"

"Haven't seen him. I think a nurse comes in a few times an hour, but, well, I've kind of been sleeping, you know?"

"Then you have no idea how she is."

Nate took a moment before he answered. "I know she seems to be resting peacefully. I know none of the machines she's hooked up to are making funny noises. I know there hasn't been any sudden rush of doctors into the room responding to some kind of crisis. I'd say she's doing exactly what she's supposed to be doing. Resting and getting better."

Quinn forced himself to take a calming breath. It was as early there in Isla de Cervantes as it was in Virginia, after all. Dr. Montero probably wasn't even at the hospital yet. And Nate was right. If she was resting comfortably, that was a good sign.

"How, um, how are you doing?" he asked.

"Peachy. My back still hurts, but if I keep it stretched, I do okay."

"That's good. What about Lanier, Berkeley, and Curson?"

"They're a bit worse off, but on the mend."

"Best that we can expect, I guess."

"Quinn, Liz said you were trying to find who gave Romero the list," Nate said. "How's that going?"

Quinn felt a slight tinge of guilt for not having told Nate himself. "It's been…interesting."

"Interesting how?"

"I'll tell you when we come back."

"When will that be?"

"I'm hoping tonight. If not, then tomorrow."

Nate was quiet for several seconds. "I don't want to be cut out. Whatever you're doing, I want to be a part of it."

"I know. You will be. It's just—"

"I'm fine," Nate said. "It's not the first time I've been injured. I can do what needs to be done."

"I promise I'll brief you when I get back."

"I'm holding you to that."

A big rig rattled down the interstate, its engine bellowing as the driver downshifted. "If anything changes with Orlando, call me right away."

"Don't worry so much," Nate said. "I'll keep an eye on things here and call if there's anything you need to know."

IT WAS ANOTHER hour before the others were up and dressed. They grabbed a quick breakfast at the café next to their motel before heading back into DC.

Even with traffic, they arrived at the John Adams building of the Library of Congress fifteen minutes before its 8:30 opening.

"You two cover the outside," Quinn said to Daeng and Howard. "I don't want trouble showing up without us knowing about it."

Both men nodded.

"You're coming with me, though, right?" Misty asked Quinn.

"I'll be right next to you the whole time."

At 8:30 on the dot, they exited the car. While Daeng and Howard went to find lookout spots, Quinn accompanied Misty inside to one of the available public computer workstations.

"You're the driver," he said, motioning for her to take the seat.

Once she was situated, he leaned in behind her so he could have a better view of the monitor. She pulled the keyboard forward and extended her fingers above it, but they remained there, hovering, unmoving.

"What's wrong?" Quinn asked.

"I shouldn't be showing you this. Peter was very clear that no one but he and I could know."

Her loyalty to Peter was as annoying as it was admirable. "He's not here anymore."

"I don't care. I promised him. Please."

"Fine," he said, rising back up. "Wave me back once you're in."

Looking relieved, she said, "Thank you."

Quinn wandered several terminals away, and used the opportunity to scan the room in case someone had been able to bypass Daeng and Howard, but none of the library's patrons triggered his alarm.

When his gaze returned to Misty, she motioned that it was okay for him to return. He resumed his position behind her, and saw that the Library of Congress screen had been replaced by some sort of index.

"This is it?" he asked.

"Yes."

"How do you search?"

"Here." She clicked on a small circle near the top. Instantly, a text box opened, ready for input. "Should I try it?"

"That's what we're here for."

Quinn, having taken possession of the card from Peter before they'd left the motel, pulled it out of his pocket and handed it to her.

Misty looked around, as if what she was about to do was a crime. On the surface, it probably was. The Library certainly wouldn't be happy to learn its servers secretly housed the archives of a former intelligence agency.

Slowly, she typed in the first line from Peter's note.

Y7(29g)85KL/24

When she hit ENTER, the cursor blinked several times, then the screen went blank.

When it remained that way for more than ten seconds, Quinn said, "That can't be right."

"That didn't happen last time I was here," Misty said, looking equally concerned. "What should I do?"

"Maybe we should try closing the database and bringing it back up."

"How? The screen's blank."

Behind them, someone said, "Is there a problem?"

They both turned to find a woman in her early thirties, dressed in slacks and a nice blouse, standing a few feet away. Her name tag indentified her as Carole Barnes, Librarian,

Interactive Media.

"No, we're fine," Quinn said.

But she was already looking past him at the monitor, her eyes narrowing. "Is the terminal frozen?"

Misty hesitated, then said, "It seems to be."

"Here," Ms. Barnes said. "Move out of the way."

"I'm sure it's just running slow," Quinn said.

The librarian looked at him, an eyebrow raised. "And I'm sure you're not the one in charge of the equipment. Now, please, step back."

Short of rendering the woman unconscious, Quinn didn't know what else to do. So he gave Misty a subtle nod, and they moved away from the station.

Ms. Barnes immediately took the vacated seat and reached under the desk. A second later, the computer powered down.

"Let's see if that does the trick," she said without moving from the chair.

Ten seconds passed before Quinn heard the computer fan kick back on. A moment after that, the monitor sprang back to life. Once it cycled through, they were greeted once more with the Library of Congress screen.

"There," Ms. Barnes said, finally relinquishing the chair. "Let me know if it acts up again."

Quinn and Misty thanked her as she left.

"I'll turn my back, but I'm not walking away this time," Quinn said when they were alone again.

"So turn already."

Once more, Misty logged in to the Office's archive and brought up the search box.

She retyped the characters and said, "Here goes nothing," as she pressed ENTER.

The result was a repeat of last time.

"Dammit," she said.

Quinn frowned at the screen. "Try typing. Maybe it'll allow you to navigate back."

She hit a few keys. Surprisingly, characters started appearing right where the text box had been.

"Wait," Quinn said. "Erase that and type in the message again."

She did what he asked. When she hit ENTER, the screen went black again, but only stayed that way for a second before a column of several short lines of type appeared. The first line contained an address—number and street only. The ones below it appeared to be a short list of cryptic directions.

"Does the address mean anything to you?" Quinn asked.

Misty shook her head. "No."

Quinn pulled out his phone and took a picture of the screen.

"Is there another page or is this it?" he asked.

She moved the cursor across the screen. "Nothing is linked."

"What if you try typing it in again?"

As she put her fingers on the keyboard, a small box labeled TIME UNTIL LOG OFF appeared on screen, with numbers below it counting down from thirty.

Misty went ahead and typed in the characters anyway, but none of them appeared. As the countdown clock reached fifteen, she said, "You want to take another picture, just in case?"

Quinn checked the one he'd already taken. It was clean and readable. "We're good," he said.

When the clock hit zero, the screen faded first to black, then to the home screen for the Library.

"I guess that's it," Misty said, staring at the monitor. "At least we know the message *was* a password."

"Yeah, but to what?" He looked around and noticed that Ms. Barnes was heading their way again.

"Everything okay?" she asked.

"Worked fine," he said. "We just finished up."

"Great. Well, enjoy your day."

Quinn and Misty rendezvoused with Daeng and Howard back at the car.

After everyone was in the vehicle, Daeng said, "Well?"

"It worked. Gave us an address," Quinn said.

"An address to where?"

“Good question.”

Quinn looked at the photo he’d taken, memorized the street and number, then entered them into the search box of his map app. He expected to get at least half a dozen matches across the country, but only three choices popped up. All were on the East Coast—one in Maine, another in New Hampshire, and a third only a few miles away.

“Arlington,” he told Howard.

CHAPTER TWELVE

SAN FRANCISCO, CALIFORNIA

AS WAS HER habit, Helen Cho arrived at her office at five thirty a.m. That was a price she was happy to pay for being able to run her various organizations from the West Coast instead of back in New York or DC.

The East Coast had hurricanes and blizzards and humidity. San Francisco had earthquakes—though not nearly as often as people living elsewhere thought—and that was about it. She didn't mind a good ground shake anyway. She'd been born in Los Angeles and had lived through more than her share of tumblers.

Between six and six thirty, while she was invariably on a call to someone in the CIA, NSA, FBI, or the Pentagon, her assistant David—who was not a fan of early mornings—would bring in hard copies of reports that had come in overnight, and place them on her desk. If she was on a conference call that only needed her presence but not her attention, she would begin perusing them. Otherwise she would wait until the call had ended.

The call this morning had been an example of the latter, a one-on-one with an assistant director at Langley. After she hung up, she buzzed David to bring her a fresh cup of coffee, and began sorting through the pile.

The first document was a status report on field operations being run directly out of her San Francisco office. Everything seemed to be going smoothly. Next up was a lengthy breakdown of a mission that had finished up two days prior. There had been a couple problems on this one, but it had all worked out in the end. This was followed by reports on wiretapped conversations, shadowing operations, and asset acquisitions.

Near the bottom was a document from O & O. The DC security agency was a recent addition to her responsibilities. For years it had been run semiautonomously, which, it seemed, turned out to be a problem. The powers that be within Homeland Security suspected the agency of flagrant abuse of both authority and budget, but they needed proof, and had installed Helen to evaluate and clean up any messes. It wasn't a task she'd been thrilled to undertake, but she also knew no one could do it better than she. So far, her biggest problem had been getting everyone at O & O to understand *she* was the one in charge.

As she read the report, her face hardened in anger. Here was another example of information coming to her long after it should have. According to the document, yesterday someone had broken into an apartment in Georgetown, and one of O & O's agents had been shot trying to detain one of the intruders. Thankfully the wound had not been life threatening, but that didn't matter. She should have been informed immediately.

Her anger almost caused her to miss the most important detail, one that resonated with her both professionally and personally—the address of the break-in.

I must be remembering incorrectly.

She checked her private contact list, glad she had not deleted the entry she was looking for. Nope, she hadn't remembered wrong. The apartment that had been broken into—the apartment O & O had been hired to watch, for some reason—belonged to Peter.

Reading on, she saw that a tip had later come in that the intruders were using a Virginia safe house, but after another team had been dispatched to check, it turned out that though someone *had* been at the house, he or she or they were no longer there.

She put the file aside and buzzed David. "These reports are all from this morning?"

"Yes, ma'am."

"You're sure none of these came in yesterday."

"No, ma'am. They were all from this morning."

"Get me Stone at O & O." Gregory Stone was O & O's managing director, and the biggest pain in the ass of the bunch.

Thirty seconds later, David called. "I have Mr. Stone for you."

As soon as he hung up, Stone was on the line.

"Gregory, what the hell is going on over there?" Helen asked.

"Good morning to you, too, Helen."

"I asked you a question."

"I'm afraid you'll have to be a bit more specific."

"I just read the report about the apartment break-in yesterday. The one where one of your men got his fingers blown off? How come I'm just hearing about this now?"

"Let me pull up the info," Stone said, sounding as if he were doing her a big favor. She could hear him typing. "I have it here. The client requested temporary retention of the information."

This was another of O & O's annoying business practices. Some clients had been granted right-of-retention privileges they could invoke anytime they felt it necessary. When that happened, no one but the client would receive updates for the first twelve to twenty-four hours, depending on the operation. Helen had already sent a directive rescinding the rule, but apparently Stone had ignored it.

"I don't care *what* the client requested. The retention rule is no longer valid and you know it."

"This is a grandfathered client. Our hands were tied."

She bit back a response, knowing things could spiral into a tangential conversation that would distract her from finding out more about what had happened at Peter's place. After giving herself a moment to calm down, she opened the O & O client database and said, “Who’s the client?”

“Is there something specific you’re trying to find out? Maybe I could—”

“Yes. I *specifically* want to know who the client is.”

“If you’re unhappy with how things are—”

“Dammit, Gregory! Give me the code!”

Stone read her the client code.

Helen typed it in and the client name popped onto her screen almost instantly.

DARVOT CONSULTING

Is this some kind of joke? she thought, staring at her screen.

Darvot was as gray an organization as one could get. More than a few stories had circulated through the legitimate intelligence community about the lengths Kyle Morten, president and CEO of Darvot, and his dog Griffin would go to in helping their clients. Unfortunately, they were good at covering their tracks so it was all rumor, but Helen knew they were dirty, and Helen hated dirty.

She’d thought she’d seen it all from O & O, but this had to be the biggest example of the organization’s incompetence. No proper agency would even answer Darvot’s phone calls, and here O & O was doing potential wet work for them.

Dear God.

“Helen?” Stone said. “Helen, are you still there?”

She needed to dig into this properly so that none of it blew up in her or her superiors’ faces. She bit back the riot act she wanted to read him and said, “I’ll call you back.”

CHAPTER THIRTEEN

ARLINGTON, VIRGINIA

THE ADDRESS TURNED out to be for a place called Wysocki Self-Storage in a mixed-use neighborhood. The facility consisted of several two-story buildings, some with roll-up doors along the outside, and some that Quinn guessed were entered through hallways running down the middle of the structures. There was a small office located right on the corner, with a counter inside where two employees were assisting customers.

Quinn pulled out his phone and looked at the instructions that had accompanied the address. The first two items read:

1. Bldg 6
2. 72591

He took a second look at the storage place. Painted on the side of each building was a number. The one directly across from where they were parked was labeled 2, and the building next to it 3.

"Around the corner," he said.

Howard pulled away from the curb. As they turned, the sides of three more buildings came into view. Number 4 was first, then 5, and finally 6.

Quinn pointed at a spot opposite 6. "Park there."

Howard did as instructed.

Like the other buildings that made up Wysocki Self-Storage, number 6 had an access door off the street, with a small square box mounted on the wall next to it.

"Steve, stay here and keep an eye on that door." He nodded across the street at 6's entrance. "If anyone other than us goes through it, call."

"Got it," Howard said.

"Daeng, Misty, let's go."

The square box by the door was exactly what Quinn had expected—a security keypad. He consulted his phone again, and tapped in 7-2-5-9-1.

When he heard the buzz of the lock releasing, he pulled the door open. The inside also turned out to be what he'd thought—a wide hallway traveling the length of the building, lined with equally spaced doors. Behind each would be a storage locker.

"Which one?" Misty asked.

Quinn checked the photo.

3. 6-117

He looked up. The door on the right was marked 6-130, and on the left 6-129.

"Should be down about halfway. We're looking for one seventeen."

They found the unit just shy of the middle. The door was secured by a padlock, with six side-by-side tumblers on the bottom where the combination would be input.

4. 318037

Quinn thumbed the numbers into place and pulled, thinking the door should now be unlocked. But instead of the shackle disengaging from the body, a portion of the lock's outer skin slid open, exposing a surface of black glass. He immediately knew what it was.

"Place your thumb on it," Quinn told Misty.

She hesitantly pressed her thumb against the surface.

There was a *thunk* from inside the door.

Quinn pulled the lock again. Though the lock remained fastened, the whole door and frame swung out an inch. He pulled until the opening was wide enough for them to get a look inside.

The locker space was underutilized—about a dozen boxes stacked toward the back and that was it. Peter could have easily gotten away with a locker a quarter of the size. Hanging in the middle of the room was a light fixture, but Quinn didn't see any way to turn it on.

"What's the next instruction?" Misty asked.

"The combo for the lock was the last one," Quinn said.

She looked around dubiously. "So this is what he wanted us to find?"

"Apparently."

While Daeng remained in the hallway, Quinn and Misty moved into the locker to see what was in the boxes.

The first three they opened were full of books and old magazines.

"My God, do you think there's something hidden in one of these?" Misty asked. "That'll take us forever to go through."

"Let's check all the boxes first, then we can decide what to do next."

Most of those remaining also held books, while the last few contained Tupperware containers, plastic cups, and disposable plates.

"I don't get it," Misty said after they finished. "Why would he want us to come here? This is all garbage."

It wasn't quite garbage, but Quinn understood her frustration. Peter must've had some other reason for leading them here. Perhaps whatever he'd wanted them to find was already gone. Or maybe, because of the dim light, they were missing something.

He pulled out his phone and called Howard.

"Everything all right?" Howard asked.

"Do you have a flashlight in your car?"

"Sure."

"Can you meet Daeng at the door with it?"

"On my way."

Ninety seconds later, Quinn had the flashlight in his hand. He took a quick look through each of the boxes again before panning the light slowly around the rest of the space.

At first, he thought the line on the floor had been created in the dust as they'd moved the boxes around. But it was a little too perfect and a little too long. He knelt down and pushed a box of plastic cups out of the way.

Not dust at all.

A cut in the concrete.

"Help me with these," he said.

Once the boxes were out of the way, there was no missing the perfectly cut square in the floor. He noticed a small divot at one end and slipped a finger inside. Grabbing on to a lip, he pulled, but the square didn't move.

Quinn leaned back and thought for a moment. If this was the opening to a secret storage place, then Peter would probably have been concerned about someone walking down the hallway and seeing it open.

"Daeng, get in here," he said. "And shut the door."

Two things happened the moment the door clicked shut. First, Quinn could feel that the hatch was suddenly free to move. And second, the light came on.

"Would have been nice if that little bit of information had been included in the instructions," Daeng said, glancing up at the bulb.

"No kidding," Quinn agreed as he pulled up the hatch.

Daeng moved through the rearranged boxes to join them. As soon as he saw the hole, he said, "Whoa."

Quinn pointed the flashlight into the opening. This was no mere extra storage space. This was some kind of tunnel. The vertical shaft went down fifteen feet, then appeared to run off to the left, out of sight. To get there, a metal ladder had been built into the side of the shaft.

"I'll go first," he said. "If everything's all right, you guys follow me."

He lowered himself into the hole. As soon as his feet

touched the ground, a row of lights came on, revealing a tunnel extending to the side.

"So?" Daeng called down.

"Passageway. High enough to stand."

"Where's it go?"

"Not sure yet. Can't see the end. I'll be right back."

The arching tunnel was six and a half feet tall at its apex, and no more than four feet wide. Even sticking to the center, Quinn couldn't help feeling the urge to duck as he made his way along. At what he guessed was about seventy-five feet in, the tunnel took a hard turn to the left. Another fifty feet ahead, he came to a door.

This one had no lock, which wasn't particularly surprising given all the security before this point. On the other side of the door was a room outfitted with monitors, a large desk, computer keyboard and trackpad, half-sized refrigerator, and a couch. There were two other doors. One led into a bathroom, and the other into a space just large enough for the mattress that filled it.

Quite a little hideaway.

He returned to the other end of the tunnel and called up, "Come on down."

"I don't know," Misty said. "I could wait here."

"Trust me. You're going to want to see this."

With obvious reluctance, she crawled down the ladder. Once she reached the tunnel floor, Daeng followed, and Quinn led them back to the room. Misty was barely past the threshold when she gasped in surprise.

"Damn, Peter," she said. "Why didn't you tell me about this place?"

"Nice," Daeng said as he entered. "An evil lair."

Misty whipped around. "Peter was *not* evil."

"Just a joke," Daeng said.

"Not a very good one." She paused, gathering herself. "I'm sorry. I know that's not what you meant."

In typical Daeng fashion, he shrugged and said, "No problem."

The desk ran the length of the wall opposite the door.

Underneath were cabinets, and an open space in the middle for whoever sat in the chair in front of the keyboard. On the wall in front of the desk were six, identically sized monitors broken up into two rows of three.

Quinn reached out and touched the space bar on the wireless keyboard. Immediately he could hear the whir of a computer somewhere under the desk. After a short delay, the center screen on the bottom row turned on. It remained gray for several seconds, an animated dial in the middle twirling as the computer woke itself up. Finally, the dial was replaced by a rectangular text box. At the left end of the box was a blinking cursor.

"One guess what we should type in there," Daeng said.

Quinn pulled out the chair. "Misty?"

After she was seated, Quinn placed the index card from Peter next to the keyboard. Misty took a deep breath and began to type. The text box, however, remained empty.

"Try it again," Quinn said.

Misty input the password. "It's not working," she said. "Why isn't it working?"

Quinn looked at the keyboard. It had been working fine just moments ago when he'd woken the computer. He picked it up and turned it over—and revealed a small glass square inset in the desk. Another scanner, he realized.

"Try your thumb on the glass," he instructed Misty.

The instant she pressed her thumb down, the scanner lit up.

When the light dimmed again, Quinn said, "Now try the password again."

This time each keystroke appeared in the text box. When she finished, the screen went black for a moment before an image of Peter appeared, staring out at them.

"Hello, Misty," Peter said. "If you're here we both know what that means. But let's face it—it was bound to happen at some point. There is no one I trust more than you. That's why I had to bring you here. I need you to do one last thing for me. Clean up what I've left behind and destroy any physical information that I've kept here. Knowing you, you grabbed the files from my safe at the apartment when you found the note with the code I left you."

Note he *left*? Quinn thought. He hadn't left the note—he'd mailed it. Maybe he'd decided to change the procedure.

"If you did, great," Peter went on. "You can add them to the stuff here. If not, you'll need to go back and destroy them. The townhouse is another matter. I may or may not have left sensitive information there. If I did, it'll be in the safe, so once you finish the other tasks, please go there and check. I also have several other safe houses spread around the district. You'll find a list in the townhouse safe. At the time of this recording, none of them contains anything important, and I don't foresee that changing. But, as time permits, I would appreciate it if you would check each. You needn't worry about any of my digital information. That's already being taken care of."

Quinn unconsciously leaned forward, tensing.

"The archive at the Library of Congress began its wipe procedure the moment you logged off after entering the code I gave you. The computers at the townhouse began their purge when this video started. And the computer here, well, we'll get to that in a minute."

Something wasn't right, Quinn thought. Peter shouldn't be instructing them on a personal erase job, he should be telling them why he thought someone was going to kill him, right? That's what Quinn had been expecting.

"Okay, this is how I'd like you to destroy the items here. There's a safe located along the back wall behind the refrigerator. The wall there is a false panel. Push once on the top, twice on the bottom, and it will pop out. The combination is simple this time. It's your birthday. Gather everything from inside and put them on the desk. That's all you need to do."

Quinn looked over at Misty, wondering if she was as confused as he was, but she was staring rapt at the monitor, hanging on Peter's every word.

"Misty, I realize I wasn't the easiest person to work with, and I didn't tell you nearly enough how much I appreciated your help. But know that I did, and that I would have failed long ago without you."

That was another odd thing. The video seemed directed solely at Misty. So why had Peter wanted Quinn there, too? Misty wouldn't have needed Quinn to help her get rid of a few files. Granted, things hadn't exactly been normal when they'd visited the apartment, but Peter couldn't have known Misty would be in physical danger.

"I apologize for not being a better boss, but, well, I can't be someone I'm not. And I definitely can't change anything now. I'm sure you understand and forgive me. You always did."

Quinn snatched up the index card and read it again.

Y7(29g)85KL/24

I need your help.

Call Quinn. A last assignment. For both of you.

He stared at the last words. *For both of you.*

"Okay," Peter said. "Enough of the sentimental crap, huh? Now this part is very important. You're going to have to work fast, because in exactly ten minutes, this room will turn into an inferno."

Quinn jerked his head up, his gaze shooting back to the image of Peter.

"So as soon as the files are on the desk, get out of here, but remember to seal all the doors behind you so that the fire is contained to this space."

What the hell, Peter? Quinn thought. He looked down at the card again and silently mouthed the words. "For both of you. For *both* of you."

"That's all you have to do," Peter continued. "You can forget about this place after that. The rent is paid for years, so chances are no one will discover the bunker until then. When they do, it will only lead to questions with no answers."

"For both of you." This time the words slipped out of Quinn's mouth in a whisper as he realized what they must mean.

"Thank you, Misty," Peter said. "Now go—"

Quinn lunged and slapped his thumb down on the scanner. The video of Peter froze and then went black as the glass scanner lit up.

"What are you doing?" Misty asked. Her water-filled eyes stared at him in confusion and hurt. "Why did you stop it?"

It was Peter who answered as he once again appeared on the screen. Only this wasn't the same Peter from moments before. The previous video had been shot in that very room, but the new one had been taped in what looked like Peter's apartment. His clothes were different, too, and he looked more tired and…angrier.

"So you both made it," Peter said. "Thank you. I don't know how much of the other video played before you activated this one, so excuse me if some of what I say is a repeat. You have ten minutes to get out before this place is incinerated." He then gave instructions similar to those from before about the items in the safe. "There is one thing in there, though, that I want you to hold on to. This." He raised a dark-stained wooden box. It was about four inches square and an inch high. As he set it back down, he began speaking again. "We'll get to what's inside in a minute." He paused and frowned. "The fact that you're watching this means that apparently my efforts have failed. I've been poking around in something others would rather I leave alone. Now I'm asking you to poke around in it, too. You can decline. I'll never know, and if that's your decision, I understand. I'm hoping it won't be, though." He leaned toward the camera, his gaze intensifying. "A tragic injustice was done. It can never be righted, but it can be avenged. Unless I died from an obvious accident or from verifiable natural causes, you should assume that those behind this…event are responsible for my death. Hell, even if my death certificate claims I did die from an accident or natural causes, it could have been staged by these assholes. They are capable, and they have done similar things before. You'll see what I mean when you go through the file." He paused. "We should talk about that." He lifted the box into frame again. "In here you'll find the file with everything I've collected to date. It's encrypted using Hansell IV. The protocol is base seven. I need you to come at this with fresh eyes, so I'll let you read the file without any commentary from me. The thing the file can't tell you is the name or names of those I've been hunting. I'm close, but I haven't been able to uncover that yet. You have a huge advantage I didn't. My death." An ironic smile. "Find out who killed me and you'll find out who I've been looking for." He tilted back away from the camera. "Time for you two to get out of there. The clock's ticking. And don't forget to close the doors on your way out."

The screen went dark.

None of them moved, their eyes still glued to the monitor. It was Daeng who finally broke the spell.

"Maybe we should think about getting out of here."

Quinn nodded, his gaze lingering a moment longer on the screen before he turned and darted across the room.

The small refrigerator was easy enough to move out of the way, and the wall panel came off like Peter had described. With the safe exposed, Quinn said to Misty, "What's your birthday?"

He heard her chair scrape across the floor as she scooted it back, then her steps as she approached.

"Can I open it?" she asked, kneeling next to him.

Leaning out of the way, he said, "Go ahead."

She input a series of numbers, turned the safe's handle, and opened the door. Most of the inside was taken up with files and large manila envelopes, while the wooden box was sitting on its end, squeezed between the edge of the files and the safe wall. Quinn reached in and pulled it out. Given its light weight, he figured it must contain only a thumb drive or memory stick. Resisting the urge to open it, he slipped it snuggly into his coat pocket and stood up.

Misty, in the meantime, had started pulling out the files and envelopes.

"No," Quinn said. "It's time to go."

She shot him a disapproving look. "Peter *said* put them on the desk. So that's what I'm going to do."

"I'll do it," he said, then looked at Daeng. "Get her out of here."

"Come on," Daeng said, moving over to help her up.

She pulled back from his outstretched hand. "No. I'm fine. I can take care of it."

"Misty, go," Quinn said. "Now."

Together the two men lifted her to her feet.

"I'll take care of it," Quinn told her. "I promise."

Reluctantly, she allowed Daeng to lead her out of the room. Quinn started grabbing files and moving them over to the desk. He wondered for a moment if maybe they should take the files with them, but he knew Peter would have said something if there were something important inside they could use.

Once the files and envelopes were all piled where Peter had wanted them, Quinn decided to do a quick search in case they had missed something. He had just flipped over the mattress in the second room when the overhead lights started to flash on and off. There was no mistaking their meaning.

He ran back through the main room and out the door, stopping long enough to shut it before heading down the tunnel.

He was ten feet from the stairs when the lights flashed twice, then cut out completely.

"Quinn! Hurry!" Misty yelled down from the storage locker.

In the tunnel behind him, Quinn could hear a muffled growing roar, and knew Peter's self-destruct system had kicked in. He sprinted the rest of the way to the ladder and scrambled up, making it almost to the hatch before the heat reached him.

Daeng extended a hand to him. "Take it!"

Quinn grabbed it and let Daeng yank him up to the safety of the locker. The moment he rolled out of the way, Daeng shoved the hatch down until it snapped in place.

Quinn lay on the floor, panting. "That was…*not* ten…minutes," he growled between breaths.

"It was, if you take it from when the first video said it

was starting," Daeng said.

Quinn pushed himself up, annoyed. "Well, Peter certainly didn't make *that* clear, did he?"

"No, my friend, he did not."

"You're all right, though, right?" Misty asked.

"Yeah. I'm fine."

"Good." She punched him in the arm.

"Hey, what's that for?"

Glaring at him, nostrils flaring, she said, "You could have gotten killed!"

"You were the one who wanted to stay," he said.

"It shouldn't have taken that long."

"I wanted to make sure we didn't miss anything, so I took a quick look around."

"Well?" Daeng asked. "Did we?"

Quinn shook his head. "No."

Misty hit him again.

CHAPTER **FOURTEEN**

ZURICH, SWITZERLAND

THE MEETING WAS held at the Hotel de Grasse, District 1, in an out-of-the-way room on the third floor. Morten had used the location multiple times, the hotel's underground parking garage and private elevator that exited directly across from the meeting room perfect for maintaining his clients' anonymity.

While a table and chairs were at one end of the room, Morten, as always, chose to use the sitting area at the other end. He was sitting in a blue, cloth-covered chair while his client—his *potential* client—was sitting on the matching couch.

This was their second meeting. The first had been four days earlier in Berlin. A meet-and-greet set up by the client's chief of staff. This second meeting was the proof-of-concept meeting, where Morten would explain exactly what Darvot Consulting could do for the client.

"This is what I mean," Morten said.

From inside his briefcase, he pulled out an eight-by-ten photograph.

"I'm not sure I want to see that," the man said.

"Oh, I'm sure you will."

Morten laid it on the coffee table. The picture showed two people in mid-copulation.

Despite his earlier protest, the man leaned forward and

picked it up. "Is that…"

"Yes." The male half of the couple in the photo was the popular sitting parliament member against whom Morten's potential client was running in an upcoming election.

"That's not his wife."

"It most decidedly is not," Morten agreed. "She's the daughter of one of his constituents."

The man was having a hard time hiding his revulsion. "How old is she?"

"Seventeen."

Morten reached over and plucked the picture back.

"So what?" the man said. "You propose to release that? Is that the idea?"

Morten looked at the picture for a moment before putting it back in his briefcase. "What would that do? Yes, it might win you the election, but there would be a very good chance your own credibility would be undermined. People would assume you had something to do with releasing the picture. At best you'd last no more than one term. Is that what you want?"

"Of course not. Then what are you proposing?"

Morten smiled. "Your opponent would be approached. A quiet meeting, much like this one. He will learn of the pictures, and trust me, there are more than just the single shot. In fact, there's more than just this one girl. He will then be given a choice. He will either do as we say, or the pictures will be released."

"But you said if the pictures are released, I'll get the blame."

"Not if they're released *after* the election. He'll be forced to resign and a special election will be held, where you will then be the favorite."

"And if he takes the deal?"

"Then he'll throw the election for us."

"How?"

"This is where you need to trust me. This is not the first time I've done this."

By the time Morten headed back upstairs to his room, the

man had moved from potential client to paying client. There had never really been any doubt. Morten had been doing this for a long time, and knew exactly how to hook the greedy. At least it wasn't like the early years, when he had to be a little more involved in the execution of jobs. Now his focus was almost entirely on cultivating new business, instead of leaking stories or identifying bodies at an "accident" scene, or luring targets to faux meetings that would put them in the wrong place at the wrong time.

Of course, there were a few exceptions, like having to worry about old jobs that seemed to have risen from the dead.

As soon as he entered his suite, he activated the electronic bug jammer, and put in a call to his enforcer.

"So?" he asked.

"Nothing new," Griffin replied.

"What do you mean, nothing?"

"Forensics swept the apartment, but whoever was there left no fingerprints."

"Cameras?"

"Several security cameras were identified in the area, but none had a good angle."

Morten's jaw tensed. "Anything more on the house in Virginia?"

"Not yet," Griffin said. "I'm going to call them as soon as we finish, and have them do a forensic check there also."

"If O & O can't come up with anything, pull the job and do it yourself."

"Exactly what I was planning."

"Good," Morten said.

He hung up, grabbed the bottle of thirty-year-old Macallan whisky from the bar, and poured a generous amount into a tumbler. He took a drink.

Old. Goddamn. Jobs.

This one in particular shouldn't have been a problem anymore. Peter was dead. They'd made that happen. *Morten* had made that happen. And with the son of a bitch's death, that should have been it. No more chances of exposure.

Done. Finished. Completed.

Morten took another drink. As the whisky trickled down his throat, he could finally feel his body calming, and his thoughts becoming more reasonable.

There was no way to know if the people who'd been in Peter's apartment knew anything even loosely connected to Morten or his boss. Peter had been involved in a multitude of things over the years, all potential reasons for why someone would've wanted a look inside his flat.

Yes, Morten needed to stay vigilant, but he didn't need to get worked up. This was merely another project. Find the trio, figure out why they were there, then, no matter the reason, eliminate them.

Keep it simple. Get it done.

He smiled as he raised the glass back to his lips.

CHAPTER
FIFTEEN

VIRGINIA

WITHIN MINUTES OF driving away from the storage facility, Misty was slumped against the back door of Howard's car, staring out the window. The chaos of the past twenty-four hours—twice being hunted by armed assault teams, seeing Peter again, the near immolation in the bunker—had clearly taken its toll on her.

Quinn tried to get her to talk, but it was as if she didn't even hear him. Turning to Howard, he said, "Any place around here to get a room? Doesn't have to be flashy."

Howard thought for a moment before he said, "Yeah, I know a good place."

He drove them to the Homestead Studio Suites just north of the tollway, and arranged for a room in the back wing. Once inside, Misty immediately lay down on the bed and closed her eyes. The others settled into the sitting area by the window, where Quinn pulled the wooden box out of his pocket.

"So that's it, huh?" Howard asked.

Quinn turned the box, taking a good look at it for the first time. The lid was hinged and clasped shut. Carved across the top were two rows of vines paralleling the edge. More vines were carved into the sides, while the bottom was smooth and unadorned.

Quinn flipped the clasp and opened the lid. Almost the

entire interior was taken up by black packing foam, like the kind used in cases that carried electronics and musical instruments. Cut in the very center was a small round hole, and in that hole a chrome metal cylinder.

He pulled it out. It was no more than a half-inch long, and flat on each end.

"That doesn't look like a thumb drive to me," Daeng said.

"No," Quinn said. He looked closely at the top and saw it was a movable lid, pinned at the edge. "It's a canister."

Gently, he moved the top away so he could look inside. Tucked within the cylinder was a roll of something that looked like thin plastic. He turned the canister over, and the roll fell easily into his palm.

"What is it?" Daeng asked.

Quinn held it out so the other two could see it. "Microfilm."

"Microfilm? That's kind of old school, isn't it?"

"Very."

Quinn twisted the roll around, examining it. There were no signs of age, and it felt flexible between his fingers. Still wary that it might be a relic from Peter's past, he carefully took hold of the end and unrolled the first inch. It felt strong and gave no sign it might break, so he held it up to the light. All he saw was black, so he unspooled another inch and raised it again. There were brighter frames now, with little black squiggles running through them.

Words, he guessed. Documents or notes.

Instead of unrolling only another inch, he kept going until the entire strip was open. More documents. Then frames with color. Pictures, maybe? He couldn't make out anything.

He lowered the film. "Either of you have glasses? Reading? Prescription? Anything?"

Daeng and Howard shook their heads.

"I do," Misty said, raising her head off the bed. Apparently she hadn't been asleep, as he'd thought. "Reading glasses. They're in my purse." She started to sit up, then stopped and closed her eyes, her shoulders drooping. "Which is under the seat in my car."

Her car was still parked near Peter's place.

"I think we passed a Target store not far from here," Daeng said.

Quinn put the film back in the canister. "Can I borrow your keys?" he asked Howard.

"Of course." Howard handed them to Quinn. "You want some company?"

"No, you two stay here." Though he didn't expect another group of armed men to break into their hotel room, there was no sense in taking chances, and two watching over Misty was better than one.

As he headed toward the door, Misty swung her legs off the bed and stood up. "Is there something I can do? Anything?"

He stopped. "The most important thing you can do right now is rest."

"I can't sleep. I just keep thinking about Peter and the video." She looked lost, helpless. "Can I see what you found?"

"Sure." He handed her the metal canister.

She opened the top but didn't dump out the film. "Just like Peter. There were certain things he liked physical copies of." She handed the cylinder back, her eyes half full of tears.

Quinn wanted to comfort her, but he couldn't find the correct words, so he said, "I won't be long," and left.

Daeng had been right. There was a Target right around the corner. Instead of hunting for reading glasses, Quinn went directly to the office supply area and found a magnifying glass. He pulled out the microfilm and did a quick test. The glass blew up the images enough so that if the text had been readable, he should've been able to make it out. Unfortunately, it was illegible. What he saw were lines made up of tiny squares—some alone, some connected only at their corners, some side by side. It was like they wanted to be text but weren't.

He looked around to make sure he was still alone before unrolling more of the film. When he reached one of the color frames, he checked it. More squares, clearly not randomly sequenced, but impossible to decipher.

Peter had warned that the information would be encrypted, but Quinn had hoped he could comprehend *something.*

He rerolled the film, put it back into the canister, and returned the magnifying glass to where he'd found it. He would have to figure out a way to get the frames digitized so he could then have them decoded.

On his way out, he made a quick stop in the drugs section and picked up a bottle of Tylenol PM, thinking maybe it would help Misty get some sleep. At the checkout counter, the cashier had just started to ring him up when his phone vibrated. He pulled it out and was surprised the call was from Nate.

"Seven seventy-eight," the clerk said.

Quinn raised his phone to his ear. "Nate?"

"You're going to want to head back," Nate said.

"What happened? Is there a problem?"

"Sir," the cashier said. "Seven seventy-eight."

"Not a problem," Nate said. "But…"

"What?" Quinn asked as he fished a twenty out of his pocket and handed it to the cashier.

"Orlando. She just woke up."

For half a second, the world disappeared.

Awake?

As happy as the news was, Quinn was also angry. He had wanted to be there. Needed to be there. Needed to be the first thing she saw.

"Excuse me, sir."

Quinn snapped back.

The cashier was holding out his hand. "Your change?"

"Oh, thanks."

Quinn grabbed the change and the bag holding the pills, and headed for the door.

"When did this happen?" he asked Nate.

"Five minutes ago."

"Did…did she ask for me?"

"She hasn't said anything yet."

Why not? Quinn wondered. Was there something wrong? Had something affected her speech? Or worse, her mind?

But he didn't ask. The only thing important now was getting back to her side.

"Tell her I'm on my way."

AT THE CLIENT'S request, Central dispatched a second forensics team to the house in Arlington Ridge. He was sure it was a waste of time, but the client was insistent, and it wasn't Central's place to question. What *was* Central's place was going above and beyond for clients whenever feasible. In other words, if you had people sitting around doing nothing, and there was an angle on a client's job that could get done, do it. Director Stone always said showing the client they were willing to go the extra mile was a good way to make sure the client used O & O again.

As Central went over the reports from the previous day, he had noted a hole in one of their operations pertaining to this client. The assignment in question was the forensic follow-up at the Georgetown apartment. While the apartment itself had been thoroughly checked and deemed clean, the area around the building had been neglected.

Though unlikely, it was possible the intruders had left clues to their identities outside during the chases. There was also the matter of transportation. While the group had left on foot, it was not known how they had arrived. Sure, if they *had* driven there, chances were the vehicle would have been retrieved by now, but it was something worth checking.

And Central did have a two-man recon team available.

He mulled it over for less than a minute, but could think of no serious argument against doing it. So he located Teig's number on his computer and clicked CONNECT.

"Hello?"

"Teig? This is Central. I have an assignment for you."

"SHE'S AWAKE," QUINN said as he reentered the hotel room.

Misty apparently had decided not to lie back down, and had joined Daeng and Howard in the sitting area. "Orlando?" she asked.

Quinn nodded.

"When?" Daeng said.

"Within the last half hour. I…I've got to go."

"Of course. Do you want me to come with you or stay?"

Quinn thought for a moment. "I'd like you to stay until we're sure things have calmed down here, if you don't mind."

"I don't mind at all."

Quinn looked at Howard. "Is there any safe place, not connected to the business, where you all could hole up for a while?"

Howard took a moment to consider the question. "I have a friend who has a cabin in the forest near the border with West Virginia. As far as I know, he's not using it right now."

"And he's not in our world?

"Not even close."

"Good. You can drop me at the airport on the way."

"Wait," Misty said. "What about my car? My purse?"

Quinn had forgotten about the car. Before he could come up with an answer, Howard said, "We could swing by there. Probably a good idea to move it out of the neighborhood just in case, don't you think?"

Quinn knew it was risky, but leaving Misty's car near Peter's place for so long wasn't good, either. "Drop me at the airport first, then go for the car. If you spot *anything* unusual, get the hell out of there."

CHAPTER SIXTEEN

WASHINGTON, DC

"CENTRAL, WE ARE now on site," Teig reported as Holt, his recon team partner, turned their car onto the calm Georgetown street.

"Copy that, Team Seven," Central replied.

Teig set the radio down and started checking addresses. "That's it." He pointed at a building a quarter block away.

Holt pulled the sedan into an open spot. "What first?" he asked as he turned off the engine.

"Check around the building. Central said there should be a pass-through on the left side that'll take us to the alley in back. After that, we'll check the street."

"Works for me."

"HOW DO YOU want to do this?" Howard asked Daeng as they reached Georgetown.

"Once we turn onto the street, keep it slow and steady so we can scope things out. If it looks good when we reach Misty's car, then we'll stop. If not, keep going."

"Sounds good."

Daeng turned so he could see Misty in the backseat. "Let me have your keys."

"Why?"

"So I can drive your car."

"I can do it."

"I'm sure you can, but I think it would be better if I did."

Reluctantly, she handed her keys to him. "The driver's door can be tricky. My car is old so it doesn't have keyless entry, and the lock sticks."

"No problem."

A few minutes later, they turned onto Peter's street. Like the previous day, cars were parked up and down both sides, but since it was still the middle of the workday, plenty of spots were available. Howard kept the speed of his BMW down as they scanned for trouble.

Daeng saw five people total—seven if you included the occupants of the two strollers a couple women were pushing. He worked his way from one person to the next, quickly assessing and then dismissing them as threats. He sensed that all five either lived on the block or worked there in some kind of domestic function—nannies, most likely.

"Anything on your side?" Howard asked.

"Not yet," Daeng said.

"How do things look to you?" Howard asked Misty.

"I don't know," she replied. "Everything looks normal."

As they continued forward, Peter's building came into view. It looked quiet, no one out front, just a man with another stroller a few buildings down, and a woman walking a small dog a dozen feet behind the man.

"There's my car," Misty said, pointing at her Camry. It was parked on Peter's side of the street, right where they'd left it the day before, and looked untouched.

"What do you think?" Howard asked.

Daeng looked around. The street seemed quiet enough. "Okay. Let's do it."

THERE WAS NOTHING of interest along the side of the building, and as far as Teig could tell, the alley was also a bust. Central had told him he might not find anything, but that did little to ease Teig's annoyance. He was a goal-oriented person, so when assigned a task, he felt a hell of a lot better when he accomplished it.

"Let's go back to the street," he said. "Central wanted

photos of the plates on all the cars parked around here."

"How far do we go?" Holt asked.

"Both sides of the street, a block each way. I think that should do it."

THERE WAS AN empty spot at the curb two cars in front of Misty's. Howard drove to the end of the block, made a U-turn, and then drove back and eased his sedan into the spot.

Daeng once more scanned the street in both directions.

Nothing new. Nothing unusual.

He opened the door and hopped out, phone in hand. Walking casually along the road, he looked down at the cell's screen like he was checking e-mail or texts. Just another busy local doing what everyone else did.

He didn't look up again until he was only a few feet from the Camry. He quickly examined the door, checking for any signs that someone had tried to break in—scratches around the lock, loose weather stripping at the base of the window—but all looked good.

He slipped Misty's key into the lock, but it only turned a quarter of the way. He jiggled it, thinking that would loosen it up, but it would go no farther.

Fine, he thought. He'd get in on the passenger side. But when he tried turning the key to extract it, it wouldn't come back out, either.

Behind him, he heard a car door open, and looked over to see Misty heading in his direction.

"I told you it was tricky," she whispered as she walked up.

She jiggled the key until it turned all the way and the door opened. "There you go," she said, taking a step back.

But Daeng barely heard her. His attention was focused on Peter's building, where two men in suits looking very much like the ones from yesterday had just emerged from the side access way.

"Get in the car," he said.

"What?"

"Get in. Now. And move over to the passenger side. I'm

driving."

He glanced over at the BMW, and shared a quick look with Howard through the side-view mirror. Daeng could tell Howard had seen the men, too.

"Go," he mouthed, and climbed into the driver's seat of the Camry.

TEIG AND HOLT walked over to the cars parked directly in front of the apartment building.

"You take this side of the street. I'll take the other," Teig said. "Frame it so you get the license plate and a partial of the car so that they can see make and color."

"All right."

Teig stepped between the bumpers of the two closest cars, planning on crossing to the opposite side, but paused when he noticed the BMW heading in his direction. By the way the car was angling onto the road, Teig was pretty sure it had pulled out of a spot at the curb. Best to get a picture of it.

When the BMW neared, he raised his phone to take the shot. That's when he noticed the second car pull out of a parking spot.

This one a Toyota Camry.

DAENG WANTED TO pull a quick U-turn and head in the other direction, but the parked cars on the other side made the street too narrow. They had no choice but to drive by the men in front of Peter's building.

As they pulled away from the curb, Misty gasped.

"That man. Is he—"

"Act like you live here," Daeng told her.

One of the men Daeng had seen was now standing between two parked cars, pointing his phone at Howard's BMW. There was no doubt in Daeng's mind he was taking a picture.

Daeng could feel Misty's tension across the divide between their seats. "It's going to be okay," he said.

She made no reply.

As soon as Howard passed Peter's building, the man

standing on the street turned his phone toward the Camry.

"Keep it casual," Daeng said, his lips barely moving. "Make him think this is our neighborhood."

He chanced a quick look at her, and knew they were in trouble. Her forced smile screamed, "I'm hiding something."

When they were only a dozen feet away, the man lowered his phone. He'd taken his shots, and by the look on his face, he knew something was up. As they passed him, he was turning to his colleague.

Daeng heard him shout, "That's them!"

Glancing at the rearview mirror, he saw both men running in the same direction, and knew they were going for their vehicle.

So much for staying under the radar.

He shoved the accelerator to the floor.

"THAT'S THEM!" TEIG shouted to Holt.

Both men started running to their Audi sedan.

"Are you sure?" Holt asked, not breaking stride.

Just then the Camry's engine roared.

Teig glanced back and saw it racing away. "Hell, yeah, I am," he said.

AS THEY REACHED the end of the block, Daeng slowed only enough to take the turn without flipping the Camry, then sped up again until they were right behind Howard's BMW.

He checked the rearview mirror. For a moment, he thought perhaps the others had decided not to pursue them, but it was only wishful thinking. Before he even had a chance to move his gaze back to the road, a dark Audi sedan skidded around the corner.

Following Howard's lead at the next intersection, Daeng turned again, right this time. As the Camry's tires screamed in protest, Misty's arms shot out, bracing herself against the dash.

"Oh, God," she muttered more than once.

They went up the block and turned again, causing a car coming in the other direction to screech to a halt and blare its horn. Unfortunately, Daeng knew that it didn't matter how many turns they took. While Misty's Camry was fine for everyday life, the ancient vehicle was nowhere near the same performance class as the BMW or the Audi.

"You have your phone?" he asked.

"It's in back," Misty said, her hands still pressed against the dash. "It's in my purse."

"Take mine. It's in my pocket." He twisted his hips so that she'd have easier access to his jeans pocket on the right, but she didn't move. In a calm voice, he said, "Misty, please get my phone. We need to call Steve."

It took a few more seconds, but she finally reached over and worked the phone out. After he talked her through unlocking it and finding Steve's number, she placed the call, putting it on speaker.

Howard answered right away. "You guys okay back there?"

"This Audi's got us beat," Daeng said. "No way I can lose him in this. We need a diversion and I'm open to ideas."

The line went quiet for a few seconds. "I have one. You guys hang tight."

"You want to give me a hint?" Daeng asked.

Howard had already hung up, but he gave them a hint nonetheless as his BMW suddenly shot ahead in a burst of speed the Camry couldn't even dream about matching.

"Where's he going?" Misty asked.

Since Daeng had no idea, he didn't answer.

They watched as Steve turned down another street. When they reached the intersection, they turned, too.

All they could see ahead of them was empty road.

HOLT WAS BEHIND the wheel, while Teig was on his radio, filling in Central.

"Not sure if it's two or three," he said. "We think the Camry the woman and the man are in is following another car driven by a male alone. A BMW. He passed by us a few seconds before they did. I was able to get pictures of all three."

"Send them to me," Central said, as if this was the first thing that should have happened.

Teig retrieved his phone and sent the images in a single e-mail. "You should have them any second," he said as the message left.

There was a pause. "All right. I'm going to see what I can find out from here."

"What do you want us to do? Follow or capture?"

"Do they know you've made them?"

Teig hesitated. "Uh, yes."

"Then just following is out of the question, isn't it?"

"Yes, sir."

"Teig, do *not* lose them."

"We won't."

Teig replaced the radio in its harness and looked down the road. The Camry was about three quarters of a block away, the BMW still in front of it.

"Don't worry about being seen," he told Holt. "Close in."

As Holt increased their speed, the BMW turned onto a new road. As soon as the Camry reached the intersection, it turned, too.

That cinched it. They had to be together.

For the next several minutes, Teig and Holt zigzagged through the neighborhood as the others tried to lose them, but that was a contest the Camry could never win.

Suddenly the BMW, which had been driving only fast enough for the Camry to keep up with it, zoomed ahead and took a turn. It was several seconds before the Camry and the Audi followed suit.

"Looks like the other guy took off," Holt said.

The BMW was nowhere in sight.

Smart man, Teig thought.

"Do we stay on the Camry or go try to find him?" Holt asked.

"The Camry," Teig ordered.

DAENG CHECKED THE mirror again. The Audi had moved in

close, and was now a mere half car length behind them.

Daeng kept taking turns, hoping they'd catch a break, but so far that hadn't happened.

"You doing okay?" he asked Misty.

"Not really," she said. She had one hand still on the dash, while the other was now gripping the handle above the door.

He hoped whatever Howard had in mind was going to work, but he knew he couldn't count on it, and needed to come up with his own solution. Shooting the other driver would have been the easiest thing. Unfortunately, he didn't have a weapon.

No, he realized. That wasn't exactly true.

There was always the Camry itself. What he needed to do was create the opportunity for the Audi to come alongside. If he did it right, a quick whip of the wheel would send the other vehicle smashing into a parked car.

He eased back on the accelerator a bit.

"Come on," he whispered as he looked in the mirror. "Come take a look."

TEIG KNEW IT was almost over.

Without the BMW to guide it, the Camry was starting to slow, the driver no doubt realizing he didn't have a chance. If Teig really wanted to, he could have Holt bump the back corner of the Toyota and spin it out right now. The only drawbacks were potential injuries or deaths. Orders were to bring at least one of them in alive.

If they could get around front, they could cut off the Camry. That should do the trick.

He scanned past the other car at the road ahead. Another intersection was coming up, and after that the street widened a bit. The perfect place to perform a takedown.

He explained to Holt what he wanted to do.

"WHAT ARE YOU waiting for? Come on," Daeng said. His gaze bounced from the mirror to the road and back.

"What are you talking about?" Misty asked.

As they passed through the next intersection, Daeng

glanced over, intending to reassure her. But the car racing down the intersecting road stopped him from saying anything.

TEIG SETTLED BACK in his seat as they approached the intersection. From the holster rig under his shoulder, he removed his gun, and popped out the mag to double-check the load as he always did before going into action.

The mag had just cleared the end of the grip when he spotted something out of the corner of his eye.

It was large and black and moving much too fast.

He started to turn to take a better look.

THE SOUND OF the impact was loud and jarring.

Misty looked around. "What was that?"

"Our diversion," Daeng said as he slammed on the brakes.

Leaving the engine running, he scrambled out of the Camry, Misty only seconds behind him.

"That's…that's Steve's car," she said.

Indeed it was. Daeng had seen the BMW come down the intersecting road. Howard had timed his run perfectly, T-boning into the side of the Audi and pushing it clear out of the intersection, onto the curb.

Daeng ran toward the accident, scanning the two German sedans. No way either of them would ever be driven again.

In the smashed front cab of the Audi, he could see the two men jammed together, unconscious or dead. Which meant, at least for the moment, he didn't need to worry about them, so he angled straight for the BMW.

He found Howard slumped against his seatbelt, a deflating airbag draped on his lap. Daeng tried to jerk open the driver's door, but it had been bent in the accident and wouldn't budge. He tried the door behind it. This one popped open right away, so he crawled in and reached around the seat, feeling Howard's neck for a pulse.

It was there. Strong and steady.

He crawled over the seat and shook Howard's shoulder. "Hey, Steve. Wake up." No response. "Steve, come on. Can you hear me? Wake up. We've got to get you out of here."

He heard the front passenger door open, and looked back to see Misty sticking her head in.

"Is he dead?" she asked.

"No."

"Oh, thank God."

A fat guy in a faded Guns N' Roses T-shirt jogged up behind Misty. "Hey, is that guy all right?"

Misty, sounding surprisingly in control, said, "We're checking him now."

"Steve, it's time to wake up," Daeng said, tapping Howard's cheeks.

Howard started to blink.

"He came out of nowhere," the overweight rocker said. "Whacked right into those other guys."

"Maybe you should go check on them," Daeng suggested.

"There's somebody already over there."

"They could probably use some help," Misty said. "We've got this one here."

The man hesitated, then nodded. "Yeah. I'll see what's going on."

Misty leaned back into the cab. "Are you okay?" she asked Howard.

"Not my best day," he said, wincing. "But I'll be fine."

Daeng did a quick check for broken bones, but found nothing obvious. "We need to get out of here before any others show up. You think you can move?"

Howard nodded once. "Yeah. I just…need some help."

Daeng unlatched the seat belt, and helped Howard climb across the seats. Once they were out, Daeng and Misty got on either side of him and headed for Misty's car.

"Should you be doing that?" It was the same guy as before. "He probably shouldn't move until the EMTs get here. He might have internal injuries, you know. Don't you watch TV?"

Misty replied before Daeng had a chance. "I'm a nurse," she said. "I've already checked him over. I think it's best to get him to the hospital as soon as possible."

"You're a nurse? Shouldn't you take a look at these other two also?"

"Let me help with this one first, and I'll be right there."

As soon as they'd left the man behind, Daeng whispered, "Nice improvising."

"Thanks," she said, sounding like she couldn't quite believe what she'd done.

They got Howard into the backseat of the Camry, and started to get into the front.

"The files," Howard said, his voice weak. "In my trunk."

The files from the safe at Peter's apartment. They hadn't had time to dispose of them.

Daeng looked at Misty. "Are they important?"

"It wouldn't be good if anyone found them, if that's what you mean."

"Okay. I'll be right back."

Racing back toward the accident, Daeng could hear sirens approaching, no more than a minute or two away.

"Hey, what happened to that nurse?" the onlooker asked. "Thought she said she'd be right back."

"The other guy started bleeding. She's taking care of that first."

Mr. Guns N' Roses didn't look completely convinced. "Well, she'd better hurry. I don't think these other two are doing so well."

"I'll let her know."

At the BMW, Daeng leaned in through the passenger door, pulled the key fob out of the ignition, and pushed the button to open the trunk. When nothing happened, Daeng guessed that the electric system had been disabled in the accident, and used the actual key to unlock the trunk. The files had spilled out of the bag, so he had to waste several valuable seconds shoving them back in. As he turned for the Camry, his gaze lingered on the Audi for a moment, wondering if he should try to find the phone the man had used to take their pictures. The piercing siren only blocks away made up his mind for him, and he sprinted the rest of the way back to Misty's car.

When he got there, he saw she was in the back with Howard, so he climbed in behind the wheel and dropped the bag in the front passenger seat.

"Everyone ready?" he asked.

Misty snorted a laugh.

He took that as a good sign as he shifted into Drive and sped away.

CHAPTER SEVENTEEN

SAN FRANCISCO

"WHAT?"

If Helen Cho hadn't already been on her feet, she would have shot up as she'd yelled into the phone.

"They hadn't expected to find anyone," Central said. "The recon team was just there double-checking that there wasn't any evidence missed from yesterday that might ID the intruders."

"And *who* authorized that?"

A pause. "I did."

"Why would you do that?"

"The client has made it very clear that they want these people found. I thought in the confusion yesterday something might have been overlooked. It's standard procedure."

Helen seethed. Great, another O & O standard procedure. She bit back a response that would have been unproductive. Central wasn't the one to argue the point with. That would be Stone.

She took a moment to regain her composure, and asked, "How are your men?"

"Alive, but both will be in the hospital for a while."

"What about local authorities? Have you been able to contain the situation?"

"Yes, ma'am. We've spun the accident as being the result of road rage. It jibes with what witnesses reported seeing, so it was an easy sell. Once our men regain consciousness, they'll be briefed before they can make statements to the police."

"Any leads on the car that hit them?"

"The vehicle is registered to a corporation that doesn't exist. It's in police custody, but it's my understanding they have yet to check for prints. I have a person in place who will forward that information to me as soon as that happens."

Helen could hear a few keyboard clicks over the line.

"We do have photos of all three suspects," Central said.

"You do?" Here, at least, was some good news. "E-mail those to me right now."

"I should probably check with—"

"You should probably check with no one. Send them *now*!"

"Yes, ma'am."

Helen stormed back to her desk, woke up her computer, and waited for the e-mail. As soon as it arrived, she opened the three attached files.

The first image was of a Caucasian man behind the wheel of a BMW, the same BMW that had apparently caused the accident. The second was of another male, this one Asian. He was driving the Camry. The third was the Camry's passenger, a woman.

Helen stared at the screen. She had met this woman before.

"Shit," she said under her breath.

"Ma'am?" Central said.

"Nothing."

"Have you opened the files?"

"Yes."

"According to witnesses, the woman claimed to be a nurse. She and the Asian male helped the BMW's driver out of his car and over to theirs. While she stayed with the injured man, the other one returned to the BMW and retrieved a bag from its trunk before they left." Another click of a key. "I went ahead and ran the plate on the Camry, and came back with the name Misty Blake. The picture on the driver's license issued to that name matches the woman in the picture I just sent you. I have an address, and will be dispatching a team there momentarily. I should have more answers for you very soon."

"Have you reported any of this to the client?"

Central was silent for a moment. "Not yet."

Good, Helen thought. At least something was still in her control.

"Have your team stand down," she said.

"I'm sorry?"

"You heard me. Tell them to stand down."

"But…the woman. We should—"

"You should do as ordered. Or would you like to be relieved?"

"No, ma'am. How would you like me to proceed, then?"

"As far as O & O is concerned, this project is closed," Helen told him. "You will cease all surveillance, seal the records, and forward no more information to the client. Any inquiries from the client should be directed to me. Is that understood?"

"Are you going to tell this to Director Stone, or should I?"

"*You* will tell him. You will also tell him to get on a plane and be in my office first thing tomorrow morning. Got it?"

"Yes, ma'am."

She could tell he was eager to get off the line, so she said, "If there is anything else I should know about, tell me now, because if I find out you've kept something from me, your job isn't the only thing you're going to need to worry about."

"No, ma'am. I believe that's it."

She let him hang on the line for several seconds before she said, "All right. Good. Please keep me posted on the condition of your men."

"Of course."

Helen set her phone down on the desk, and looked once more at the image of the woman on her monitor.

Misty Blake. Helen had never known her last name. To her, the woman had only been Misty, Peter's executive assistant.

She had no idea what the hell was going on, but she knew she needed to get a handle on it. She also knew that Peter would have wanted her to protect Misty, so that's where she decided to start.

She turned to her computer, found Misty's record, and set about making the woman disappear.

CHAPTER EIGHTEEN

ISLA DE CERVANTES

THE SUN HAD just set when Quinn's plane landed at St. Renard's International Airport. He hurried through Customs and grabbed the first available cab. When it finally pulled up in front of the hospital compound, he didn't even wait until it came to a full stop before throwing open the door and jumping out.

It took all of his will not to run through the corridors as he made his way to Orlando's room. Reaching her door, he paused to catch his breath and then stepped inside.

He wasn't sure what he'd expected to find, but it wasn't seeing Orlando lying in bed, her eyes closed, and looking exactly as she had when he'd left. He stopped a few feet in, perplexed.

Liz was sitting in a chair next to the bed. She twisted around when she heard him enter, then jumped up and rushed over.

"I...I thought..." Quinn stammered. "I mean, Nate said she was awake."

His sister put a hand on his shoulder and whispered, "She was."

He looked past her at the bed again. "But..."

"She's asleep. *Normal* sleep. Not like before."

He relaxed a little. "Did she say anything?"

A gentle smile graced Liz's lips. "Not much. Just that

she was thirsty."

"That's it?"

Liz started to turn him toward the door. "Why don't we talk in the hall?"

He glanced at Orlando, not wanting to leave in case she opened her eyes again.

"We'll be right outside," Liz assured him.

With extreme reluctance, he followed his sister into the corridor. As soon as the door was closed, he said, "Dr. Montero said she wasn't going to wake for three days at least."

"Her vital signs were improving, so he eased back on what they were using to keep her under."

"You could've told me that. I would have come back sooner."

She grasped his bicep. "Jake, look at me. If I had known, I would've called you, but we only found out he'd done that after she opened her eyes the first time."

"How many times has she been awake?"

"Two more times since Nate called you."

Two more times Orlando had seen he wasn't there. "What's Dr. Montero saying now?"

"He's cautiously optimistic."

"That tells me nothing." Quinn spun around as if he might spot Montero standing nearby. "I want to talk to him. Where is he? I need to know exactly how she is."

As his voice grew louder, a nurse at a station down the hall looked up. With a frown, she patted the air, gesturing for him to lower his volume.

"Jake," Liz said, taking hold of both his arms this time, and stopping him from twisting the other way. "The important thing is that she's getting better."

"I want to talk to Dr. Montero." Until he heard the doctor tell him that, he couldn't allow himself to believe it.

Liz took a breath. "Fine. Why don't you go back inside and I'll see if I can find him, all right?"

He nodded. "All right." He paused. "Thank you."

He let himself back into the room, walked over to the

bed, and looked down at Orlando. He immediately realized his original assessment of her had been wrong. She didn't look exactly as she had when he'd left. There was color in her cheeks now that helped rid her face of the lifeless mask it had been wearing. And someone—Liz, no doubt—had combed her hair, so that it lay on either side of her head.

If he narrowed his eyes to slits and blocked out everything else but her, he could almost believe they were at her house in San Francisco. That she was taking a nap, waiting for him to return from a workout, a trip to the store, or some other unimportant task. That if he leaned down and kissed her, she would ease her arms around him and pull him onto the bed with her, where they would stay for the rest of the day.

And the next.

And the next.

Her hand was lying on top of the covers. He slipped his fingers under it, and gently moved them across her palm, tracing the familiar creases. He desperately wanted to squeeze her palm, not hard, just enough to wake her so that she would see him, so that she'd know he was there. But he knew that would only be selfish. She'd wake soon enough.

"She looks better, doesn't she?"

Quinn snapped his head around. Nate was standing a few feet away. Quinn had been so focused on Orlando, he hadn't heard the door open. That was unnerving. He always knew what was going on around him.

"Sorry," Nate whispered. "I didn't mean to intrude."

Quinn's former apprentice was wearing jeans and a black T-shirt, not the hospital gown Quinn had last seen him in. "Not intruding," Quinn said. "I was just…" He stopped as he lost the energy to explain himself, and turned back to Orlando. "Did you talk to her?"

"Only for a moment," Nate said.

"What did she say?"

"It wasn't easy for her to talk. She's still weak."

"She must have said something." Quinn hesitated. "Did she ask for me?"

A pause. "Yes."

Relief? More guilt? It was becoming hard for Quinn to separate all he was feeling. "What did you tell her?"

"That you'd be back soon."

"What else?"

"Nothing else."

Quinn looked back at him. "What else?"

"Nothing," Nate said, meeting Quinn's stare. "I think she wanted to say something more, but she drifted off. As far as I know, that was the last time she was awake."

Quinn closed his eyes. He should be happy, ecstatic even. But instead he was frustrated and angry and guilt ridden and jealous that Nate had already talked to her. He had to get a grip. He had to get himself under control.

When he opened his eyes again, Nate was still looking at him.

"I'm sorry," Quinn said. He opened his mouth to explain himself, but Nate held up a hand, stopping him.

"We're all a bit out of sorts right now," Nate said. The corner of his mouth ticked up in a wry grin. "It's been a pretty screwed-up few weeks."

Quinn felt a bit of his tension ease, and returned the half smile in kind. "It has been, hasn't it?"

"I blame you."

"Excuse me?" Quinn said, tensing again.

Nate shrugged. "If Romero's men had taken you instead of me, I wouldn't have all these welts on my back."

"But that means I would."

Another shrug. "There's give and take on everything."

Quinn suddenly felt his fingers being pressed together. He turned back to the bed. "Orlando?" he whispered.

Her eyes were still closed, and the rhythm of her breathing unchanged. He glanced at her hand. The fingers encircling his palm had relaxed, but he knew they had definitely squeezed him. Had she only been dreaming?

"Orlando?"

No response.

Quinn's phone vibrated. His first inclination was to

ignore it, but it was a patterned ring, one he used for only two people: Nate and Daeng.

He eased his hand out from under Orlando's and retrieved his cell.

"Yes?"

"We have a problem," Daeng said.

NOT WANTING TO disturb Orlando, Quinn told Daeng to hold as he and Nate relocated to an empty room down the hall. Keeping the volume low, he put the phone on speaker so they could both hear.

"What's going on?" he asked.

"We ran into a little trouble when we went for Misty's car."

"What kind of trouble?"

Daeng briefed Quinn and Nate about the men who'd spotted them outside Peter's place, and the subsequent chase that ended with Howard using his car as a blunt instrument.

"Is he all right?" Quinn asked.

"He's shaken up and bruised, and probably going to hurt for a while, but he should be okay."

"And the other two?"

"I don't know. We didn't have time to check them. All I know is that they weren't moving." Daeng paused. "There's something else."

"What?"

"They took pictures of us as we drove by. I would have searched for their phones, but the police were almost there."

Quinn was silent for a moment. This was definitely not good. "Where are you now?"

"Steve's friend's cabin. It's in a place called Trevor Hollow. I'll SMS you the GPS coordinates."

"You didn't use Misty's car to get there, did you?" After the chase and the accident, Misty's car would be white hot.

"No. We appropriated another vehicle before we left DC."

"Okay," Quinn said. "You should be safe there. Just hunker down, and let's let things cool for a few days."

"Will do." A beat. "Orlando?"

"Asleep. But…but better."

"I'm happy to hear that."

"Stay safe."

After Quinn hung up, Nate asked, "Who were these guys chasing them?"

"Probably the same outfit that sent the team to kill us last night," Quinn said.

"Wait, what? What happened last night?"

As concisely as possible, Quinn did what he had earlier promised, and brought Nate up to speed.

"Sounds like you pushed somebody's button," Nate said.

"Yeah, but whose?" Quinn asked.

"This Witten guy—he couldn't tell you?"

"He didn't know. His organization works client-blind."

Nate nodded in understanding. There were a handful of agencies that operated under client-blind rules, when only a select few—often only one person—would know who was really picking up the tabs for specific operations. "So do you at least think this unnamed client is the one Peter was worried about, and maybe the person who gave Romero the list?"

"For sure? No, I don't, but it's damn hard to ignore the connection."

WHEN THEY RETURNED to Orlando's room, they found Dr. Montero and Liz waiting in the corridor outside the door.

"Dr. Montero only has a few minutes," she said to her brother.

"Perhaps it's best if I start with an update," the doctor said.

Quinn nodded.

"Your friend's vital signs are right where we want them. And there's been no signs of infection, which was one of my major concerns."

"So she's out of the woods?" Quinn asked.

The doctor weighed his response. "I think it's safe to say she's no longer in danger."

No longer in danger. Those were words Quinn had

longed to hear, words that meant he wasn't going to lose her.

That she would live.

"She will, however, be weak for some time," the doctor continued. "It could take months or years before she reaches the level of strength she was at before being shot, if she ever does."

While Quinn knew the last part should have been troubling, all he could hear was that Orlando had years to live, not just hours or days.

"What she'll need is rest and physical therapy. Lots of both."

"How long?" Quinn asked.

"There's no way to know right now. She may need PT for the rest of her life."

"No. I mean, how long does she have to stay here? When can we take her home?"

The doctor frowned like a father disappointed in his child. "You realize she's still in very serious condition? I wouldn't consider discharging her for two or three weeks at the earliest."

"What if there's a facility closer to home we can take her to?"

Again, the frown, but this time the doctor considered what Quinn said. "I would have to know more about the place, and talk to the staff there. Even then, there is no way she can leave here for at least ten days. Any lengthy trip prior to that could jeopardize the progress she's already made."

Ten days and Quinn could take her back to California. He could live with that.

Not home at first, of course, but closer than Isla de Cervantes. Two private hospitals that catered to people in his and Orlando's world came immediately to mind. One was near his home in Los Angeles, while the other was near hers in San Francisco. He had more experience with the former, but the latter would be closer to her son, Garrett. Quinn could easily bring him to visit her every day.

He suddenly realized everyone was staring at him. "What?"

"I asked if you had any other questions," the doctor told him.

Full of thoughts about getting Orlando home, he almost said no, but as he started to speak, his hand brushed against his pocket and he felt the tiny lump of the microfilm canister. In his rush to fly back to be with Orlando, he hadn't even realized he'd brought it along.

He said, "Do you have a laboratory on site?"

THE HOSPITAL DID indeed have its own laboratory. It was located on the first floor between the in-house pharmacy and a CT scanner suite.

Quinn's knock on the locked door was answered by a woman in a white lab coat. Though she was probably in her early thirties, the pinched look on her face made her seem as if she was at least a decade older.

"Dr. Montero called," Quinn said in Spanish. "I believe you're expecting us."

The only things that moved were the woman's eyes, as she first scanned him and then Nate before moving out of the way so they could enter.

Though the room wasn't huge, it was impressive. Half a dozen workstations were split up long the walls, with four more taking up space on an island that ran through the center. The area between stations was filled with various pieces of equipment, the purpose of most known only to the specialists who used them.

There were four other lab workers present. Three were so engrossed in their work they took no notice of the new arrivals, while the fourth merely glanced up before looking back at his computer monitor.

Still silent, the woman who'd opened the door led Quinn and Nate across the room to an empty station far from the others. As Quinn had requested, a microscope—a Keyence VHX-2000—was sitting on the counter. A better machine than he'd hoped for.

"Here," the woman said in English.

She pressed a button and the monitor next to the

microscope came to life. She then demonstrated a few basic functions and started to leave.

"Wait," Quinn said. "How do we capture a picture?"

She frowned, but showed him what to do.

"We'll also want to take the images with us. You wouldn't happen to have a spare thumb drive, would you?"

She stared at him as if he were crazy, but Quinn held her gaze, smiling. After a moment, she rolled her eyes, walked across the room to one of the stations, and pulled open a drawer. When she returned, she placed a black thumb drive on the counter, and looked at Quinn, her eyebrow raised. It didn't take a genius to know she was asking if she could go.

"If we have any problems, we'll let you know."

She didn't look happy with this response, but with a grunt Quinn guessed was a good-bye, she returned to whatever she'd been working on.

Quinn pulled out the microfilm canister and Nate moved in behind him, creating a wall that would prevent anyone else in the lab from seeing the microscope's monitor. After a few aborted tries, Quinn finally got the first frame under the lens.

"That's fascinating," Nate said.

Quinn looked at the monitor. On the screen was a big blob of white, with a hint of black encroaching at the top. The microscope's current magnification setting was much too strong. As he began reducing the power, black moved in from all four sides, creating blurry lines and squares. When it was evident he had the entire frame of microfilm on the monitor, he fine-tuned the focus, sharpening the image.

Just like he'd noted when he'd looked at the frames with the magnifying glass, the horizontal lines were made up of dozens of black squares. He took a picture, then moved the film to the next frame.

"How many shots are there?" Nate asked.

"Twenty-three." Quinn took another picture and moved the microfilm again. "Eleven of them are like this." He nodded at the screen. "The other twelve look like they could be photos, but we won't know until we decode them."

He worked his way through the rest of the documents,

and started in on the colored frames.

As he was about to move from frame nineteen to twenty, Nate said, "Whoa, whoa."

Quinn sat back and raised his fingers off the keyboard.

"What's that look like to you?" Nate asked.

Quinn examined the screen.

"Right there." Nate circled the upper right corner of the monitor. "See it?"

"Looks like part of an ear."

"Yeah. That's what I thought."

"Probably just the encryption. It could be anything."

"It looks pretty real to me."

Though it was purple and gray, it did look real—like the outside ridge of an ear near the base, with a hint of the lobe at the bottom. Since there was no way to know for sure, Quinn continued working his way through the rest of the photos, neither he nor Nate seeing anything else that looked familiar.

Once he had all the images saved to the thumb drive, he switched off the monitor and put the microfilm back in the canister.

At any other time, his next step would have been to give the images to Orlando, and she'd have them decoded in no time. But that option wasn't open to him right now.

There were a few other people he thought might be able to handle it, but he wasn't sure how much he could trust them. This wasn't just some job. This had been personal to Peter, and, if it was connected to the whole Romero thing, it was personal to Quinn, too, so he had to be very careful about whom he involved.

Perhaps he could try to decode the images himself. The gear they'd had on the jet that had taken them to and from Duran Island was now in a locker in the hospital's basement. Orlando's bag would be there, and in it would be her laptop. He might not be as quick as she, but with a little trial and error, he thought he could figure out which program to use and how to work it.

He put the drive into his pocket and stood. "Let's go."

CHAPTER NINETEEN

SEPTEMBER 3rd
ZURICH, SWITZERLAND

MORTEN'S PHONE RANG softly on the nightstand. As always, he had activated the cell's DO NOT DISTURB function, so that the only calls that got through were from Griffin.

He picked up his phone and grunted.

"I apologize, sir," Griffin said. "I know it's late there, but there's been a development."

"What is it?" Morten was using the least amount of energy possible.

"I'm being ignored by O & O."

Morten rolled onto his back. "What do you mean, ignored?"

"They haven't contacted me since I requested the forensics search of the Virginia home, and they're not returning my calls."

"What? That's ridiculous. Call Stone directly. Tell him to fix the problem."

"I've tried to get ahold of Director Stone as well, even routed the call so it looked like I was phoning from CIA headquarters, but I was told he was unavailable. I think I should probably get involved personally now. Bypass O & O completely."

Morten thought for a moment. Having Griffin move into the field instead of using a government-run third party such as

O & O could expose Darvot if something went wrong, but then again, not putting a lid on this problem could be even worse.

"All right," he said. "Just be careful. And only use your team if you absolutely have no choice."

"Yes, sir. I understand."

CHAPTER TWENTY

ISLA DE CERVANTES

QUINN HAD FALLEN asleep in the chair by Orlando's bed. On the rolling table next to him was her laptop.

He'd worked late into the night, trying to figure out how to decode the images, but it wasn't nearly as clear-cut as he'd hoped. When he had set the computer to the side, he'd told himself he would rest his eyes for a few minutes, but ended up falling deep asleep.

The glare of the early morning sun through the window woke him. He covered his eyes and squirmed in his chair, attempting to get out of the light's direct path.

"Too bright for you?"

At first he wasn't sure where the voice had come from. It had been no more than a whisper, like the lingering wisp of a dream.

He looked toward the door, blinking both sleep and the afterimage of the sun away.

"You should really sleep in a bed, you know."

He twisted around and saw her. Orlando. She was looking at him, her eyes half opened. He nearly knocked the computer off the table as he pushed himself up and moved to the bed.

"Hey," he said, smiling.

"Hey."

For a moment, he couldn't get another word out and just

stared at her. Finally he managed, "How are you?"

"You tell me."

"You're alive."

"That's encouraging."

"And the doctor says you're doing better every day," he added quickly, pulling himself out of his shock.

She closed her eyes and readjusted her head on her pillow. When she opened them again, she asked, "How long have I been here?"

"A week and a half."

"That long?"

"The doctor said we can take you home soon." He hoped that would make her feel better.

She studied his face as if trying to see if he was lying. "How soon?"

"Another week or so." He leaned over the bed and brushed away a strand of her hair that had fallen over her cheek. "You need to build up some strength first, that's all."

He took her hand, and realized she was staring at him again.

"How bad?" she asked.

"How bad what?"

One side of her mouth rose in a weak smirk. "How bad am I?"

"Not as bad as you were."

"Don't do that. Please." She squeezed his hand. "Just tell me."

He smiled as best he could. "At some point soon, you're going to need to get your knee replaced."

"That sounds like fun."

He was silent for a moment. "You're missing a couple things."

She stiffened slightly, and he could see her mind racing as she wiggled the toes on her uninjured leg, and the fingers of both hands.

"Nothing on the outside," he said.

"Then what?"

"Your left kidney, and your spleen." He raised an

exaggerated eyebrow. "Apparently we're born with two kidneys. Did you know that? And the spleen? Don't need it. The things you learn hanging around a hospital."

She rolled her eyes back and let out an exasperated huff. "Dammit, Quinn. You could've just said that right off. For a second there I thought I was going to have to worry about mixing up prosthetics with Nate."

"Don't think you guys would get mixed up. He's a lot taller than you."

She clamped down on his hand, her grip surprisingly strong for her condition.

"Hey," he said. "Just being honest."

The short laugh that escaped her lips quickly turned into a cough.

Quinn grabbed a pitcher of water on the nightstand and filled one of the waiting cups.

"Here," he said, slipping a hand under her head, and moving the cup to her lips. "My fault. I shouldn't have gotten you going like that."

The warmth he'd begun to feel as they'd talked had disappeared the moment she stopped laughing.

When she had enough water, she pulled back and cleared her throat. "I'm okay. My throat's dry, that's all."

He lowered her head to the pillow and returned the cup to the nightstand. "You need to take it easy. Getting stronger is your only job now." He reached out and squeezed her hand again. "Get some more sleep. That's the best thing you can do."

Her eyelids were already half shut, the exertion of their conversation clearly having taken its toll. Thinking she was on the verge of knocking out, he took a silent step backward and turned toward the door.

"You weren't here before," she whispered.

He stopped.

"I woke up…I don't know when, but you weren't here. Liz said…you were…you were away."

He licked his bone-dry lips, his guilt thundering back down on him like an avalanche. "I'm here now," he said.

"Liz told me you were trying…to find out who was…responsible." Her volume decreased with every syllable, each new word a struggle.

"We can talk about it later." Dammit. He *knew* his sister had said more to Orlando than she'd let on.

Orlando took a couple of breaths. "I…want…"

The pause was long, and Quinn wondered if she had finally drifted off. But then she cracked her eyelids open again.

"I want…to help."

"Just sleep now," he said. "That's the best help you can give us."

But he needn't have said anything. She was already out.

TREVOR HOLLOW, VIRGINIA

DAENG LOOKED OUT the cabin window. Sometime during the night, clouds had begun rolling in. They were darker now than when he woke an hour ago, and held the promise of rain. Maybe in an hour. Maybe at the end of the day. It was hard for him to tell. In Bangkok he would have known without even thinking about it. Los Angeles, too. But this part of the States was unfamiliar to him.

Across the room, the bedroom door opened, and Misty stepped out quietly.

"How's he doing?" Daeng asked.

"I gave him some more ibuprofen, and he fell back asleep."

Daeng knew Howard could probably use something stronger than over-the-counter drugs, but without robbing the drugstore where they'd stopped, their choices had been limited.

"I made some fresh coffee," he said.

Misty allowed herself a small smile. "Exactly what I need." She walked into the kitchen and poured herself a cup. "You want some?"

"I'm fine," Daeng replied.

When she joined him at the table, she looked at the cloth

grocery bag containing Peter's files, sitting off to the side. "We should get rid of those."

"Why not now?"

Half a minute later they were kneeling in front of the fireplace, the bag between them. Using some kindling and a few pieces of wood from the holder on the hearth, Daeng got a fire going. Misty then pulled out a file, opened it, and began feeding sheets of paper one by one into the flames.

Daeng considered helping, but he could tell that for her, this was more than a simple task of getting rid of unwanted documents. This was an act of finality—a cleansing, even—one of the last things she would ever do for Peter. There was a respect to the way she placed each page into the blaze—gently, a pause as the fire caught, then the next sheet.

After a file was empty, the folder itself was burned before Misty moved on to the next. When she finished the last, she stared at the flames until the final bit of paper curled into black ash.

"Thank you," she said.

Daeng dipped his head in acknowledgment.

He gave her another moment before he stood and grabbed the bag. The heft of the bag caused him to pause. He reached inside and pulled out the wooden box. He opened the top, expecting to see the metal canister, but it wasn't there.

"Do you have the microfilm?" he asked.

"It's not in there?"

He turned the box so she could see.

"Quinn must have taken it with him," she said. "He had it last, didn't he?"

"Must have," Daeng said. Not wanting to take a chance, he sent a text asking Quinn if he took the microfilm, and then carried the bag and the box to the table.

The reply came quickly: YES.

That was a relief. Daeng had no desire to retrace their steps in hopes of locating the spool of film. He started to shove the box back into the bag, but stopped. He took his new role as the main support member of Nate and Quinn's teams seriously, and had learned to always be an asset rather than a liability. One of the things Nate had stressed was details. These were the backbone of a cleaner's job. Missing a detail could blow a whole mission and quite possibly get someone imprisoned or even killed.

He'd almost missed such a detail. It had been right there in front of his eyes as he'd looked inside the box. The black foam that had held the canister in place had not been level with the plane of the box. Rather, it was tilted, albeit just a fraction of an inch.

He opened the box again and double-checked to make sure he'd seen it right. He stuck a finger into the hole where the canister had been, and pulled up. As he'd suspected, the foam wasn't glued in place. Once it cleared the opening, he could see something underneath.

A stack of photos. Different sizes, maybe a dozen or more.

He pulled them out.

"Misty," he said after he perused them. "Take a look at this."

"What is it?" she asked, rising off the floor.

He showed her what he was holding.

She held out her hand. "Let me see." She shuffled quickly through the photos. "Where were these?"

"In the bottom of the box. That's her, isn't it?"

She said nothing until she'd looked at each one. "Yes. These were the ones in Peter's missing file. It's his wife, Miranda."

CHAPTER TWENTY ONE

WASHINGTON, DC

AS SOON AS Griffin felt a drop of water hit the back of his hand, he turned and looked up at the sky. Dark gray clouds hung heavily over the city, the leading edge of a tropical storm that, not long before, had been an early season, category-two hurricane. According to the news, rainfall in the DC area was predicted to reach an inch and a half before the storm passed further inland.

But he wasn't about to let the weather bother him. He had work to do, actual fieldwork, which was rare these days. He had started out as Morten's field enforcer years ago, but had gradually become, more and more, the coordinator of other efforts. While he was good at it, sitting in an office dealing with morons like those at O & O was at times maddening. Getting out, doing the work himself—he needed that every once in a while.

Several more raindrops hit him as he opened his car door and climbed in. Instead of starting the engine, he pulled out his phone. His first call went to voice mail after ringing five times. He disconnected and hit the number again. Same result. On the third try, the call was answered after the first ring.

"Hello?" The voice was male and half asleep.

"Good morning, Michael."

"Who is…" A pause. "Griffin?" The last was almost a whisper.

"Long time no chat."

In the hush that followed, Griffin imagined Michael Dima's heart rate increasing as he quickly considered his options, but coming up with only the final, inevitable—

"What can I do for you?"

Part of Griffin's job had been to cultivate contacts in agencies who could be potentially useful at some point. His preferred method was not one of faux friendship and cash, but of legitimate threat and blackmail. When people's carefully constructed lives were in danger of crashing down around them, ninety-nine out of a hundred would choose the path of least resistance. In other words, cooperation. The other one percent? That's where the *legitimate* part of the threat came in.

Dima's flaw was a violent streak in his past that he'd been able to hide from all but the most vigorous investigator—Griffin. While a young man, Dima had put someone in a permanent vegetative state by using an iron pipe. The authorities had never learned the perpetrator's name. Griffin, on the other hand, had discovered the truth, and it proved to be the leverage he needed to obtain Dima's attention.

It had been a while since Griffin had needed to use the man, but the moment O & O had gone silent, Griffin knew he and Dima would soon become reacquainted.

"Your organization was tasked with keeping tabs on a certain apartment in Georgetown. You know the one I mean."

"How did you…I can't talk about that."

"Please, Michael. Don't insult me. Who do you think your client was?"

The pause that followed was thick with tension. "You?"

"Of course. So are you familiar with the apartment I'm talking about or not?"

"Yes," Dima said quickly.

Griffin never doubted Dima would be aware of what O & O had been up to. Dima was one of the people at O & O who served as Central, coordinating the agency's active projects, so any answer but yes would have been a lie.

"According to the reports I received, your people found nothing that would identify the intruders at the apartment. Is that correct?"

The hesitation was slight. "That's correct. The team that responded to the incursion found nothing."

Griffin's eyes narrowed. *The team that responded to the incursion...*It was a very specific reference. "Think very carefully before you answer this question, Michael." He fell silent for several seconds, giving Dima time to worry. "How *many* teams did you send out?"

"Well, the response team, and—I assume you know about the safe house?"

"The one in Arlington Ridge. Yes, I'm familiar."

"Um, right. So there was the team that went there, but the place was empty." He paused. "Oh, and then the follow-up recon to the Arlington Ridge home to check for anything that might have been left behind. Again, nothing."

Dima was doing it again, only this time trying to confuse things by overexplaining. "Was that it? Or were there more?" Griffin asked.

The pause was long. "One more."

This was new. "Where did they go?"

"The...the apartment."

"When?"

"Yesterday. Midday."

"And?"

"Well...um..."

"Don't make me pull it out of you."

It only took another second before the dam broke and Dima spilled everything—the chase, the two men, the woman, the accident.

"Why didn't I receive a report about this?" Griffin asked.

"You...you didn't?"

"Now you're just trying to piss me off. Why didn't I get the damn report?"

"T-That decision came from higher up."

"Who higher up?"

"I'm...not sure."

Griffin let Dima drown in silence.

Finally Dima said, "Director Cho, I think. She now oversees O & O."

Griffin had heard of Cho, but their paths had never crossed as far as he could remember. He filed her name away to look into later. "Was O & O able to ID the two men and the woman?"

"Well, there's the car left behind at the accident, but that's a dead end."

"Explain."

Dima told him what they'd found, which was basically nothing.

Griffin frowned. "You're holding something back."

"No, I'm—"

"Why are you making me remind you that there's no statute of limitation on attempted murder?"

Dima stopped breathing. "The…the…the recon team…they were able to get pictures of all three."

Well, *that* was interesting. "So you were able to identify them?"

"It was taken out of our hands. We didn't have a chance."

"By Director Cho?"

Dima did not respond.

"I want the pictures," Griffin said.

"I'm at home. I don't have access to them."

"Get access."

"They've probably been purged from the system by now."

"I *want* the pictures."

"I'll, um, see what I can do."

"Do more than just see."

Dima's response was more a whine than a word.

"One more thing," Griffin said, before the other man could hang up.

"Yes?"

"Where's the BMW from the accident?"

MOST OF THE space at the city impound yard was taken up by fully functional vehicles, sitting side by side as they waited for their owners to spring them from jail for parking violations.

The group off to the left, behind a separate chain-link fence, though, was different. Many of these would only see the open road again on the back of a truck hauling them to a wrecking yard. They were leftovers of recent accidents—the bent, the broken, the totaled—kept there only as long as the police needed them.

That's where the BMW and O & O's Audi were.

Griffin stopped first at the office, and flashed the FBI badge he always brought with him. It was fake, of course, but even the most knowledgeable authority wouldn't be able to tell.

"What can I do for you, Agent?" the impound employee asked.

"I need to take a look at a vehicle in your accident lot," Griffin said, donning his well-honed, bored-investigator persona.

"Which one?"

He made a show of pulling a small notebook from his pocket and shuffling through the pages. "It's a…BMW." He gave the license number Dima had provided him.

The man looked it up on the list. "Still here. And I see you've already been okayed by Detective Marsh."

"Good. Wasn't sure if he'd contacted you yet." The real Detective Marsh had not contacted the yard. It had been Dima using O & O's system to e-mail the appropriate clearance from what appeared to be the detective's account.

"Sign here," the clerk said.

Griffin scribbled an illegible signature on the sheet.

"You know the way?"

The enforcer flashed a smile. "I do."

As he stepped outside, he pulled his collar tight to his neck, and popped open his umbrella to ward off the now steady rain. Slogging between the rows of parking violators, he made his way over to the open gate of the accident area and passed inside. It took less than a minute to locate the two vehicles from the crash. From the way the Audi's side was smashed in, Griffin could now see why the man who'd been sitting in the passenger seat hadn't died. The BMW had hit the back half of the car, containing most of the wreckage to the rear passenger area. As for the BMW, its damage was mostly limited to the front end—buckled hood, crunched fenders, and, by the way the vehicle was skewed, a bent frame.

If there had been any prints on the outside of the BMW, the storm had washed them away. So Griffin opened the back door on the passenger side, scooted onto the seat, and shut himself in.

The sound of the rain hitting the roof was almost relaxing, its intensity fluctuating in waves that could have easily lulled Griffin to sleep if he'd been in the mood. It was almost like music, something John Coltrane might play. An endless, intoxicating melody.

Griffin leaned between the front seats and scanned the driver area. An expelled airbag hung loosely over the steering wheel, but everything else looked almost normal. On the passenger's side, the glove compartment hung open, and whatever had been inside was gone, confiscated by Metro Police or O & O.

What Griffin was looking for, though, was not registration papers or discarded receipts or stray fingerprints. In fact, he wasn't hunting for anything a search of all the normal places would turn up. He was looking for things not easily found, things that would clearly indicate these intruders were pros.

He ran his fingers across the carpet covering the rear footwells, and checked under the front seats. Both were clean. The ceiling liner was next. There he made his first discovery, above the front passenger's door. Evenly spaced, and situated so that he almost thought it was part of the vehicle's frame, was a four-piece set of lock picks.

He continued his search.

Tucked under the front dash where only his fingertips

could reach, and held in place by pressure brackets, was a collapsible, four-inch hunting knife. Not far from it was an extendable baton. There was no question now. Pros for sure.

He checked the air-con vents, the radio speakers, and the door panels, but the three items he'd already found were apparently all that was hidden in the cab. He stuffed his discoveries into the pockets of his overcoat, and climbed back out of the car.

The crunched hood of the BMW had been turned into an inverted V, creating a gap that allowed him to look inside the engine compartment. Nothing jumped out at him, but he knew any thorough inspection would necessitate using equipment to rip the hood off first. He had neither the time nor the inclination for that.

He moved around to the back of the car. From the scratch marks along the lip of the trunk, it was clear the police had used a crowbar to dislodge it. He gave the lid a test, and was happy to see it rise.

The trunk was messier than the car had been. There was no cargo to speak of, but the carpet that had covered the cargo area had been ripped away and pushed to the back. He revised his earlier thought and decided it probably wasn't the police who had searched the vehicle, but O & O. At least they saved him having to rip the damn carpet out himself.

Leaning inside, he studied the metal surface, his hand darting out on occasion so that he could rub his fingertips over anything he found suspect. It was along the wall on the driver's side that he discovered a trap—a vehicle hidey-hole.

The seam delineating it was nearly imperceptible—the paint and molding jobs top-notch. He moved his fingers along it, hoping the release would be in the same area, but knowing it wasn't likely, given the quality of the workmanship. He finally discovered the release several feet away, right below the taillight, disguised as a rubber electrical system cap.

To be sure he was right, he turned it so he could see the backside. Embedded into the rubber was the thick, braided wire he knew from experience would be connected to the latch holding the trap closed. He was about to give it a pull when he spotted something else. Another wire had been braided into the main one, clinging to it like a remora on a shark. Together they disappeared behind one of the metal brackets.

Griffin frowned. There was no reason for them both to go to the latch.

He pulled his mini flashlight out of his pocket, closed the umbrella, and crawled all the way into the trunk. Moving as close as he could to the inside wall, he followed the wires around the corner by the taillights to the sidewall. There they split—the bigger wire continuing toward the trap, the smaller wire heading down into a metal tube that ran along the junction of the wall and the trunk floor. The tube was welded into place and painted to look like it was standard issue. It had even fooled Griffin when he first saw it, but now he was sure it hadn't been manufacturer installed.

He traced the tube all the way to the back of the trunk, where it disappeared behind a metal plate and didn't reappear again. Either the wire stopped there, or went through the wall into the back of the car.

With extreme care, he slid two fingers along the tube where it ducked under the plate. He didn't get far before he hit an obstruction. He pulled his fingers out and tried again from the other sides. He closed his eyes as he traced the shape and drew a mental picture. It was some kind of junction, or relay, or…

Son of a bitch, he thought as he pulled his fingers out.

A fail-safe switch. If he had pulled the trap's release cable, it would have triggered some kind of self-destruct system, destroying anything that was hidden inside. Okay, so how would the owner open the compartment without losing the contents? There had to be a bypass somewhere.

He searched around, his fingers hunting in the spaces he couldn't see into.

It took him twenty minutes to finally locate it. Thank God for the rain. If it had been a clear day, one of the yard employees would have probably wandered by and wondered what he was doing.

The bypass switch was hidden under an inspection sticker along the edge of the trunk's lid. It was a tiny, two-position switch. He moved it into the opposite position, and crawled out of the trunk, hoping he'd disarmed it instead of arming it. The only way to find out was to pull the release.

Not one to waste time contemplating the unknowable, he grabbed the rubber cap and yanked. At first it resisted, as if it were rooted in place, then there was a *thunk*, and the cap moved away, bringing the wires with it. There was no sudden burst of flames or smell of dissolving chemical, only a second *thunk* as the top of the trap door swung open.

With a satisfied smirk, Griffin lit up the interior with his flashlight. The space was filled side to side by a black nylon bag. He carefully removed it, and looked into the trap again. Held in place by metal clips attached to the wall were a Walther PPX pistol, three preloaded magazines, and a suppressor.

Griffin reached into the compartment and searched around. There were no more loose items inside, but he did find two dome-shaped, incendiary devices fixed to the bottom, each one more than enough to destroy what had been in the trap.

Overkill. Which meant the owner had really wanted to make sure the black bag's contents didn't fall into the wrong hands.

Oops.

Griffin unzipped the bag.

Not surprisingly, it was a standard dump-and-run kit: an envelope full of cash—about five grand, a change of clothes, and two passports, US and Canadian. The names were different, but the pictures were the same.

The driver, no doubt.

"Hello there," Griffin said.

He pulled out his phone and took a picture of one of the passport photos. He then opened his e-mail, but before he could create a new message, he saw two e-mails waiting for him. One was from Morten, anxious for a progress report. The other was from Dima—no message, only three attached files.

Griffin opened them. The first was a picture of the woman. The second of the Asian man who had been in the car with her. And the third was the same man pictured in the passport.

Perfect.

Griffin opened a new e-mail, attached the photos from Dima and the one he'd taken, then wrote:

> Identify. You have one hour.
> Griffin

He addressed it to the best researcher he knew, a man who, like Dima, Griffin controlled. In this case, it wasn't from knowledge of past criminal activities or some deviant sexual behavior, but merely by fear of Griffin himself.

Once the message was sent, he confiscated the Walther, its mags and suppressor, put them all in the black bag, closed the trap, and shut the trunk.

His work at the yard was done.

CHAPTER
TWENTY TWO

SEATTLE, WASHINGTON

AN ICON FLASHED in the corner of the Mole's monitor, letting him know a new e-mail had arrived. At the moment, though, he was busy trying to coordinate his online team as they attempted to clear another street of the alien soldiers trying to invade Earth.

"Red Dog, what the hell are you doing?" he said into his headset microphone. "I said left side, dipshit. You're with Monty, not Jasmine."

"Why do I always get stuck with Monty?" Red Dog whined.

"What's wrong with me?" Monty asked, his voice deep and booming. It wasn't his actual voice, the Mole knew. The guy was a squirrelly, twenty-five-year-old grad student in the UK who'd purchased a vocal synthesizer. He'd be surprised that the Mole knew this, but then again, the Mole knew everything about his entire team.

The Mole was an info guy, a researcher, so looking into the people he gamed with was not something he even thought twice about. For instance, while Jasmine *was* a female, she wasn't the kickass twentysomething she pretended to be online. Instead she was a sixteen-year-old honor student going through what he considered a prolonged awkward phase. Not that he was one to talk.

"I've got movement! I've got movement!" Ivan yelled.

The Mole, as team leader, had the ability to observe what each of his team was seeing. He switched to Ivan's view. "Dammit! Everybody, left, left! Behind the building. There's a whole squad of Jellys heading our way."

The team scrambled down the street, but it was already too late. The Jellys—nicknamed for the way their guts poured out when shot—had seen them and opened fire. Warning lights started popping up on the Mole's screen as members of his team were hit.

"What's wrong with you people?" the Mole yelled.

"They came out of nowhere!"

"That wasn't my side to watch!"

"Ah, crap!"

"I don't think this is realistic! They wouldn't have just shown up like—" The game cut off Monty's voice the moment a Jelly's plasma ray ripped through his combat suit. Once killed, a player was dead until the end of the battle.

The Mole looked around. Only two others had made it to the safety of the building with him, and one of them was badly hurt. The Mole had played the game so many times, he knew it was impossible for his team to finish this level with so few members.

Five minutes later, he was proven correct as his screen flashed white and his voice was cut off. Since he'd been the last man standing, there hadn't been anyone to talk to anyway.

With the whole team dead, the game reset, putting everyone back in the ready room and reactivating communications.

"Well, that sucked," Red Dog said.

"Way to state the obvious, asshole," Jasmine shot back.

There were a few other choice comments before Monty said, "So are we going again, or what?"

The e-mail icon on the Mole's computer was still flashing. He frowned, wanting to keep playing, but he did have a business to run.

"Five-minute bathroom break," he said. "Then we go."

He pushed his headset down around his neck, minimized the game, and brought up his inbox. It contained several unread messages. Two were notifications from his bank about payments he'd received—nice! One was an auto-generated message, from a bot he'd sent out to dig through some secured servers in Texas for some information a client wanted. The rest appeared to be requests for his services. He was always ambivalent about new work. While he usually enjoyed the process, the people asking for his help were, more times than not, pains in the ass.

He checked through the requests to make sure nothing was pressing, and made it three quarters of the way through before a sender's address caused him to stop.

Griffin.

Shit.

The Mole could go for months without thinking about that asshole. Months when he could just do his thing, and not worry that he'd find Griffin sitting in his room with a big knife in his hand, ready to slice the Mole's throat from ear to ear.

But not only did Griffin know where he lived, he also knew the Mole's real name. None of the Mole's other clients had any idea. Well, Orlando did, but she was a friend, probably the only true one the Mole had, and she'd never used her knowledge against him.

Griffin, on the other hand, was all about using what he knew.

A sound of scratchy voices coming out of his headset broke the Mole's trance. He pulled it back on.

"—keeping time?" Ivan said.

"Come on. Let's go. We're losing daylight." This came from Red Dog.

"Change of plans," the Mole said. "You'll have to go on without me."

"What are you talking about?" Jasmine asked. "I thought we all cleared our schedules."

"Yeah, well, mine just got busy."

"Serious, man?" Ivan said. "You're going to screw us up."

"Red Dog can step up to team leader," the Mole said.

"Uh, sure. I can do that," Red Dog responded.

Of course he could, the Mole thought. Red Dog had been dying to lead a mission ever since they all teamed up. Well, here was his chance. "Try to stay alive," the Mole said.

He quit the game, and set his headset next to the vocal modulator box he plugged into anytime he talked to a client. It was light years better than the one Monty used, and gave the Mole's voice a deep, haunting monotone that he augmented with a slow, uneven speech pattern. No need to use the unit at the moment, though. He didn't want to talk to Griffin until he had the information the man requested. Besides, Griffin knew what his voice sounded like.

As he opened the e-mail, he automatically started up the familiar daydream of ways he could remove Griffin from his life. Most involved scenarios viable only in video games, but the truth was, the virtual world was probably the only place he could ever beat Griffin. The Mole was not a physically imposing individual. He could probably outthink the asshole, but—

He shook it off. He just needed to get the damn work done, and Griffin would be out of his hair.

For a while, anyway.

He read the message.

> Identify. You have one hour.
> Griffin

Four image files were attached to the e-mail. The first picture was of a woman in the passenger seat of a car. A Toyota Camry, by the looks of it. The second was of a man driving the same car. This one included a shot of the license plate. The subject of the third was another man behind the wheel of a BMW, and the fourth was the same man again, only this time he was looking directly into the camera in what was most likely a passport shot.

Identify.

No problem, that was right up the Mole's alley. It was the second part of the message—the "you have one hour" part—that concerned him.

A good fifteen minutes of that hour had been wasted while his team of dweebs had offered themselves up for slaughter to the Jellys. Still, with clear photos, license plate numbers, and three quarters of an hour left, he should be able to get enough information to keep Griffin from getting angry.

Both license plates were from Washington, DC. Utilizing a hack he'd used a million times, he entered a national motor-vehicle database that linked information from all states and US territories. He selected DC, and decided to start with the BMW. Turned out it was registered to a corporation with a New York City address. He minimized the database window, opened a new one, and did a search on the company. It didn't take him long to realize it was a dummy corporation.

"Wonderful," he muttered. While he had no doubt he could eventually track down the real owner, it would likely take more time than he had left. Best, he decided, to save the BMW for later.

He went back to the database and typed in the number for the Toyota. A part of him expected it to be owned by the same phony company, but when he hit ENTER, the response he got was:

NO MATCH

The Mole gave the database the benefit of the doubt, and reentered the plate number in case he'd mistyped.

NO MATCH

That couldn't be right. He highly doubted the car's owner had hammered out replica DC license plates. Perhaps the number had been altered in some way.

He brought the picture back to the front of the screen, enlarged it until the license plate filled the window, and examined the image. The magnification caused a loss of resolution, but he could still make out the letters and numbers, and, as far as he could tell, none of the characters had been tampered with.

So why wasn't the plate in the database? A glitch, perhaps?

He accessed the source code, and quickly determined that while the software was not even close to being the best written one he'd ever come across, there didn't seem to be anything blocking him from finding the info on this particular plate.

He checked the clock and cursed. No way was he going to make the deadline.

He switched over and checked the logs, not only the ones associated with the national database, but also those that were DC specific. With his trained eye, he rapidly scrolled through the data, looking for anything unusual.

He stopped on an entry from the previous day. A file deletion notice. In and of itself, that wasn't unusual, but what had caught his attention were the last four characters of the file name. They corresponded exactly to the license number in the picture.

He followed the trail and realized the deletion had gone a lot deeper than just the DC and national databases. The worm that had removed the file had also gone through backup servers for both systems, destroying all previously saved versions.

The Mole's fear of Griffin started to fade into the background as his curiosity grew. Why had someone felt it necessary to make this car disappear? He leaned back in his chair, thinking. There had to be somewhere else he could find what he was looking for.

Pistol, he realized.

He pulled his headset on, plugged it into the vocal modulator, and used one of his anonymous Skype accounts to make an audio-only call.

"Yay?" Pistol answered, his rough, smoker's voice making him sound twenty years older than he actually was.

"It is…me," the Mole said, falling easily into his work persona.

"Hey, buddy. What's going on?"

"I…have a…question for you."

"Shoot."

"Motor vehicle databases…do you have?"

Pistol was a collector, only he didn't collect baseball cards or *Star Wars* action figures. He was interested in digital information, illegally obtained by hacking into databases and downloading them onto his own server farm. One never really knew what might capture Pistol's fancy. Some things the Mole was sure Pistol would have? Turned out to be of no interest to him. While other things, esoteric crap no one would ever need, took up large chunks of space on Pistol's drives.

"Depends," Pistol said. "Are we talking in or out of the States?"

"In."

"Hmm. Hit or miss. I got some, not all, though. Now, if you were interested in India, I got you covered. Of course, not everyone there registers their car." He laughed.

"My interest is specific…to…Washington, DC."

"DC, huh? Hold on."

He was gone for less than a minute.

"You're in luck," Pistol said. "I do have it, but it's about a year out of date."

The car in the picture was considerably older than that.

"I…need you to…run a plate…for…me." He gave Pistol the number.

"Hey, it's not like I'm just sitting around, you know."

"I will pay…you."

"It's a grand per request."

"Understood," the Mole said. Last time it had been only five hundred bucks, but a check of the clock told him he only had ten minutes left before Griffin's deadline, so quibbling over fees was not a luxury he could afford. If he at least had the name of the woman, that might mollify Griffin.

He could hear Pistol enter the number on his keyboard. After a pause, the man said, "Here we go. You got a pen?"

The Mole had already opened a blank document on his computer screen. "Go…ahead."

"The license plate belongs to a 1994 Toyota Camry.

Color dark gray, no reports of accidents."

"The owner," the Mole said, impatient.

"Let's see. It's registered to Misty Blake." He read off an address that was located in the Dupont Circle area of DC. "Anything else?"

"Hold...please."

The Mole brought up the national auto database again, changed the search parameters from vehicles to licensed drivers, and entered the woman's name.

Three seconds.

NO MATCH

Surprise, surprise.

"Is your...information...limited to vehicles...or do you have...driver...data also?"

"I got both," Pistol said.

"Please...retrieve Misty...Blake's information."

"That's another grand."

"I am...aware."

Pistol's illegal database copy came through again. Instead of writing down the information, the Mole requested that Pistol make screen grabs of the data, and e-mail it all to him.

"That's not covered under the retrieval cost," Pistol argued.

"Two thousand...you are getting...I...believe...it is covered."

Pistol grumbled for a few more seconds before saying, "Fine."

The e-mail containing the screen grabs arrived four minutes before the hour was up. The Mole quickly opened them and confirmed that the woman in Griffin's picture was the same one on the driver's license for Misty Blake. He still had no idea what this woman did or why she would be important, but he did have a name and address.

When the final minute ticked off, he expected ringing to blare from his computer speakers, but they remained silent.

He waited a full sixty seconds before deciding he should use his time to see if he could find out anything more. He thought about starting in on the second man, but now that he had the woman's license picture and name, he could check several other databases.

Since she lived in DC, he thought there was a decent chance she was a government employee. So that's where he went first, typing her name into a system that would tell him if the US government paid her salary.

He found three Misty Blakes in public service. Two were on the West Coast—one in the forest service in Washington State, and the other an FDA inspector in Bakersfield, California. The third had switched jobs within the last year, moving into a support role at the Labor Board in DC. But her new position wasn't the most interesting detail. It was the fact that the title of her previous role and the division she'd worked for had been redacted.

The Mole glanced down at the phone icon on his screen to make sure he hadn't accidently turned off the ringer and missed Griffin's call, but it was on.

He looked at Misty Blake's picture again. *So what exactly were you doing before?*

He ran her name through a couple of the other databases he had access to, but came up with nothing new, so he decided to use his photo recognition software. It would search criminal, military, and intelligence databases for likely matches. To cut down on the search time, he limited it to Caucasian females between twenty-eight and thirty-six, living in the DC area.

After he started the search, he got up to take a leak.

He'd just flushed the toilet when his computer rang. He ran his hands under some water, and grabbed the towel to dry them as he sprinted back into the living room. Plopping down into his seat, he pulled on his headset.

"Hello?"

"Turn that crap off," Griffin told him.

"What are you talking about?"

"That voice crap. Turn it off."

The Mole realized he was still plugged into the vocal modulator. "Just a second."

As he was shoving the jack into the direct connection at the bottom of his computer screen, his monitor dinged. He looked up. His face recognition software was designed to notify him whenever there was a hit, even if the search was ongoing. Apparently, a potential match had been found.

"Okay, I'm back," he said as he clicked on the link to see what the program had come up with.

"Your hour's up," Griffin said.

"I realize that. These aren't exactly…" He paused. How about that? The search had found her. He started to read the information under her name.

"Something wrong?" Griffin asked.

"What? Oh, no," the Mole said. "I was just saying these aren't easy searches."

"Tell me you at least found something."

The Mole opened his mouth to say he had, but the words died in his throat.

"Hey! Are you listening?" Griffin said, growing angry.

"Yes, sorry. I've been concentrating mainly on the woman, but, well, there's a problem."

"What kind of problem?"

"I ran the car through the DMV database, but it appears that it has been completely removed from the records. Even the backups."

"There's got to be something there. The files can't be completely written over, can they?"

"Whoever did the removal was pretty thorough." So far everything the Mole had said had been true. The next part, though, wasn't. Which was why he hesitated before he spoke. "I'm optimistic that I'll be able to dig something up, but it might take me a little while."

A pause. "And nothing on the men."

It took all of the Mole's will to keep his voice from cracking. "The men, no. The BMW, though, is registered to a—"

"I know about the BMW. I need to know who the *people*

are."

"I understand that. I was just thinking—"

"How much more time do you need?"

"Uh, well, a day would be good."

"A day?"

"Like I said, these aren't easy searches."

"You have four hours," Griffin said, then hung up.

What the hell am I doing? the Mole thought.

He knew he should have told Griffin what he had learned, but his gaze strayed back to the facial match result on his monitor. Misty Blake had indeed worked for the government several years before transferring to the Labor Board. The agency she had worked for, however, had been a semiautonomous one. It was this agency's demise that had undoubtedly necessitated her moving to a new job.

The Office.

The Mole knew it well. While he had never worked directly for them, he'd done enough tangential jobs through third parties—mainly Orlando, and once for her partner Quinn—that a fair amount of the Office's cash had passed through his accounts. He had talked once to Orlando about the sudden dismantling of the organization, and she'd been very sympathetic toward those who worked there, telling him they'd been given a raw deal.

Hey, maybe one of the men in the other pictures is the guy who used to run the place. What was his name? Paul? Peter? One of those apostle names.

He tried to concentrate on what he should do next. He had never met or talked to Misty Blake. He'd never had any contact with the guy who had run the Office, either. So, technically, he had no reason at all to protect either of them.

But they were Orlando's colleagues, maybe even her friends. And Orlando was definitely his.

The Mole didn't have a huge conscience, but he did have one. And before he sold anyone out to Griffin, he knew he had to talk to Orlando first.

He adjusted his headset and opened Skype again.

WASHINGTON, DC

GRIFFIN SAT WAITING in his Lexus sedan, his demeanor darkening with each passing minute. He had hoped to have some good leads by now, and while he did have the photos of the intruders, they didn't seem to be getting him anywhere.

The Mole had so far proven useless. Griffin had given him a deadline that had been completely ignored, and he knew if he let that go unchecked, it would likely happen again. Which meant once this project was over, he would have to make a trip out there. But the more pressing matter at the moment was, what if the asshole didn't even come through in four hours? That would be a huge problem. Not only for the dumbass techie, but also for Griffin. What Griffin needed to do was branch out and get some others working on this.

Several names came to mind. He finally settled on three, and sent them all identical e-mails with the images attached. He'd barely set his phone down when it rang. The name on the display was one of the people he'd just contacted.

"This is Griffin."

"It's Keenan. I got your e-mail. I'm happy to do what I can."

Griffin sensed a "but" coming, as in "but I don't have time right now," so he said nothing.

"It's…um, I don't know who the woman or the guy in the car with her are, but the other one, I know him."

"You do?"

"I worked with him once, maybe eighteen months ago. Also seen him a couple times since. Parallel projects."

"So he's in the business?" Like Griffin thought.

"Yeah. Been in longer than I have, I think. His name's Howard."

"Howard what?"

"No, no. That's his last name. First is…uh, crap, um…" Keenan went silent for a moment. "Steve," he said, blurting out the name. "Steve Howard. That's it."

CHAPTER
TWENTY THREE

ISLA DE CERVANTES

NOT LONG AFTER Orlando had fallen back asleep, Liz had come into the room and offered to stay for a while so Quinn could freshen up and get something to eat. Once she promised to call him if Orlando woke again, Quinn allowed himself to leave.

After a quick shower and change of clothes, he went to the small cafeteria and took a table in the corner, where he could work on Orlando's laptop without anyone looking over his shoulder.

The problem was, Orlando had dozens of different decrypting programs. He'd gone through as many as he could the night before, looking for any that mentioned a code called Hansell IV, but had struck out.

For the first thirty minutes he sat in the cafeteria, he was having more of the same lousy luck. Then he opened a program called Juniper Lemon 23. What the title meant, he had no idea, but under the selection menu was the option: HANSELL IV.

When a nurse at a nearby table looked over, he realized he must have grunted in triumph, so he smiled his apologies. She returned a disapproving scowl, but turned back to her meal and seemed to forget he was there.

He imported the first image he'd taken of the microfilm into the program and clicked the START button. As the computer was doing its thing, Nate entered the cafeteria and joined him.

"Still at it, huh?" Nate said as he sat down.

"Think I might have it this time," Quinn told him.

"Really?"

Though the program was still processing, Quinn turned it so Nate could see the screen, too. A status bar lay across the center of a white page, the progress marked as the bar filled with red. The bar disappeared when the red hit the end, and a finished image took its place.

"Uh, not sure that's right," Nate said.

"Stow it," Quinn told him.

While the image was no longer rows of what appeared to be randomly placed black squares, it was not a readable document, either. The decrypting had produced a few places where words could be teased out—"play," "window," and "might" were the easiest—but most were still indecipherable blobs.

There must have been a wrong setting, or—

Protocol is base seven.

"I'm an idiot," Quinn whispered to himself.

"Well, if we're taking a poll..." Nate said.

"One more word and I'll put you back in that hospital bed permanently."

Quinn opened the program's options, searching for a place to input the correct protocol, but nothing looked right.

"You want me to try?" Nate asked.

"You think you could do better?"

"I was thinking maybe a fresh pair of eyes? You know."

Quinn scooted the laptop in front of Nate. "Go ahead. Be my guest."

Nate had just begun to hunt around when Quinn's phone vibrated. He pulled it out, thinking maybe Orlando had woken up. But the caller ID read:

UNKNOWN

What the hell? UNKNOWN was not something that

usually appeared. Thanks to some software additions Orlando had installed, Quinn's, Nate's, and Daeng's phones were able to read every number that came in, even if it was blocked by more than the standard phone company setup.

"Who is it?" Nate asked.

Quinn showed him the screen.

"I didn't think that was possible," Nate said.

"It's not supposed to be."

"You going to answer?"

Quinn shook his head, and pushed the button sending the call to voice mail, sure that the person on the other end wouldn't leave a message. After a few seconds, the phone began vibrating again with another call.

UNKNOWN

This time, he sent it to voice mail right away.

"Same again?" Nate asked.

Quinn nodded. Ten seconds later, UNKNOWN called for the third time. He considered sending the call away again, but he was curious now.

"Who is this?" he said, his voice low and emotionless.

"I did not…want…to call you, but…I…have no choice."

Though it had been a few years since he'd heard the voice, Quinn immediately recognized the halting pattern and electronic monotone. It was one of Orlando's sources. A guy, or maybe a girl, who went by the name the Mole. The last time Quinn had talked to him was when Orlando went missing in Berlin and Durrie reappeared.

"What do you mean, you have no choice?"

"I tried to call…Orlando…but she…has not answered and…I don't…have a lot of…time. I need to talk…to…her."

"Well, you can't right now," Quinn said.

"Where is she?"

"Unavailable."

Silence for several seconds. "Is she…dead?"

Though the Mole's monotone made the question sound detached, Quinn sensed concern.

"No, but she's not exactly doing great right now, either."

Another pause. "I need…to talk…to her."

"I told you, you can't. If you need to talk, you can talk to me."

"I need…to talk…to her." Before Quinn could repeat his response, the Mole added, "This is very…important…deadly important. I need to talk…to Orlando." Desperate, almost pleading now.

"I don't even know if she's awake."

"Please…please can you check?"

Against his better judgment, Quinn said, "Call me back in five minutes," and hung up without waiting for an answer.

CHAPTER TWENTY FOUR

WASHINGTON, DC

GRIFFIN WAS READING through a digital file full of information about Steve Howard when Dima called.

"Metropolitan Police found the woman's car," Dima reported.

"Where?"

"Parking garage near the Mall. A manager called it in because it had been parked there overnight."

"Empty?"

"Yes.

Of course they had dumped the vehicle. After studying Howard for the last twenty minutes, Griffin knew the man was smart. He had to be, to last as long as he had as a freelance operative.

"Were there any reports of stolen vehicles from either the Mall or the surrounding area yesterday?" he said.

"I knew you'd ask that so I checked, and there were two. One on the street three blocks away somewhere between three and four pm."

"And the other?"

"At 2:46 p.m. From inside that very garage."

Well, well, well. "What kind of car was it?"

"A Volvo S60 sedan. Blue."

Griffin stared out the window, his mind processing the new information.

"If there's nothing else..." Dima said, his voice tentative.

"Of course there's something else. You're going to help me find that car."

"How are you expecting me to do that?"

"Don't pretend you don't have access to traffic cameras. You know the car now, you know what they look like, and you know the approximate time they must have left that garage. Find their trail. Tell me where they went. You have forty-five minutes."

"But—"

Griffin hung up.

CHAPTER TWENTY FIVE

ISLA DE CERVANTES

Liz was asleep in the chair when Quinn and Nate reentered Orlando's room. Orlando, though, was awake. So much for relying on his sister.

Quinn walked quietly up to the bed and whispered, "How are you feeling?"

"You don't want to ask that."

"Are you in pain? I could get the nurse."

With effort, she reached out and put her hand on his. "No. It's okay."

He looked her over, concerned. "Is there something I can do?"

"Relax, maybe. You're stressing me out."

He forced himself to smile. "Sure. Sorry."

"Ugh. That's even worse," she said.

As he moved his other hand onto the bed, he realized he was still holding his phone.

The Mole.

He thought for a moment. If his offering to get the nurse had stressed Orlando out, he couldn't imagine what talking to the Mole would do to her, so he slipped the phone into his pocket.

Nate moved in behind him. "Hey, how are you doing?"

"I hear that I'm better than I was," Orlando said.

"Well, yeah. That wouldn't take much, though."

"I see you came to cheer me up."

"My official capacity today is Quinn's Sherpa." He raised the laptop.

Orlando looked confused. "That's mine, isn't it?"

"Um, I guess," Nate said.

"It is," Quinn told her. "Hope you don't mind I was using it."

"No, it's fine. Have something to do with why you went to see Misty?"

"Yeah, partly."

She watched him for a moment. "Are you going to share?"

"It's not important."

"Actually, maybe you can help," Nate said.

Quinn glared at him. "It's *fine.* Not important."

Orlando looked back and forth between them. "Tell me, for God's sake."

Nate opened his mouth to speak, but Quinn said, "Stop. I'll tell."

"Sure," Nate said. "No problem. Just trying to help."

"Thanks," Quinn told him, the sarcasm thick and heavy. As concisely as he could, he explained about the files and trying to decrypt them using her computer.

"What program did you use?" she asked.

"I looked through almost all of the ones in your encryption file. One called Juniper Lemon 23 came closest to working, but I couldn't figure out how to input—"

With a groan, she rolled her eyes, a look of utter disgust on her face. When she looked at him again, it was as if she were wondering whether he was worthy of her attention. "Two problems. A) I don't have a specific encryption file, and b) you're not even using the right program." She looked at Nate. "Give that to me."

She tried to lift her hands toward him, but had to settle for turning them palms up.

Quinn stayed Nate's arm with his own hand. "I don't think so," he said.

"Do you want it done or not?" she asked.

"Just tell us how. You don't have to do it yourself."

"It'll be faster if I do it."

"I said no."

"I don't care what you said. I'm not a child."

Quinn's phone vibrated in his pocket. *The Mole. Dammit.* He reached in and sent the call to voice mail as he said, "You're not in any condition to help. Just rest. That's your job right now, remember?"

"I'm fine," she said.

"Oh, really." He let his gaze trace some of the wires and tubes that connected her to the devices surrounding her bed. "When you can sit up on your own, maybe we'll talk."

Her mouth pressed into a hard, thin line, her eyes narrowing to match it. "Okay. If that's how you want it, good luck figuring it out."

"Oh, so *now* it's all right to act like a child?"

His phone vibrated again.

"If you're going to treat me like a child, I might as well act like one." In the pause that followed, the cell vibrated again. "Are you going to answer that?"

Quinn pulled out the phone. UNKNOWN again. "I'll deal with it later," he said as he sent the Mole once more to voicemail.

Before Quinn could even put the phone away, the Mole called back.

Orlando's eyebrows rose, her anger partially replaced by curiosity. "What's going on?"

He looked at her, and then at the phone. "Hold on," he told her.

Turning for the exit, he pressed ACCEPT. "Yes?"

"Orlando…can I talk…to her?"

"Not right now. She's—"

"Who is that?" Orlando said.

Two things happened at the same moment. Liz's eyelids cracked open. She sat up and said, "What's going on?"

And on the phone, the Mole said, "I heard…her voice…this is important…please…I need…to…talk to…her."

Quinn stood unmoving in the doorway for a moment

before stepping back into the room. With extreme reluctance, he said to Orlando, "It's for you."

"Who is it?"

"A friend of yours." Walking back to her bed, he said into the phone, "Do *not* upset her."

"That is not my…intention," the Mole said.

"Fine. I'm going to put you on speaker, and I *will* hang up if I think there's even a chance of that happening."

Liz looked at him, clearly confused. For half a second, Quinn considered asking her to leave the room, but she would probably find out from Nate what was discussed anyway.

He put the phone on the bed next to Orlando, and pressed speaker. "Okay. You can talk to her now. But don't forget what I said."

"Who is this?" Orlando asked.

"It's me," the Mole said. "I understand you aren't well." While his distinctive monotone was still there, his usual lethargic pacing had disappeared.

"It's been a rough week," she said. She was still obviously perplexed that the Mole had called her.

"Better now?"

"Getting there."

"Good." The Mole paused. "There's something I think you need to know."

"What?"

"Does the name Misty Blake mean anything to you?"

Quinn looked at the phone, his eyes widening. "Misty? What about Misty?"

"I was not talking to you."

"It's okay," Orlando said. "We both know Misty. You can answer him."

"There was a car accident in Washington, DC yesterday. Misty and two other men were involved."

"How did you know about them?" Quinn asked.

"I was asked to identify them from photographs."

Photographs? "Who asked you to identify them?"

The Mole said nothing.

"*Who*?" Quinn asked again.

"Someone who wants to find them."

"That's not an answer."

"For now it's my answer."

"You've got to give us more than that."

"All right. An individual."

"An *individual* who works for a security and retrieval firm in the DC area, I'll bet."

"DC, yes. But he does not work for any kind of security and retrieval firm."

That was not the answer Quinn had been expecting. The only photos this "individual" could possess were the ones taken by the men who'd been outside Peter's place when Daeng, Misty, and Howard had been there. It hadn't been a stretch to assume the photographer worked for the same place as Witten and his team. Was this the unnamed client Witten had mentioned?

"Why does this person want to find our friends?" Orlando asked.

"He wouldn't tell me, but he deals in dirty work, so I'm guessing what he wants can't be good."

"Lovely client you have there," Quinn said.

"He is *not* my client!" The software controlling the Mole's voice could not contain his anger.

"Then why are you helping him?"

Several seconds passed before the Mole finally answered. "Sometimes we have no choice."

"So you've given him this information already?"

Another flash of annoyance. "No! I've put him off for now." The Mole took a breath. "When I figured out who the woman was, I knew you might know her, Orlando, so I thought it best to talk to you first."

"But at some point you're going to have to tell him," Orlando said.

"I will have to tell him something. But I'm open to suggestions."

Orlando looked at Quinn, perplexed. Quinn, too, wasn't sure what the right answer was.

"When are you supposed to let him know?" Quinn asked.

"He gave me four hours. That was seventeen minutes ago."

Good, Quinn thought. There was still more than three and a half hours left until the deadline. "We need to think this through. Can we call you back?"

"Don't wait too long."

CHAPTER
TWENTY SIX

WASHINGTON, DC

"WELL?" GRIFFIN SAID.

Dima was on the other end of the phone, his call coming twelve minutes ahead of the forty-five-minute deadline. "They left the city right after they stole the car."

"You're sure it was them."

"Have them on a traffic camera. The Asian guy was driving. The woman was in the backseat, but I couldn't see the other man."

"Where were they headed?" he asked.

"Toward Arlington."

"That opens a lot of possibilities. Tell me you were able to narrow it down more than that."

"I was. I used our access to the Virginia Department of Transportation's traffic-cam system, and tracked them east on I-66. When they reached I-81, they went south for a few miles before exiting. I followed them to a block away from the off-ramp, but there were no more cameras after that."

"Where did they exit?"

"A place called Trevor Hollow."

CHAPTER TWENTY SEVEN

ISLA DE CERVANTES

AS SOON AS the Mole hung up, Quinn called Daeng.

"We just received a call from a source," he said. "Someone's trying to track you down."

"I assume the same people as before, right?"

"I'm not so sure about that. Apparently this is a single operative. I think he could be the client Witten mentioned. I'm going to do some digging and see what I can find out. The thing to worry about right now is that he might be able to figure out where you all are."

"I'll keep an eye out."

"Okay. Let me know if anything happens."

"Wait," Daeng said before Quinn hung up. "I called you because I found something."

"You called? I called you."

"And I called you a few minutes ago."

It took Quinn a second before he realized it must have been Daeng calling the first time his phone vibrated. It hadn't been the Mole.

"What is it?"

"I was looking inside the box the microfilm was in. Under the packing foam I found several photographs."

"Of what?" Quinn asked.

"Not what, who. Miranda, Peter's wife. Misty says these were the ones in that other file he kept."

"Miranda?"

"It seemed odd to me that he would keep them with the microfilm."

It seemed odd to Quinn also.

"I asked Misty what she thought," Daeng went on. "And, well, maybe I should let her tell you." There was a click, then a more distant Daeng said, "Can you hear me?"

"Yeah, hold on. I'm putting you on speaker here, too."

Quinn switched over and placed his phone back on the bed as he shared with the others in the room what Daeng had found.

"Okay, Misty," he said. "Go ahead."

"Well, I was thinking the thing Peter said he'd been poking around in might have something to do with a project his wife could have been working on."

"She was in the business, too?" Quinn asked.

"No. She worked for the State Department."

"In what capacity?"

"Her specialty was eastern Europe, but she was rising fast and becoming one of the go-to people for difficult negotiations, no matter who was involved. You've probably heard of her."

"I told you, Peter never mentioned her."

"Not through Peter," Misty said. "On the news when she died. Miranda Keyes. Does that help?"

It took Quinn only a second or two to remember why the name sounded so familiar. "*She* was Peter's wife?"

"Yes."

"I had no idea."

"Few did. They kept their marriage quiet for obvious reasons."

Quinn nodded to himself. Peter was in the intelligence business, often spying on the very nations his wife was negotiating with. Best to keep their union private. In the end it didn't matter. An accident had ripped them apart.

The crash had been all over the news. It had occurred in Turkey, and because it involved Miranda and three other "rising stars" of the American diplomatic corps, at first it had been speculated that it wasn't an accident at all, but an act of terror. The news ran with that for several days, making Miranda Keyes, the lead negotiator in the group, a household name. But it was soon revealed the crash had been caused by an unexpected mechanical issue—a tire blowout, failed brakes, something like that. He couldn't remember the exact details. Whatever the cause, the result had been the deaths of everyone in the car.

"Nate," Orlando said. "Give me the laptop."

Nate shot a look at Quinn, who frowned but nodded his consent.

"Do you know what she might have worked on that Peter would be looking into?"

He could almost hear Misty shaking her head across the line. "No, I'm sorry. And I might be completely wrong. It was just the first thought that came to mind."

"All right. Thanks, Misty. We'll touch base with you guys later." Once the call was disconnected, he said to Orlando, "Did you find the image files?"

"You didn't exactly hide them," she said.

"Will you be able to decrypt them?"

"We'll know in…"—she looked at the screen—"a tad under seven minutes."

"Now you're just showing off," he said.

Though she looked tired, her eyes sparkled as she grinned at him. If it weren't for the hospital bed and the monitoring equipment, she almost looked like her old self again.

Thirty seconds short of the seven-minute mark, she said, "Here we go."

They crowded around the side of her bed so they could all see the laptop's screen. Centered on it was a document, and to the side a vertical column of the other files.

"That's not English," Nate said.

"I believe it's Turkish," Quinn said. Though he didn't speak the language, he'd seen enough of it in his travels to recognize it.

"There's a date in the upper right," Orlando said.

It was written European-style—day first, month second, year last—and was over a decade old.

"Miranda Keyes," Liz said, pointing at the screen.

Typed on a line that ran the width of the paper was not only Miranda's name but three other names—Morris Tate, Gerald Yamada, and Brenda Samson.

"It's the accident report," Quinn said. "Those are the people who died with Miranda. I remember the names."

"So Peter was looking into his wife's death?" Liz asked.

"Let's see what else is here first." He nodded to Orlando. "Next page."

Documents two and three were the rest of the report, while four and five were condensed English translations. According to these last two, the four passengers had been on a break from the international conference they were attending in Bursa, and had taken a drive into the national park toward Mount Uludag. While there, on a windy mountain road, the driver—Morris Tate—lost control of their car, drove off the side, and their vehicle tumbled down a slope approximately one hundred fifteen meters long. No other cars had been involved, and the cause was determined to be a combination of high speed and brake malfunction. Pretty much like Quinn remembered.

When Orlando moved on to file six, they were all surprised to see that it looked to be a copy of the very first file—page one of the Turkish report.

Orlando flicked back and forth between the two. Same dates, same names, same ink marks in the margins. She moved on to document seven. A copy of the second page of the Turkish report. Only…

"The last two paragraphs," Nate said. "Look."

As Orlando toggled between documents seven and two, it became clear that while most of the information in each document was identical, the last two typed paragraphs were completely different.

Moving on to document eight, they could see that the five signatures at the bottom were the exact size and in the exact same position as those on doc three. The paragraphs above them, however, did not match.

Files nine and ten were the English version again, but they looked nothing like the previous translations. Just from the format, it was obvious they'd been prepared by someone else entirely.

The new version did not tell the story of a driver who'd lost control of his car, but rather of a driver who'd been shot in the head and died before the car even reached the edge of the pavement, leaving the passengers unable to prevent the crash. An investigator found the bullet lodged in the backseat of the car. Given the angle it would have had to travel from the man's head into the cushion, the investigator was able to determine the likely spot the gunman had fired from. A search of the area revealed only ground that had been brushed clean.

"Dear God," Liz said. "Is this the correct report? Or is it the other one?"

"Depends on what you mean by correct," Quinn said. "Official? That would be the first one." He left the rest unsaid and told Orlando to keep going.

Files eleven and twelve were typed notes—addresses, names, thoughts—ending with a list:

N. Lionel
Kablukov
BJD
Mossad
Jude Eisner
Lon/Tec
Darvot
SVGX
Klaus Pounder
Herman Raver
P12

Most of the names were familiar to Quinn. Many referred to intelligence agencies, some associated with a specific country and some not, while the individuals he recognized also played in their world. So what was this? Peter's suspect list? That was the first thing that came to Quinn's mind.

They could come back to it later, though, so he nodded to Orlando that he was ready to move on.

File thirteen was the beginning of the pictures. The first five had an embossed stamp in the lower right corner that Quinn guessed meant they were official. Each was a different shot of the crash, victims and all. Miranda had apparently been sitting in the backseat on the passenger side, which was probably the only reason she remained recognizable. In contrast, the face of the woman who had been sitting in front of her was a bloody and unrecognizable pulp, most likely because it had been bashed repeatedly against the dash and windshield.

Not surprisingly, the picture featuring the driver avoided any angles that would reveal his fatal wound, and instead concentrated on his crumpled form.

File eighteen was another crime scene photo, only this one was missing the official seal. It showed the center section of the backseat cushion, complete with bullet hole. To either side of the picture, you could see a portion of Miranda and the woman who'd been sitting beside her, leaving no doubt the picture was from their accident. The next two photos were of the driver, each showing the entry wound above his right eye, and confirming what Quinn had already suspected—the second report was the accurate one.

Next came a map with a circle around the area where the accident had occurred, while the final two files were pictures again. The first was a wide shot of the crash scene, also without a seal. Several people were looking through the car, while more huddled in smaller groups, talking. The last image was a close-up of the group that had been farthest from the camera. It wasn't a new shot, but a blowup of the previous one, which, because of the magnification, meant the subjects were blurry. The main focus seemed to be on the man in the center. He had short brown hair and appeared to be more Caucasian than Turkish, but that was pretty much all Quinn could make out.

"Go back," he said.

Orlando clicked back to the group image. Though the area blown up in the final image was considerably smaller now, it was actually easier to make out some details. No, the man was definitely not Turkish. He was talking to an official-looking man in a suit. Perhaps the lead investigator?

"Anybody recognize him?" he asked.

"I don't," Orlando said.

Nate shook his head. "Me, neither."

"Who do you think he is?" Liz asked.

"Someone Peter was interested in, I guess," Quinn replied. "But other than that, I don't know."

"Maybe he was from the US delegation, there to ID the bodies," his sister suggested.

"That would be done in a morgue, not while the bodies were still in the car. Besides, I doubt they would leave the bodies there very long anyway, so the pictures had to have been taken shortly after the police arrived on scene."

"Maybe he's with the police," she said.

"I don't think so."

"Because he's white? I'm sure there's some fair-skinned Turks."

"I'm sure there are. But look at his haircut. Look at what he's wearing." The man was dressed in khaki pants and a black polo golf shirt. "If he's not American, then he's pretending to be one."

"Then he *could* be from the delegation," Liz argued.

Quinn shook his head. "If he were, Peter would have known, and wouldn't have blown this picture up. Whoever this guy is, I'd bet he's tied to what happened to Miranda and her friends."

"I might be able to clean the picture up some," Orlando said. "Then maybe…send it around. See if anyone recognizes…him."

"Yeah, maybe after you take a twelve-hour nap," Quinn said.

"I'm okay. Just need to rest for a minute."

"I'll help her," Liz said. "She can tell me what to do."

Quinn disliked that idea only slightly less than having Orlando do it on her own, but the truth was, getting that picture would help. He nodded. "E-mail me copies of all the decrypted files first, then see what you can do."

He motioned for Nate to follow him, and left.

In the corridor, he said, "Peter said it in the video I saw. Whoever's responsible for killing him killed Miranda, too."

"It would be a hell of a coincidence otherwise."

"Exactly. You saw the list in Peter's notes, right?"

Nate nodded.

"I'd bet everything that the person or group we're looking for is on there. We need to pull the pieces together, and figure out which one it is."

"And how are we going to do that?"

To answer, Quinn pulled out his phone and called Daeng.

"News?" Daeng said.

"Nothing yet," Quinn replied. "I need to talk to Misty."

"Sure. Hold on."

A short pause, then Misty said, "Hello?"

"How you holding up?"

"Well, you know. Okay, I guess."

"I have a question for you. Peter once mentioned there was an organization that took over for the Office. I'm pretty sure he knew the person in charge."

"Yes, he did."

"I had the impression Peter trusted him."

"Very much. But it's not a him. It's a her."

CHAPTER
TWENTY EIGHT

SAN FRANCISCO

HELEN CHO GRABBED the pot of coffee off her credenza and filled her cup.

When she was settled behind her desk, she pushed the intercom button and said, "Send in Director Stone."

Across the room the door to her office opened, and Gregory Stone, current director of O & O, stepped in.

"Good to see you, Helen," he said as he walked up to her desk and extended his hand.

"Sit," she said, not taking it.

"All right." He pulled his hand back and sat down. "Now what's so important we couldn't have dealt with it over the phone?"

"First off, you're fired."

He leaned forward. "Excuse me?"

"I don't see a need to repeat myself."

"You can't fire me. You don't have the authority."

"You mean even though your organization now falls under me?"

"Yes. Check my job description. You may be able to order O & O around, but I can only be removed from office by the secretary of Homeland Security or someone above him. Which, I believe, is only one person."

"Two if you count the vice president."

"No one counts the vice president," Stone said.

"Fair enough. I've read the details of your employment parameters. Needless to say, they will be removed before your successor takes office."

Stone snorted a laugh, leaned back against his chair, and crossed his legs. "Dream on."

She held his gaze for a moment before she reached over and tapped one of the buttons on her phone. "Are you still there, sir?"

"I am," the secretary of Homeland Security said.

"And I trust you heard everything."

"I did indeed."

The blood drained from Stone's face. "I, um, wasn't aware someone was listening in. I should have been informed."

"Does it matter?" Helen asked.

"Yes, former Director Stone, that's a good question," the secretary said.

"It's not fair, sir. This is an ambush."

"What this is," Helen said, "is an overdue spring cleaning."

"You cannot—"

"Stop right there," the secretary said. "I would think very long and hard before you open your mouth again, Mr. Stone. You've made a mess at O & O. Helen is only doing what needs to be done."

"Sir, I don't know what stories you may have heard, or what Director Cho had chosen to tell you, but—"

"Director Cho has *chosen* to tell me nothing. She merely asked that I look into O & O for myself, which I have." He paused. "I am embarrassed that this agency exists under my umbrella. Who knows how long it's going to take us to unravel everything you've done there? Starting right now, you will answer everything Director Cho asks you. You will answer truthfully without hesitation. But it doesn't end when you walk out of the room. Consider the rest of your life one gigantic exit interview. If and when Director Cho has questions for you in the future, you will answer those immediately. You will also answer any questions your successor has, if we decide it's worth keeping O & O going. Lie one time, put off one answer, and you might as well kiss your life good-bye, because I can assure you, where you'll be taken, you will not see the light of day for quite some time. If I'm particularly annoyed, like I am right now, I'll arrange it so you *never* see it again. Am I understood?"

"Yes, sir."

"Are there any questions?"

"No, sir."

"Good. Then Director Cho, I will leave matters in your hands."

"Thank you, sir," Helen said, and touched the button that disconnected the call.

For several seconds, Stone stared at the phone, as if he were sure the secretary was still on the line.

"Darvot Consulting," Helen said.

He looked at her, confused. "What?"

"Darvot Consulting, the client for the Georgetown job we talked about on the phone. Who is your main contact there?"

"That, um, would be Kyle Morten."

"So Mr. Morten is the one who hired you to watch the apartment?"

"Actually it was arranged by his associate, Mr. Griffin."

As she suspected.

"What was the purpose of this job?"

"To detain anyone trying to enter the apartment."

"And how did that go?" She paused only a second before saying, "Never mind. Your failure on the mission isn't important at the moment. It's the mission itself I'm interested in. What were the reasons for detaining anyone found there?"

"I assume you've read the project brief," he said. "Likely terrorist activity?"

"You believed the brief?"

"My job is not…*was* not to question a brief, but to render services to clients on our approved list. Darvot is on that list."

"Who put them on that list?"

"They've been there for as long as I've been with the

organization."

"Let me broaden that a bit. Who approves anyone for that list?"

His hesitation was probably enough to get him sent to Guantanamo, but she made no mention of it.

"The director of O & O."

"So, you."

"Yes. But I do my due diligence, and my predecessor would have done the same."

"I'm sure. What you're telling me is that your job is not to question a brief from a client approved by the director of O & O, and yet you are the director of O & O. Help me out here."

"My predecessor, in this case," he said.

"The director of O & O," she countered.

In the corner of her eye, she saw a message from her assistant David flash onto her computer screen. She glanced over.

> I have a Jonathan Quinn on line three. He insists on talking to you.

Jonathan Quinn? It took her a moment to place the name. He was an operative, a…cleaner, if she wasn't mistaken. Why in God's name would he want to talk to her?

She typed a quick reply.

> Take a message.

David responded almost immediately.

> He said he'll hold.

She wrote back:

> Tell him I'm tied up.

Then she turned her screen so she wouldn't see it if

another message appeared.

"Apologies," she said to Stone. "Let's keep moving forward. Mr. Griffin answers to Mr. Morten. Do you know if Mr. Morten answers to anyone?"

"How should I know that?" Stone said. "They haven't shared their corporate structure with me."

"It's not in the file O & O has on Darvot?"

"You must have looked at it yourself. You know if it's there or not."

"It's not."

"Well, then, there's your answer," he said defensively.

She stared at him until he blinked and looked away. "You want to know what I've learned about your organization since it came under my control? O & O and due diligence are not synonymous. I have no doubt we're going to find numerous examples of O & O activities that border on the criminal, if not cross the line entirely."

"I don't know what you mean. I have no knowledge of anything remotely like that."

"Of course you don't." She clasped her hands, set them on the desk in front of her, and leaned forward. "What I'm telling you, Mr. Stone, is this. You will never look for another job again. Not in the government. Not in the private sector. Not even serving coffee at Starbucks. You will live off the money you have now, and the retirement package you are due. And that's it."

He jerked forward and slammed his palms down on the front of her desk. "What? You can't do that! I don't have enough to—"

"Actually, I can. If you break this rule, you will find yourself in one of our secret courtrooms, where you'll be convicted and sentenced to life."

"On what charge?"

She smiled. "We'll think of something." She stood. "Now get your ass out of my office."

"I want to talk to the sec—"

"Don't embarrass yourself. Get out, Gregory. We're done."

It was several moments before he finally pulled himself to his feet and left her office, looking shell-shocked.

Before the door could close again, David slipped inside. "Excuse me, Director, but Jonathan Quinn has called back again."

"For God's sake, David. Run interference. I don't have time to deal with him."

"He said to tell you it has to do with Peter." He said the name almost like it was a question, as if he wasn't sure he was pronouncing it right.

Helen froze. "He said Peter?"

"Yes, ma'am."

That's right. That's how she knew Quinn. He was Peter's go-to cleaner. But why would he be calling now? What the hell was going on? "Give me a minute, then put him through."

When her phone rang, she was sitting again, looking at her computer. She picked up the receiver and said, "Mr. Quinn."

"Director Cho, thank you for taking my call. I'm—"

"I know who you are," she said. On her monitor was a surprisingly short dossier for one Jonathan Quinn. "You're a cleaner."

"That's correct."

"As you can imagine, my schedule is rather full. I only have a moment. If we could make this quick?"

"Of course. I'm hoping you can help me with a few questions."

"I'm not an information service."

"I'm asking as a favor to Peter."

As a test, she said, "If Peter wants a favor, he can call himself."

"Ma'am, I have no doubt you already know Peter was killed in the Caribbean early last week."

She said nothing.

"I was standing less than fifty feet away from him when it happened."

Helen seldom found herself at a loss for words, but this was one of those moments. When she finally found her voice, she said, “Tell me how it happened.”

Quinn told her a story of kidnapping and torture and murder and escape. His details so neatly filled in the holes in the report on Peter’s death that she knew he was telling the truth. Her analysts were right. It had been an act of revenge gone wrong.

“The rest of you survived, though?” she asked.

A hesitation. “Yes.”

Neither said anything for a moment.

“You said you had questions, Mr. Quinn.”

“Peter left some unfinished business that he wanted me to take care of.”

“And what might that be?”

“What do you know about Miranda Keyes’s death?”

“Miranda Keyes?” Helen said. “Who is Miranda…” Her voice trailed off as she remembered. “You mean the woman from the State Department killed in that car accident?”

“It wasn’t an accident. Someone murdered her and her colleagues.”

“That was a long time ago. I don’t remember all the details, but I seem to recall that there was a thorough investigation and no determination of foul play. So that’s quite an accusation.”

“It’s not an accusation. The original report was suppressed.”

“Who would do that?”

“That’s one of my questions.”

“Well, even if it’s true, I obviously have no idea.”

“Maybe not. But you’re in a position to help me find out.”

“And why would I do that?”

“It’s my understanding that you and Peter were close, or at least as close as Peter would let anyone get. I thought you’d be interested in bringing his wife’s killers to justice.”

“Wait, are you saying Miranda Keyes and Peter were married?”

“Yes.”

“I don’t believe it.”

"That's not my problem."

She considered the possibility. It would have been the kind of marriage better kept secret, for the obvious, diplomatic reasons. But still… "I knew Peter. If he wouldn't share that with me, he wouldn't tell you, either."

"You're right. He never said a word to me. But he did tell his assistant, Misty Blake."

Misty Blake. For a second time, Helen found herself unable to speak.

"I need your help narrowing down who might have wanted her dead," Quinn said. "I'll take it—"

"It was you, wasn't it?" she said, the pieces falling into place.

"Excuse me?"

"You were with Misty at Peter's apartment."

Now it was Quinn's turn not to say anything.

She decided to push again, using what she knew to get more information out of him. "Yesterday photos were taken of Misty and two other men outside Peter's place. One of them is you, isn't it?"

"No," he said cautiously. "I…I left before they went back there."

"But you were there for the break-in the day before, weren't you? I'll bet you're even the one who shot my man in the hand?"

"*Your* man? Sorry I bothered—"

Sensing he was about to hang up, she said, "Hold on. While the team does work at one of the agencies I oversee, I had no knowledge of the operation, not until it was over."

Silence.

"Mr. Quinn?"

The silence continued for another second, then, "You sent men to a house in Arlington Ridge, too."

"Again, my people, but not by me. Once I found out what was going on, I canceled the entire job."

Dead air, long and empty. If the display hadn't shown that the connection was still active, Helen would have thought Quinn had disconnected.

"Director Cho," he said after nearly half a minute. "This agency of yours—what's it called?"

"That's not important," she said.

"Really? You're dodging that question? You don't think I could find out some other way?"

"All right, it's called O & O."

"Ah, so that's O & O. I've heard of them, but have never had the pleasure until now. Not the kind of place I'd ever do work for. They don't exactly have the best rep."

"I'm aware of that."

"My understanding is that O & O does work for hire."

"If you've heard of O & O, then you know it does."

"Then don't you see? The client who sent them after us is most likely the one who sold Peter out to prevent him from looking into his wife's murder. Whether they pulled the trigger or not, they're the ones responsible for his death. Now they seem to be interested in taking out my friends and me. So what I need you to do is tell me who this client is."

"You'll forgive me for declining to give you that information," she said.

"Actually, I won't."

"Let me rephrase. Decline to give you that information at the moment. You understand that I can't just give you a name without doing some due diligence on my end." The irony of her statement was not lost on her.

"I believe I can help you with that. Expect an e-mail from me. You'll want to examine the attached files very carefully."

"You have my e-mail address?"

"Of course," he said. "Do you have a pen?"

"Yes."

He gave her a phone number. "I expect to hear from you very, very soon. And know this. I'm going to find out who these people are one way or the other, and you'd much rather be on board now than have me look later into why you were unwilling to help."

"Is that a threat, Mr. Quinn?"

"It is."

CHAPTER
TWENTY NINE

SEATTLE

THE MOLE HAD no idea what he was going to tell Griffin if Orlando and Quinn didn't provide him direction. He could go ahead and give up this Misty Blake woman, but he had a pretty good idea what Griffin would do if he found the woman, and the Mole couldn't bring himself to be a part of that.

Perhaps he could generate a fictional identity. He could easily seed data all over the place to support it. He played it through in his mind, and grimaced. With enough time, he could do it, but that he didn't have. One little glitch and it would be a house of cards tumbling down right on top of him.

So…what? Keep lying and say he couldn't find anything? Griffin would never go for that.

The only real solution was if he didn't have to worry about Griffin anymore.

He folded his arms and pursed his lips. Now there was an idea. He couldn't execute it himself—not the physical part, anyway—but he could help someone else achieve that goal.

Quinn, for instance.

Griffin was already moving into the cleaner's crosshairs. If the Mole could make sure Quinn had a clear shot, that would be problem solved.

All right. So what's the first thing Quinn would want to know?

Where Griffin was, of course.

The Mole woke his computer and opened Slime, his self-written tracking software. Slime was a constant work in progress. He tweaked it sometimes two or three times a week, improving its capabilities and success rate. It could employ a variety of methods, the most common being the ability to track a cell phone.

The Mole didn't try inputting Griffin's number, though. He was sure the phone would be untraceable via traditional methods. That was fine. There was another, backdoor route he could try. He'd used it before, after the last time Griffin paid him a visit, when the Mole had wanted to make sure the man had actually left Seattle. It meant sending Griffin an e-mail, but as long as he had a legitimate reason for it, there shouldn't be a problem.

Using the tracking program, he opened a blank e-mail with an embedded bot that would travel to Griffin's phone and report back. Until the message was deleted, it would act as a tracking bug.

In the body, he typed:

> Quick update. Making progress on woman. Looks like she's former intelligence but will have more info when I contact you later.
>
> M

He read it again, felt it would stand up to scrutiny, and hit SEND. He then switched to the tracking control screen and waited.

With the exception of the blinking cursor in the upper left corner, the box was empty.

"Let's go, baby. Show me where he is."

The cursor continued to blink, unmoving.

"Come on, you son of a bitch. Where are you?"

Blink.

Blink.

Blink.

There was at least one other time, with a different target, when the bot had not sent a message back, but the Mole was confident he'd taken care of that error. So why was this one not—

Suddenly the cursor began to move, spitting out a set of GPS coordinates. Once the line was complete, the Mole copied it, pasted it into Google Maps, and was almost instantaneously provided with a location.

For the first time since he'd been shooting aliens with his team, the Mole smiled.

CHAPTER THIRTY

ISLA DE CERVANTES

ORLANDO WAS ASLEEP when Quinn and Nate reentered her room. Liz was sitting in the chair, working on the laptop.

"How is she?" Quinn asked.

"She's okay," Liz said. "Just tired."

Quinn's gaze lingered on Orlando for a moment longer before moving down to the laptop screen.

"That's a little better," he said.

The blurry picture of the man at the Turkish accident scene had become more defined.

"I tried another pass," she said, "but there was no visible change, so I think this is as good as it's going to get."

Quinn took the computer from her so he could get a better look. While the man's face was still hazy, it was clear enough to be recognizable, especially to someone who knew him. Unfortunately, Quinn didn't.

He showed Nate. "Ever seen him?"

"No," Nate said after he scanned the face.

"Okay, let's get this out to some people we trust. See if any of them can ID the guy. Can you two do that?"

Nate and Liz looked uncomfortable, but Nate said, "Sure."

Quinn considered them for a moment. "Something going on here I need to know about?"

"No," Nate said.

"Yes," Liz countered.

Quinn raised an eyebrow. "And that would be…?"

Liz glanced at her boyfriend and then at her brother. "Nate's not exactly fond of sharing information with me."

"It's not that," Nate said. "It's—"

"He thinks I can't handle it. There's also the whole keep-the-secrets-in-the-club thing you've all got going." She pointed at her brother. "That's your fault." To Nate, she said, "I have news for you. I'm *in* the club now. Have been since the moment I arrived in Los Angeles and found you missing. You want this to work out between us? Don't coddle me, and don't keep things from me."

Only three weeks ago, Quinn would have argued in Nate's favor, telling his sister she didn't need to know certain things. But she was right. She'd played a valuable part in the search for Nate and Peter, and had handled herself exceptionally well. And then there was Orlando. He didn't need her to almost die for him to know how important she was in his life, but it reinforced the point nonetheless. Being with her—their loving each other—made everything better, but their relationship would have never lasted if they'd kept secrets from each other. As much as he hated to admit it, Nate and Liz were good together. He loved both of them, and knew they deserved what he and Orlando had. If they could get past acting like idiots.

He took a deep breath and said, "Dear God, are you kidding me? Nate, sometimes there's an exception that trumps any of the rules I've taught you. Can you not see that Liz is that exception? Don't screw it up. And Liz, there's a club of secrets. And yes, you're in it now, but sometimes both Nate *and* I will forget that and balk before telling you something. It doesn't mean we don't trust you. It just means we want to keep you safe. Point it out to us when it happens, then move on." They both gaped at him. "Are we good? Great, then let's get those e-mails sent."

While they got started, he walked over to Orlando and ran his hand lightly over the top of her head.

"Nice speech," she whispered, her eyes still closed.

"Oh, you were listening, were you?"

"Kind of hard to sleep with all the noise."

His playful manner disappeared. "Oh, sorry. We'll move down to the cafeteria."

"Don't you dare. I like having people here."

He swept his finger past her temple. "Are you sure?"

When she didn't answer, he realized she'd fallen back asleep. He was half tempted to go ahead and tell the others to take it out of the room, but he knew that wasn't what Orlando wanted.

A few minutes later, his phone vibrated. He pulled it out and saw the call was from UKNOWN. He moved over near the door and answered.

"Where are your friends hiding?" the Mole asked. The machine-like monotone was still there, but his halting speech pattern was gone.

"I don't think I need to tell you that."

"Then let me tell you. Western Virginia, or perhaps West Virginia."

"What makes you think that?"

"Because my client is heading in that direction as we speak."

Quinn tensed. "Where exactly is he?"

"At the moment, on I-66 ten miles west of Marshall, Virginia."

Quinn didn't have a map in front of him, but if the Mole's client was still on I-66, he had to be at least forty-five minutes to an hour away from Daeng and the others. "Are you going to tell me his name now?"

"That depends. Can you promise me he won't be a problem for me anymore?"

"If he's involved in what I think he is, then yes."

"That's not a guarantee."

"It's the best I can do at the moment."

A pause, then, "Griffin. His name is Griffin."

SAN FRANCISCO

HELEN CHO STOOD at her office window. She could see all the way to the Bay Bridge and Treasure Island. But she wasn't looking at the sights. She wasn't looking at anything at all.

On the desk behind her, her computer screen still displayed the crime scene photos from the car wreck in Turkey. It was definitely a crime scene, not an accident, as she and almost everyone else believed for so long.

She had met Miranda Keyes once, at some sort of DC function, its purpose unremembered. She could tell from that one encounter that Miranda was destined for great things. That's what made what Helen had thought was an accident so much more tragic. A strong, charismatic, intelligent woman struck down long before her full potential was realized. That was the extent of what she'd known of the woman then, but that wasn't the case now.

Her intercom buzzed. Reluctantly, she tore herself from the window and answered. "Yes?"

"Mr. Quinn is on the line again," David said.

Of course he is. "Put him through."

She sagged into her chair and stared at the display screen of her office phone before touching the blinking line. "I believe I said *I'd* be in touch with you."

"You've had plenty of time to read what I sent you, and check what you needed to check," he said. "But let me help you. Your client's name is Griffin."

"Where did you learn that?"

"Not important. I just need you to confirm."

She clicked through the pictures until she found the one she was looking for. "Griffin is not the client," she said, looking at the photo.

"You're lying to me."

"Griffin is not the client, but he does work *for* the client."

A pause. "Then who is his boss?"

"You have a picture of him. It's the enhanced close-up of the man at the crime scene."

"You know him?"

"I do."

"Who is he?"

"A story first," she said.

"I don't have time for stories."

"It'll be quick, I promise. It's an age-old tale of ambition, jealousy, and greed." The story she told was one she'd read in an archived FBI report she'd dug up after reading what Quinn had sent her.

When she finished, he said, "How reliable is this story?"

"I'll need to check sources, but given what you…well, I guess it's more what *Peter* unearthed, I would say very."

He was quiet for a moment. "The enforcer. Griffin, right?"

"Yes."

"And the second man—he's the one in the picture?"

"Correct."

"You want to tell me his name now?"

"Kyle Morten," she said.

"And the third person? Morten's client?"

"That, Mr. Quinn, is a bit trickier."

CHAPTER THIRTY ONE

TREVOR HOLLOW

THE RAIN HAD started an hour earlier. For the first few minutes, it had been an on-again, off-again sprinkle, but then the storm began to assert itself, and the smattering of rain became a downpour. The water beat against the roof in an endless series of crescendos, while the accompanying wind howled past the windows.

Daeng was used to hearing storms like this. In Bangkok, the clouds would roll in most afternoons and soak the city in minutes. But those storms were gone as fast as they came, and Daeng had the sense this one would last for a while.

"Did you touch anything over here?" Misty asked.

She was in the kitchen near the counter where the dishwasher was located, in one hand a bottle of bleach, in the other a wad of paper towels.

"I didn't, but wipe it down anyway."

While she splashed bleach onto the counter, Daeng finished removing any fingerprints from the chairs around the dining table.

Their cleaning frenzy was initiated by a call from Quinn ten minutes earlier.

"He's definitely on his way to you," the cleaner had said.

"How did he find us?" Daeng asked.

"The only way is if he figured out what kind of car you left in and traced it somehow."

"How long do we have?"

"Assume no more than thirty minutes."

"Okay," Daeng had said. "We can be out of here and in a new car well before then."

"Actually, I have something different in mind."

Quinn's plan started with their current task of destroying anything that might be used to identify them.

"I got it all, I think," Misty said a few minutes later.

Daeng looked around, and nodded. They'd wiped down everything they'd touched and more.

"Let's do the bedroom," he said.

Daeng entered, hurried over to the bed where Howard still slept, and gave him a gentle shake. "Steve, sorry to do this, but we've got to go."

Howard's eyes cracked open.

"Come on, buddy. Time to leave."

It seemed to take a moment for Daeng's words to register. Then Howard tried to push himself up, but only made it partway before he paused, wincing in pain.

"You okay?" Daeng asked.

"Give me a second."

Daeng looked back and saw that Misty had already started wiping down the dresser. That left the chair, the bed, and the nightstand. After that, the cabin would be clean.

"Okay," Howard said. "I think I'm all right."

"Let me help you." Daeng slipped an arm around Howard's back and helped him stand up. "Do you want to hang on to me, or do you want to walk on your own?"

"I can make it on my own. Just stay close. We're going to the car?"

"Yeah."

As they neared the bedroom door, Daeng said to Misty, "If you finish before I get back, grab the sheets and blankets, and come on out."

Daeng escorted Howard through the cabin and outside.

"So what happened?" Howard asked.

"We're going to have unwanted company soon if we stay here."

"How much time do we have?"

Daeng opened the back door of the Volvo. "Enough."

GRIFFIN TRANSITIONED ONTO I-81 and drove for another nine minutes before taking the Trevor Hollow exit.

Unfortunately, Dima could only point him in the direction the Volvo had taken, but after that, there were no more cameras to track the car's movements. If it weren't for the stupid storm, they could have used satellite links to follow the car all the way to its destination. Now Griffin would have to hunt and peck.

At least Trevor Hollow was considerably less populated than Arlington or DC.

"YOU THINK YOU guys can walk from here?" Daeng asked.

He'd pulled the Volvo to the side of the road, about a quarter mile west of the collection of buildings that officially represented the town of Trevor Hollow.

"Should be okay," Howard said.

"I'm not sure this is such a good idea," Misty said. "You're hurt, Steve. You can't—"

"Not the first time I've had to work injured." Howard opened his door, and used the frame to leverage himself out of the backseat into the rain.

Misty hurried out her door, popped open the umbrella they'd appropriated from the cabin, and raised it above Howard.

Daeng lowered the passenger window a few inches and leaned across the seat. "I'll call you when I'm ready to be picked up. Until then, stay out of sight. If you don't hear from me in ninety minutes, get someplace safe and call Quinn."

While Misty looked scared and uncertain, Howard nodded and said, "Good luck."

Daeng swung the Volvo in a U-turn and headed back toward the cabin. The rain was coming down so hard now that the wipers, even at full speed, were barely effective. But as much as his instincts told him to slow down, he knew he couldn't. Every second could be crucial, so he powered past where the main road turned to dirt, and slogged through the mud to the cabin turnoff.

He had a fleeting thought that this Griffin person might somehow already be waiting for him, but the parking area in front of the cabin was empty. He parked the Volvo at an angle so that someone driving up the access road would not only see it, but know what kind of car it was. He then wiped down the interior.

Before getting out, he padded his pocket to make sure Howard's now data-wiped cell phone was still there. The coat he was wearing had also come from the cabin—a black jacket complete with hood. A bit warmer than he needed this time of year, but at least it would keep some of the rain out.

Pulling the hood on, he climbed out and jogged down the road away from the cabin. When he was about a hundred feet away, he stopped and looked back, examining the tableau he'd created.

Satisfied that nothing seemed amiss, he turned to his left and disappeared into the woods.

GRIFFIN CRUISED THROUGH the tiny village of Trevor Hollow, looking for a blue Volvo S60. He knew it was possible Howard and his friends had already ditched the vehicle, but it was the only lead he had at the moment. Even if they had switched cars, finding the Volvo meant he could have Dima tap into local law enforcement records and see what vehicle might be missing in the vicinity. So far, however, no Volvo.

He headed west into the mountains on the only road leading out of town. Dima had dug up an older satellite image of the area, taken on a clear day, that showed where homes were located. He'd even overlaid a map onto it, no doubt hoping to earn some bonus points from Griffin. Too bad for him. Griffin didn't hand out bonus points.

The first two houses he checked were empty. Before he reached the third, the asphalt covering the road gave way to what was fast becoming a muddy sluice. Houses three and four were both occupied by families—neither, apparently, owning a Volvo.

According to the satellite image, the fifth house was a small place tucked down a private road. Griffin reduced his speed so he wouldn't miss the turnoff. That turned out to be a mistake. One of the back tires plunged into a particularly muddy dip, and the car lurched to a stop.

Griffin immediately punched the gas. The car rocked up, but then fell back again.

"Shit!"

He shoved the accelerator all the way to the floor. The engine roared, temporarily drowning out the sound of the rain. This time, when car reached the top of the dip, it slowed but didn't fall back.

Griffin eased back on the pedal, and glared out at the clouds. A little foul weather was always good for cover, but this storm was a bit more enthusiastic than he needed.

The road he was looking for appeared on the right a few minutes later. He slowed to make the turn, and was happy to see that though the access road was also dirt, it was narrower, the trees creating a canopy over the top. So while the ground was wet, few puddles had developed.

Reaching what he judged to be the halfway point to the small house, he let his car roll to a stop on a firm part of the road, and killed the engine. Ideally, he would have liked to turn the car around in the event he had to get out in a hurry, but there was no room.

He extracted his gun from his shoulder holster, attached the suppressor, and donned his knee-long raincoat over his suit. When the coat was buttoned, he quietly opened his door and moved outside.

The trees might have been blocking a lot of the rain, but there was still enough getting through to soak him before he'd gone a dozen yards. The mud was a problem, too. Though it was probably only a half-inch deep, the muck pulled at his shoes every time he took a step. Even when he moved into the trees along the left side of the road, it wasn't much better.

It took five minutes before the house came into view. With its wood siding and small size, it was more a cabin. And sitting right in front of it, parked near the front door, was a blue Volvo S60.

Keeping under the cover of the trees, he moved in until he could see the license plate. It was a match.

The corners of Griffin's mouth twitched up.

He focused on the cabin. Though at least two lights were on inside, he couldn't see anyone through the windows. He circled around, scanning each side of the building, not stopping until he reached the front again on the other side of the driveway.

There were only two exterior doors—in front, and in back. Windows were limited, too. Two on either side of both doors, and a small one on the right side of the cabin, probably a bathroom. The left side, where the chimney was located, had none.

He crouched and looked through the windows once more.

"Come on," Griffin whispered. "Let me get a look at you."

The occupants of the house weren't cooperating. Maybe they were asleep. Howard had been hurt—that much was clear from the witnesses at the accident—and the other two might have been exhausted from taking care of him. Getting a little rest wouldn't have been out of the question.

He watched for another minute before deciding it was time to take a closer look.

IF IT WEREN'T for the pounding rain, Daeng would have heard the man's footsteps long before he did. The problem was twofold: in addition to the noise of the storm, Daeng had been listening for a car, not someone on foot. So when he heard the sound of mud sucked up by a shoe only a few feet away, he froze.

The man who passed by the rock Daeng was crouching behind was no taller than Daeng, but he had a much broader chest, and a harder, chiseled face.

It had to be Griffin. There was no other reason for someone to be walking through the woods toward the cabin at that time. Still, Daeng knew he needed to be sure.

He let the man get a good lead, and then quietly followed.

All doubt was erased when he watched the man survey the house from a distance, before looping around it without leaving the safety of the trees. If that wasn't enough, the suppressor-enhanced weapon in the man's hand was.

Daeng backed away.

GRIFFIN MOVED SILENTLY up to the window and peeked inside. A living area—couch, a few chairs, a table for eating—and in the back, jutting off to the side, the sliver of what was probably a kitchen. The only thing missing was people.

On the wall opposite the kitchen were a couple of closed doors. The bedroom and a bathroom, he guessed. That's where they must be.

He eased over to the front door and tried the handle. Locked. He figured the back door would probably be the same, so instead of wasting time checking, he pulled out his picks, selected the appropriate implements, and inserted them into the lock.

Moments later, the door swung open with a faint squeak. He waited at the threshold for someone to come out and check, but the cabin remained still.

Too still.

He stepped inside.

And smelled the distinct odor of bleach.

Son of a bitch.

Though he knew he was alone, he moved quickly over to the two doors. The first led into the bathroom, and the second the bedroom. Both empty. Both smelling of bleach. In the bedroom, the bed had also been stripped, leaving only a bare mattress.

They must have found another car, he realized.

Shit! Shit! Shit!

This Steve Howard and his friends were really starting to piss him off.

WHEN DAENG WAS confident he wouldn't be heard, he picked up his pace and raced through the woods back to the access road. Griffin's vehicle had to be somewhere alongside. The only question was, had he brought someone with him?

Keeping in the trees, Daeng paralleled the road until he caught sight of the vehicle—a black Lexus LS 460. The sports model, if he wasn't mistaken. It appeared to be empty.

He crept forward, his eyes scanning the area for any movement. When he was sure no one else was around, he stepped out from the woods and approached the vehicle.

Given the type of person Griffin seemed to be, Daeng knew the door would be unlocked before he even pulled up the handle—easy access for a quick getaway. The trick, though, was to not get the interior so wet that Griffin would suspect something. While the passenger side might have seemed like the smartest bet, it was actually the driver's side that would get less scrutiny. Griffin would be in a hurry to get in, and even if he did see some water, it could easily have happened when he'd opened the door.

Daeng crouched next to the door, opened it, and quickly slipped his gift under the driver's seat.

Seconds later, he was back in the trees, moving south toward the main road.

THE FIRST THING Griffin did when he climbed back into this car was call Dima.

After giving him the location of the cabin, he said, "Find out every vehicle the owner has. If he has family, find out what cars they have, too. Then check and see if any of them were left here."

"I'll do what I can," Dima said.

"*Find* out and call me back."

He disconnected the call, tossed his phone on the passenger seat, and considered his next move. He could stop at the café he'd seen in Trevor Hollow and wait until Dima called back, but even then there was no guarantee they'd know where the others had gone.

No, staying around here was a waste of time. Best to head back to DC. Morten was due in later that evening anyway, and would want a briefing.

Griffin started the engine, and drove all the way to the cabin so he could turn around before heading for the main road.

DAENG WATCHED FROM his hiding place at the end of the access road as the Lexus made the turn back toward the interstate.

He tapped SEND on his phone. When the call connected, he said, "He just left."

"Good," Quinn said.

CHAPTER THIRTY TWO

GRIFFIN HAD EXPECTED Dima to call already, but here he was, nearly back in DC, and no word from the useless stooge.

While he knew it was only a matter of time before he caught up to Howard and his friends, in the interim Griffin would have to report his short-term failure to Morten. That would not go over well.

He had just taken the Rosslyn/Key Bridge exit when the phone rang.

His first thought was, *Finally.* His second was, *That's not my normal ringtone.*

Even odder, it wasn't coming from the seat next to him, where his cell sat. The sound was muffled and…under him.

Keeping his eyes on the road, he reached under his seat and searched for the source of the ring. As the tone stopped, his hand encircled the familiar shape of a phone, and pulled it out.

How the hell did it get into his car?

As he contemplated the question, it rang again. The display read: UNKNOWN. He debated for only a second before answering. "Yes?"

"Mr. Griffin, how's the drive?"

There was a small empty parking lot ahead on the right. Griffin pulled into it and stopped. "Who is this?"

"From what I understand, I'm someone you want to talk to."

The tension that had engulfed Griffin moments before

suddenly disappeared. Maybe his report to Morten wouldn't be as gloomy as he'd thought.

"Do I have the pleasure of speaking to Mr. Howard? Or are you the other one?"

The silence was short, but unmistakable. Griffin had scored a point. "Call me Steve," the man said.

"I'm glad to see that you've recovered from the accident, Steve." No response on the other end. Another point scored. "What is it I can do for you?"

"You can tell me why you're so interested in me and my friends."

"I would be happy to. Perhaps we can meet somewhere and discuss it."

The man laughed. "Right. That's not going to happen. I'm not a fool."

"If you're not a fool, then you must know why I'd like to talk to you," Griffin said, hoping to find out if Howard was even worth worrying about.

"It obviously has something to do with the apartment in Georgetown. Peter's apartment."

"Obviously."

"Specifically, I would say it has something to do with two things."

Here was the potential prize. "And what would those two things be?"

"You'd like me to tell you, wouldn't you? I'll say this much. One has to do with a tiny island in the Caribbean, and one with a leisurely mountain drive in Turkey. Does that help?" Before Griffin could come up with a response, the man said, "I'll call again."

Griffin continued to hold the phone against his ear after the line had gone dead.

A tiny island in the Caribbean. A leisurely mountain drive in Turkey.

They knew. Not only about Miranda Keyes, but also about the connection to Romero.

It was the worst-case scenario, and if he didn't clamp down on it now, he'd never be able to control it.

He had to restrain himself from throwing the phone on the floor. He needed it, needed Howard to call him back. He set it on the passenger seat next to his own cell, and put the car in Drive.

There were things he needed to do before the phone rang again.

ISLA DE CERVANTES

QUINN WALKED BACK across the room to where Nate, Orlando, and Liz had listened in on the call over Orlando's computer.

"I'd say that was a direct hit on Miranda Keyes and Peter," Nate said.

"Absolutely," Quinn agreed. Griffin had known exactly what Quinn was talking about, which meant there was no question now that the man and the people he worked for were involved in both deaths.

These were the people Peter had been hunting. These were the people Quinn wanted.

"He knew Steve's name," Liz said. "He knew about the accident. How could he?"

"The photos taken in front of Peter's place," Orlando said.

Quinn nodded. "He must have gotten his hands on them and somehow ID'd Steve that way."

"I thought Helen Cho had shut down contact between her agency and Griffin," Orlando said.

"That's what she told me." He lifted his phone and tapped the director's number. As soon as he had Helen on the other end, he said, "Either you lied to me, or you have a leak."

WASHINGTON, DC

DIRECTOR CHO ORDERED an immediate lockdown of O & O. Cell phones were confiscated, and all nonessential communications were forbidden.

Computer techs began looking through logs that tracked

not only landline calls but all cell-phone activity within the facility, searching for the specific unusual activity outlined by Director Cho.

It took only eight minutes to identify a potential suspect, and another three minutes to comb through his personal cell-phone records to confirm that more suspicious calls had occurred when he was away from the building.

When the security detail entered the suspect's office, Michael Dima—the current Central—looked up from his computer screen in surprise. "Excuse me, but you're not allowed in here."

Clyde Witten, head of the detail, took a step forward. "Sir, you will come with us."

"I will do no such thing. I'm Central. I can't leave my desk."

"Relief is on the way, sir. You will come with us."

Dima made a great show of being outraged as he reached for his phone. "This is ridiculous. I'm calling Director Stone right now."

Witten stepped forward, yanked the phone out of Dima's hand, and put it back in its cradle. "You will come with us."

He grabbed Dima by the arm and pushed him firmly toward the door.

"What's this all about? You can't do this! I want to talk to Director Stone."

"I've been told that Director Stone is no longer with O & O," Witten said. He'd received word of Stone's "early retirement" straight from Direct Cho when she gave him his current orders.

"What?" Dima said. "Then…then, I, uh, I want to talk to who's in charge."

"That won't be a problem."

DIMA WAS DEPOSITED in one of O & O's interrogation rooms, and told to wait in the chair.

A television monitor on a rolling stand was at the other end of the room. Three minutes after he sat down, it flickered on. Staring back at him was Director Helen Cho.

"Good afternoon, Mr. Dima," she said.

"Director Cho," he said, his mouth dry. Though he and everyone at O & O knew what she looked like, he'd never talked to her before.

"I have a few questions for you."

"How can I help you?" he said, hoping to God this was a mistake and not what he feared it was.

She smiled. "I'm happy to hear you're willing to cooperate. Why don't we start with this? Tell me about your relationship with Mr. Griffin from Darvot Consulting."

Not a mistake.

Exactly what he'd feared.

ISLA DE CERVANTES

DIRECTOR CHO'S NEWS that the leak had been detained solidified the plan in Quinn's mind. When he told her what he wanted to do and how she could be of assistance, he half expected her to order him to back off and leave the whole mess alone. He would have ignored her, of course, but it didn't come to that. Her response instead was to make no response at all.

After the silence had gone on for more than twenty seconds, he said, "Does this mean we can count on you?"

More dead air.

"Director?

He heard her take a breath. "We may be many things, but the US government is not in the habit of sanctioning the death of law-abiding citizens, especially for personal gain. Provisionally, you can count on us."

"Provisionally?"

"There are…others who need to be informed."

"I don't know if letting more people in on this is a good idea."

"It's the only way you'll have my support, something you and your people will need. And trust me, the ones I need to talk to won't say anything."

"How long do you need?"

"Thirty minutes. An hour at the outside."

"I'll be waiting for your call."

THEY GATHERED IN Orlando's room.

Present were Quinn, Nate, Liz, and the other men who'd been rescued from Duran Island—Lanier, Berkeley, and Curson. Daeng, Howard, and Misty were conferenced in via Orlando's phone, while the Mole was listening in on Nate's.

The medical staff had not been happy to see everyone piling into the room, but Quinn had squelched the protest after a quick, pointed conversation with Dr. Montero. Unless one of Orlando's medical alarms went off, no one would enter.

Quinn laid out the details of his plan, then said, "Now is the time for you to tell me if you are unable or unwilling to participate."

His gaze lingered on the three men who'd been held captive with Nate and Peter. While they had started to recover from their wounds, none of them was at full strength yet. But not one opened his mouth. Instead, they all looked determined and ready.

Quinn glanced at his sister. There was a hint of uncertainty in her eyes. "You okay?" he asked.

After a second, she nodded. "Yeah."

"If you have a problem with any of this, speak up."

"No, it's just you've all lived in this world for a long time. I'm still getting used to it. To most people, something like this would be handled by, I don't know, I guess the FBI."

"And in that world, an FBI investigation would be long and complicated, and probably turn into a media fiasco that would affect everything for months or perhaps even years. Chances are, some good people would be taken down because of it. You understand that, right?"

She nodded.

"Personally," he said, "I don't give a damn whether there's an investigation and scandal or not. What I do give a damn about is them." He gestured at Lanier, Berkeley, and Curson. "And about Nate, and Orlando, and Peter. And Peter's wife. In our business, we don't wait years for justice that may or may not come. We deal with it ourselves." He paused. "I understand if you have a problem with this. If I were you, I'd probably have a problem, too. So if you'd rather not help out, that's okay."

Liz looked at him with eyes that matched his own intensity, and her hand slipped into Nate's. "I never said that. You know I'll do anything you need me to do."

He wasn't sure how to feel about her support. He had never wanted to expose her to his life of secrets and death, but ever since they had reconnected, it seemed that was all he'd done. He was saved from saying anything else by the vibration of his phone.

"You can remove the provisional," Helen told him. "You have our support."

"How high does that support go?"

"High enough."

A beat. "I guess it's time to get things rolling."

CHAPTER THIRTY THREE

WASHINGTON, DC

GRIFFIN WAS BEGINNING to lose his patience.

The first thing he did when he'd arrived back at his office was to assign one of his local computer-geek contacts the task of figuring out the phone number Steve Howard had used to call him, so they could then establish the phone's exact location. But after two hours, the geek was no closer to knowing the number than when he'd started. Howard was apparently using some pretty advanced security software.

The Mole was proving useless, too. The only contact Griffin had from him was a brief e-mail saying he was making progress on the woman but basically had nothing solid yet.

And if those two things weren't enough to cause him to lose his cool, Dima wasn't returning his calls. Dima had told Griffin he was on duty that night. Even if he was monitoring several active O & O operations, he still should've had time to talk to Griffin.

Griffin checked the clock—8:37 p.m. Morten's flight was due to land in an hour and a half. He would expect Griffin to be waiting in the back of the car when he was picked up, which meant Griffin would have to leave in forty-five minutes. He would much rather wait at the office for his boss, but he knew that wasn't acceptable.

The cell phone on his desk began to ring—the one that

had been waiting for him in his car. It was now hooked up to his computer, so that call data would be instantly sent to the geek.

He snatched it up.

"Mr. Howard," he said.

"Mr. Griffin," said the same caller from before.

"Are you calling because you're ready to meet now?"

"I'm calling to see if you've had time to think about what I shared with you."

Griffin picked up some additional noise on the line that hadn't been there the last time the man called. He couldn't be sure, but it sounded like the man was in a car or some other type of vehicle.

"Why would I do that?" Griffin said. "I have no idea what any of that meant."

"You're not a very good liar."

"Perhaps there are misunderstandings all around, which I think is a good reason for us to get together and talk. Don't you?"

"If you're unwilling to admit the truth now, then why would talking in person be any different?"

"Mr. Howard—Steve—you're being unreasonable. It's a simple sit-down. I'll even let you choose the place."

"When I call back, rethink your earlier answer."

The man hung up.

Griffin immediately grabbed his desk phone and called the geek.

"Were you able to trace it?" he said.

"No," the guy said. "The call was bounced all over the place."

Fuck!

"But," the geek said, "I may have broken through the firewall. I've got the first two digits of the phone number, and should be able to get the rest. Just need a little time."

"Then do it," Griffin said, and disconnected.

He told himself to relax. Everything was going to be fine. The kid would get the number, Griffin would find Howard and his friends, and that would be that.

The past would stay where it was supposed to.

THE SECOND QUINN hung up, he glanced over at the laptop Nate was holding. Looking back at him from a video chat window was Orlando. He could see his sister, too, hovering at the edge of the picture.

"So?" he said above the drone of the jet flying him and the other men north to Virginia.

"Give me a second," Orlando said.

He hated how weak her voice still sounded, but she did seem to have more energy than before, and as hesitant as he was to admit it, she did look better.

She typed something on her computer, then smiled. "I made four numbers available. They've gotten two so far." She looked into the camera. "*I* would have gotten all four by now, by the way, but they'll tease them out soon enough."

"And you're sure they won't get the rest yet?"

Her smile turned flat. "I'll pretend you didn't ask me that."

"I was just checking," he said.

He saw her reach toward the camera a split second before the video call cut out.

GRIFFIN'S CELL PHONE rang as he was climbing into the back of Morten's car for the drive out to the airport.

"Finally," he said under his breath when he saw it was Dima. He looked to make sure the divider separating him and the driver was all the way up before answering. "Where the hell have you been?"

"I…I'm sorry," Dima said, sounding justifiably nervous. "There have been several meetings. I couldn't get out of them."

"Meetings? You missed my call for *meetings*?"

"Director Stone was relieved of duty today, but we only found out a few hours ago. Director Cho's been holding video conferences with everyone, going over, um, status of jobs, uh, what our responsibilities are. I, I think there's going to be a shake-up."

Stone was gone? That wasn't good. The guy was a jackass who didn't know what he was doing, but that's what made him useful to Griffin and Morten. He was an easy way into the intelligence community, kind of like a back door a coder might put into a piece of software. They could get things through him without anyone knowing what they were really doing—including Stone. The intelligence they'd been able to acquire had been incredibly useful to their work. But that was more a long-term problem that could be figured out later. Right now, Griffin needed to stay on point.

"If something like that ever happens again, I expect you to contact me either through e-mail or text, at the very least. It's for your own benefit. I wouldn't want to think that you were purposely ignoring me, and have to release the information I've been holding on to for you."

"I wasn't ignoring you. I swear."

That's what Griffin liked to hear. Desperation. "I understand that, Michael. Just wanted to make sure we were clear."

"We're clear."

"Good. Then we'll put that behind us. Now, can I assume you've made progress identifying what vehicle our friends left the cabin in?"

"Yes," Dima said quickly. "Yes, I have."

"Well, this is good news. Tell me."

"You were right. The owner of the cabin has a car he keeps there. A Jeep Wrangler. It's ten years old. Dark blue with a black hardtop. Did you see it there?"

"No. Is there a chance the owner had taken it somewhere else?"

"I checked myself, claimed to be with his insurance company. The…the owner said it was still at the cabin."

"Excellent work. You know what I'm going to ask you to do next, don't you?"

"See if I can find out where it went?"

"Very good."

IMMIGRATIONS AND CUSTOMS was always Morten's least

favorite part of a trip. Thankfully, his plane arrived at Dulles right before three other international flights landed, putting him and his fellow passengers at the head of the line.

Passport stamped and bag collected, he headed outside to where his car was waiting for him at the curb. While the driver put his luggage in the trunk, Morten climbed into the back.

"Good evening, sir," Griffin said. "I hope you had a good flight."

"It was fine, thank you."

"I'm happy to hear that."

The trunk slammed shut, the driver slipped into his seat, and within seconds, they were driving away.

"So, are we buttoned up yet?"

"Not quite," Griffin said. "But I anticipate it won't be long now."

Morten scowled. This was not the news he wanted to hear. "Explain."

Griffin told him what had happened that day, ending with the revelation that apparently this Steve Howard character knew about Miranda Keyes, and their connection to Peter's death.

Morten's mood darkened. That son of a bitch Peter. Why couldn't he have left his wife buried?

"Tell me how you're planning on solving this…problem," he said, teeth clenched.

"By locating Howard, which is in progress as we speak. Once that occurs, I'll pay him a visit, find out who else knows and where they are, then eliminate all the problems."

Griffin's confidence didn't make Morten feel much better. This problem should have never reached this point. "How long until this is finished?"

"A day, two at most."

Morten settled back in his seat and said nothing for the rest of the trip.

THE CHARTER JET carrying Quinn, Nate, Lanier, Berkeley, and Curson landed at 10:18 p.m. Waiting for them at the private hangar were three black Suburbans. Two of the vehicles were already full. The third had only a driver and passenger, the latter standing near the front of the SUV, his hand clasped behind him.

As Quinn and the others approached, the man stepped forward, meeting them halfway, and held out his hand to Quinn.

"Witten," Quinn said, shaking.

"Quinn," Witten said. "Sorry I never got back to you."

"You kept your men from shooting us, so I'm willing to forgive and forget."

"Mighty big of you."

Quinn turned to the others. "Everyone, this is Clyde Witten. I'll let you introduce yourselves." He looked past Witten to the vehicles. "And I suppose this is the famous O & O?"

"Out for a final hurrah," Witten said.

"Final?"

"We've been told to expect reassignment."

"Sorry to hear that."

"It happens."

Quinn glanced at the trucks again. "Any of your people know I'm the one who shot your colleague the other day?"

"Just me."

"And I trust you won't shoot me in the back?"

"Not planning on it." He stepped to the side and motioned to the vehicles. "Shall we?"

CHAPTER
THIRTY FOUR

GRIFFIN HAD JUST returned to his office when UNKNOWN appeared on the display of the found cell phone for the third time. He rushed over to his desk and plugged it into his computer.

"Hello?" he said.

"How do I know you won't have me killed if we agree to meet?"

Griffin smiled. The mere fact that Howard was even contemplating a meeting meant Griffin had him. He only needed to reel Howard in. "As I told you before, you can choose the location."

In the silence that followed, Griffin sensed the other man thinking over his options.

"Are you back in DC now? Or are you still in Trevor Hollow?" Howard asked.

"DC. Where are you?"

The man laughed. "Not DC." A pause. "But I'll be there tomorrow. Perhaps something can be arranged."

"Tell me the time and place."

"I'll call you in the morning."

As soon as the call disconnected, Griffin phoned the geek.

"I think I might have cracked it," the geek said.

"You got the rest?" Griffin asked. To this point, the kid had only been able to identify four numbers, leaving six to go.

"Give me, like, five minutes."

It ended up taking the geek seven to call back.

"So? Did you get it?" Griffin asked.

"Hell, yeah, I did. Told you no one could hide anything from me."

After writing down the number the kid rattled off, Griffin hung up. On his phone was the customized application allowing him to pinpoint cell-phone location. He input the number, and was rewarded thirty seconds later with a glowing blue dot in the middle of a map.

A low chuckle escaped. *You're a liar, Howard.*

Unlike what the man had told him, it appeared Howard *was* in DC. Not only that, he was only a few miles from where Griffin was.

For two minutes, he stared at his phone, waiting for the blue dot to move, but it remained anchored in place.

Excellent.

Griffin had made a career of not only recognizing opportunities, but acting on them. Leaving the tracking app running on his cell, he picked up his desk phone and called Dima.

"I need your assistance."

"What do you want me to do?" Dima asked.

"I want you to dip into that wonderful armory you have there at O & O, then meet me." He gave Dima an address two blocks away from where Howard was.

"Are you kidding me? I can't leave here. I'm on duty."

"I'm sure you can arrange it."

"I can't come—" Dima paused. "Hold a second. I have a team calling in." It was nearly a minute before Dima came back. "Mr. Griffin, I am not a field agent."

"You were once."

"Yes, but that was years ago."

"I just need your presence. I don't need you to kill anyone," Griffin said. While the second part was true, the first was only partially so. Yes, he needed Dima's presence, but that was because he'd decided Dima's usefulness had come to an end, and it was time to eliminate the weak link. If he could get Dima to help him in the process, all the better.

"Okay, okay," Dima said, defeated. "I'll get someone to cover the rest of my shift. But it'll take at least thirty minutes for me to get there."

"Make it twenty. Oh, and Michael?"

"Yes?"

"There's one other thing I'd like you to bring."

"S2 TO S1," one of Witten's men said over the radio.

"Go for S1," Quinn replied. Unlike the others, he was the only one not wearing a radio in his ear, and had to rely on the Suburban's dash-mounted unit.

"Griffin is on the move," the spotter reported.

"Copy that."

THE BLUE DOT on the tracker led Griffin to a twenty-four-hour diner called Mama Jo's. Arriving ten minutes before his scheduled rendezvous with Dima, he did a slow drive-by so he could peer in the windows, but while he could make out several people sitting at tables and a handful of customers at the counter, the layout of the restaurant made it impossible for him to see all the diners.

He checked his phone again. The blue dot had not moved, so either Howard had left his cell at Mama Jo's, or he was inside.

Griffin picked up his speed, intending to turn down the next block and head over to the meeting point, but he saw something that caused him to bring his car to a quick stop. Parked at one of the metered spots, a full half block beyond the restaurant, was a Jeep Wrangler, dark blue with a black hardtop. He checked the license number against the one Dima had given him. It was a match.

Howard was definitely here.

Griffin hurried over to the meeting point and was pleased to find Dima waiting for him. A honk of the horn prodded the O & O man out of his vehicle and into Griffin's.

"Did you bring what I asked?" Griffin said.

Dima removed an inch-wide, rectangular box from his pocket, and tried to hand it to Griffin.

Griffin kept his hands on the wheel. "Prep it, please."

"Oh, uh, okay."

Dima fumbled with the box before finally getting the top off. Inside was an empty syringe and a small glass bottle.

"How long are you going to want the subject knocked out for?" Dima asked.

"Not long. Twenty minutes should do it."

Dima consulted the chart on the inside of the box cover before filling the syringe from the liquid in the bottle. "They only give a range. It, um, could be as long as forty minutes."

"That's fine," Griffin said.

Dima capped the needle and, his hand slightly shaking, gave it to Griffin.

"Relax," Griffin said. "This is going to go nice and smooth."

"What are we going to do?"

"Have a little chat with someone."

"With who?"

Griffin sneered, and shifted the car into Drive. "One of the people your men were supposed to catch two days ago."

"S3 TO S1."

"Go for S1," Nate said. With Quinn now in position, Nate had assumed command.

"Rendezvous with Dima complete." The way the spotter pronounced Dima's name left no doubt how the O & O team felt about a leaker in their ranks.

"Copy that, S3."

GRIFFIN SPED BACK to the block Mama Jo's was on, and parked at the curb two spots in front of the Jeep. Once they exited the sedan, Griffin took a look around. It was a mixed-use street, businesses with some apartments above. At this hour, though, the only place open was the diner, and the lights in the majority of the apartments were off.

He checked the tracker. The blue dot was still centered over the restaurant.

"Do you remember what the driver of the BMW in the

pictures you sent me looked like?" he asked Dima.

"Well enough, I guess."

"I want you to go down to that restaurant and see if you can spot him inside from the window. Don't stay long, though. If he's moving, I need you back here."

"Sure," Dima said. He was clearly still nervous.

"Are we going to have a problem, Michael?"

"What? No. Of course not."

"Then get it together."

"I'm together. Don't worry."

As Dima headed toward Mama Jo's, Griffin stepped back into a recessed entrance to a closed hair salon about thirty feet past the Jeep on the restaurant side. He could stand within its shadows and watch Mama Jo's, then move farther back where he wouldn't be seen by anyone walking by.

Keeping an eye on Dima, he pulled out his phone and called the head of Darvot's own five-man special ops team. With O & O in chaos, he'd had no choice but to bring them in.

"Status," he asked.

"Everything's ready," Reynolds said. "Team's in place."

"Good. I'll let you know when we're on our way."

As soon as he hung up, he checked the tracking app again. The blue dot was still in the restaurant, but it was moving through the building toward the exit. He shot a quick glance at Dima. Though Howard should be visible to him, the man from O & O seemed to still be searching the interior.

When the blue dot reached the front entrance, Griffin slipped his phone into his pocket and watched the door. A couple seconds later, it opened, and a man stepped out. A few feet away, Dima glanced over at him, but almost immediately returned his attention to the interior of Mama Jo's. Griffin was starting to think Dima was a complete moron when their target stepped into the halo of the nearby streetlight.

The man wasn't Howard.

Griffin snatched his phone back out and checked the screen. The dot was definitely traveling with the man. Had Howard dumped his phone on this guy? Perhaps planted it on him? Or had it not been Howard calling him at all?

He slipped into the back corner of the entrance. What should he do? He couldn't just grab innocent people off the street. That could get very messy. He needed to be sure. He uncapped the syringe, and positioned it in his hand in a way that it wouldn't be seen. As soon as the man walked by, he stepped out.

"Brian?" he said. "What are you doing here?"

The man stopped and looked back. "Sorry. Think you have the wrong guy."

"Sorry about that."

But Griffin knew he didn't have the wrong guy. He'd recognized the voice immediately as belonging to caller UNKNOWN.

As the man turned away, Griffin stepped forward and jabbed the needle into the base of the guy's neck.

The drug worked quickly. The man had barely gotten a surprised, "What…" out of his mouth before he stumbled against a parked car. Griffin grabbed him around the waist to keep him from dropping all the way to the ground, and drunk-walked him to Griffin's sedan. With his free hand, he opened the back door and manhandled the guy inside.

He looked around and made sure there was no one else on the street before putting his fingers to his lips and whistling. Dima jerked around in surprise.

"Get over here!" Griffin yelled.

THE HOUSE WAS in a wooded suburb northeast of the city in Maryland, on a cul-de-sac with three other homes, all owned by Darvot Consulting.

Reynolds opened the garage door as Griffin drove up, and immediately closed it behind him. The other four members of his team were spread out around the outside of the house in case of trouble.

Griffin, Dima, and Reynolds lugged the prisoner into a special room in the basement designed for circumstances like this. There was a single piece of furniture in the room, a chair in the center. Though it couldn't move, it wasn't bolted in place. It was cemented into the floor.

The unadorned walls and the only door were soundproof. There were no windows. The only other thing of note was the drain in the floor directly under the chair.

Using pre-sized straps that hung on the wall outside the room, they secured the man to the chair and stepped back out. Reynolds was dismissed to join his men, while Griffin and Dima sat in front of the table that was outside the room to wait for the prisoner to wake up.

Nearly fifteen minutes passed in silence before Dima asked, “What are you going to do to him?”

“I told you before. I’m going to talk to him.”

Dima looked like he wanted to ask, “And then what?” but he kept his mouth shut.

Griffin flipped on the computer sitting on the table. From it, he could control the five cameras inside. If he wanted, he could record everything, or, as he was doing now, simply look in.

Mr. Unknown was still unconscious, his chin hanging against his chest.

“Keep an eye on him,” he said. “If he so much as twitches, come get me.”

THE THREE SUBURBANS sat empty two blocks away from the target house, the vehicles’ former occupants having moved silently down streets and through backyards until they were in position.

Nate, Daeng, and Witten were crouched near the open end of the cul-de-sac. In Witten’s hand was a mini tablet computer displaying a detailed map of the area, including property lines and house footprints. As it had been since they’d arrived in the peaceful neighborhood, the glowing white dot they’d followed from Mama Jo’s restaurant was contained within the diagram denoting the house in the middle of the curved end of the road.

“S1, this is S3,” a voice said over the comm.

Nate turned on his mic. “Go for S1.”

“Five guards. Two in back, three in front.”

"Your status?" Nate asked.

"S2 and S3 ready and willing."

"Take them down," Nate said. "Nice and quiet."

CHAPTER THIRTY FIVE

"KEEP AN EYE on him," Griffin said. "If he so much as twitches, come get me."

Dima nodded his understanding, but it was a wasted gesture. Griffin had already turned away.

Dima remained where he was until the door at the top of the stairs closed. Sure now that Griffin was gone, he entered the interrogation room.

"He went upstairs," Dima said. "Not sure how long he'll be gone."

QUINN LIFTED HIS head. He didn't know the name of the man in front of him, only that he'd been O & O's leak. When he'd been told what was going to happen to him unless he agreed to help, he had jumped at the chance, knowing it would give him at least a few years of freedom before he died.

So far Dima had performed exactly as instructed. He had provided Griffin with the syringe loaded only with saline, and had not tipped off the other man that something was up.

"Radio?" Quinn said.

Dima walked over and attached the sticky side of a small microphone under Quinn's collar. In Quinn's ear, he stuck the equally small receiver.

"Nate?" he said.

"I'm here," Nate said.

"There's at least one other person here."

"We count five additional, total."

"As soon as you hear Griffin back in here with me, you are free to take them out. Then I'll give you the word when to begin phase two."

"Copy that."

Quinn looked at the O & O man. "Straps."

GRIFFIN TOOK THE stairs to the ground floor, and locked himself in the den to avoid any chance that Dima might overhear him. He pulled out his phone and called Morten.

"I have him," he told his boss.

"That's a step in the right direction. What has he told you?"

"Nothing yet. We had to drug him, but he should wake up soon."

"We must wrap this up. We're wasting far too much time dealing with ancient history. We have paying jobs that I need you to focus on, not this crap. Get him to tell you the names of everyone who knows, then you need to root them out and dispose of them tonight."

Griffin knew it would take more than the night, but he understood his boss's sense of frustration. "I'll call you as soon as I finish interrogating him," he said.

"I'll be waiting."

When Griffin exited the den, he found Dima standing at the base of the stairs to the second floor.

"What are you doing up here?" he asked.

"I was looking for you. The…prisoner, I think he's waking up."

Griffin headed down the stairs, Dima following a few steps behind. Instead of heading straight into the interrogation room, Griffin checked camera feed first. The prisoner's head was now up, his eyes half opened.

"Has he talked?" Griffin asked.

"Not when I was down here."

That's about to change, Griffin thought, before he strode into the room. He walked right up to the prisoner, grabbed his chin, and slapped him hard.

"Wake up, asshole," he said.

The man groaned as he winced from the blow.

Griffin jerked the man's head up. "Look at me." The prisoner's eyes remained half closed. "Look at me!"

The man's lid opened only a fraction of an inch more, but his eyes focused on Griffin's face. "What?" he said.

"Who the hell are you?"

A grin spread across the man's face. "I'll tell you one thing. I'm not Steve Howard."

Another slap. "I'm not afraid of hurting you. So if you want to mess around, go ahead. But if you'd rather pass on the pain, tell me who you are."

"I'll make a deal with you."

"Sorry. No deals. Answer my question."

"Can you take your hand off my chin? That's not part of the deal, but it's kind of weird talking with you hanging on to me like this."

Griffin slapped him again, but then let go of the guy's chin.

"Thanks." The prisoner worked his jaw for a moment. "So here's what I was thinking."

"I said, no deals. Here's what I—"

"Just hear me out, okay? What could it hurt?"

Griffin stared at him, not saying a word.

"The deal is this. I don't want to say what I have to say twice. Know what I mean? Yeah, you have your fancy video system." As the prisoner said this, he glanced past Griffin at one of the cameras mounted in the room. "So you could record it and show that, but we both know your boss is going to want to hear it from me."

Griffin remained silent.

"This is the part where you say you don't have a boss," the man said. "And then I say, 'Actually, you do. I mean, unless Kyle Morten fired you.'"

Griffin locked eyes with the man. "You think you're a smart guy, don't you? You think you can trip me up with your little name-dropping?"

The prisoner shrugged. "I was trying to do you a favor."

"I don't need your favor." Griffin leaned in close. "So let me tell you the deal I have for you. Which, by the way, is nonnegotiable. You will talk. You will tell me who you are. You will tell me everything you know. You will tell me who else knows. And you will start right now."

"You mean how you and your boss murdered Miranda Keyes and her colleagues for one of your clients? A bullet to the head of the driver. Very subtle. Or do you mean how you guys handed over a list of names to Javier Romero in an attempt to keep the truth from coming out, thinking he'd take care of your problem for you?"

Griffin took a step back. "Who are you?"

"Remember, I gave you a chance."

"How many others know?"

The prisoner stared past Griffin, stone-faced.

"Answer me! How many?"

No response.

"Your silence won't save anyone. I'll find them like I found you."

The man grinned again as he looked at Griffin. "What makes you think *you* found *me*?"

Stop it! You're letting him get under your skin, Griffin told himself. This was his interrogation, not the prisoner's. He glared derisively at the man, his lips parting as he was about to start in on the questioning again.

"Now," the man whispered.

NATE NODDED AT the O & O man standing by the power box, and a second later all electricity to the building was severed.

"Perimeter team neutralized. Power out," Nate said into the radio.

EVERYTHING WENT BLACK.

As Quinn whipped his arms out of the restraints Dima had loosened for him, and leaned down so he could pull the straps away from his legs, he heard Nate's report. He could hear the door open and shut across the room.

"Dima, dammit, get the lights back on!" Griffin yelled.

No response.

"Dima, where are you?"

While Quinn freed his left leg, he heard the movement of cloth, like someone rubbing their hands across their clothes. The moment the strap dropped from around his right leg, a bluish, rectangular light flicked on. Griffin's cell phone.

Quinn couldn't see the man behind the phone, but he heard Griffin curse as he realized Quinn was free. Immediately, the light moved with the man rushing at Quinn.

Quinn dove to the side, rolling on the floor before popping back up on his feet.

Behind him, he heard Griffin skid to a stop. As Quinn turned, he saw a flash of metal, and knew the man was holding a knife.

When Griffin came at him again, it wasn't in a run but a deliberate stalk.

"You're not getting out of here," Griffin said.

"Who said I wanted to?"

"Who the hell are you?"

"Me? I'm the man who's going to take you and your partner down."

"Oh, really? I don't see that happening."

"Of course you don't."

Quinn feigned to his right, then left, heading around Griffin toward the door. Griffin was only partially fooled, and lunged, his knife leading the way. Quinn saw it coming, twisted out of its path, and lashed out with his own hand, knocking the phone out of Griffin's grip.

The moment the cell hit the floor, the light went out.

Quinn made it all the way to the door, but knew he couldn't get it open before Griffin would get there, so he crouched low against the wall and waited.

An unsettled silence fell over the room.

"It's only a matter of time," Griffin said. "I'm going to find you, and I'm going to cut you up. And then I'm going to find your friends and no one will ever know what happened to any of you."

The man was about eight feet away, straight out from the

door.

"You think you scared me with what you found out?" Griffin said. "You think you're the first problem I've ever had to deal with?" A quiet step closer to the door. "Don't kid yourself. I've dealt with far worse problems than you, and I'm still here. Just like I'm going to still be here after we're through."

Another step. Griffin was five feet away now.

"What I think I'll do is leave you locked in here for a while. If you're ready to talk when I come back, I may be willing to let you live a bit longer."

Griffin took a step toward the door.

"Enjoy the dark. I'll see you in a—"

Quinn grabbed Griffin's ankles and yanked them out from under the man. Griffin fell backward, tumbling to the floor.

Quinn followed right behind, his hands searching for Griffin's wrists, mindful of the knife the man still held.

"You son of a bitch!" Griffin yelled, pain in his voice. "Is that how you want to play?"

Quinn found the knife hand and tried to pin it against the floor, but Griffin jerked and twisted and squirmed, making it impossible to hold down. The best Quinn could do was keep the knife from plunging into him.

Griffin smacked Quinn in the shoulder with his other hand, and then popped him in the jaw. Quinn's grip on the man's wrist slipped. Griffin immediately took advantage, and shoved Quinn off to the side.

Quinn heard the man jump to his feet and run for the door. Pushing himself up, he followed right behind. Griffin opened the door and exited the room, and tried to pull the door closed again. But Quinn yanked it out of Griffin's grasp before the other man could shut it all the way.

There were two windows high on the walls of the area beyond the interrogation room, so while the lights were still off, it wasn't pitch-black, and he could see Griffin was already at the base of the stairs.

"You're not going to want to go up there," Quinn said.

Griffin sneered, and started up the steps.

“Let him know you’re there,” Quinn whispered loudly enough for Nate to pick up.

Over the radio, he heard Nate say, “Light ’em up!”

Griffin was halfway to the top when the upper door opened and three handheld HMI spotlights blazed down on him, stopping him in his tracks.

“Drop the knife and stay where you are,” Witten ordered from behind the lights.

Griffin, an arm held in front of his eyes to keep him from being blinded, swiveled his head back and forth, looking for a way out.

“Drop the knife,” Witten repeated.

Some people never knew when to give up. Griffin was one such person. As was Quinn.

In a sudden burst of motion, Griffin leaped down the stairs, bypassing the treads, and landed bent-kneed on the basement floor. As his gaze fell on Quinn, he rushed forward, fury radiating from every pore.

Quinn had his own fury stored up. After the first swipe of the knife passed harmlessly in front of him, he grabbed Griffin’s wrist and slammed it against the metal doorjamb of the interrogation room, following it up with a right hook into Griffin’s ribs.

When the knife finally fell to the floor, Quinn twisted Griffin’s arm back and rammed it into the jamb again. There was a satisfying double crack as both bones in Griffin’s forearm broke.

The man cried out in pain and tried to pull away. Quinn pretended to struggle with him for a moment longer before letting go.

Griffin’s momentum knocked him back against the wall. He took a step, ready to run, but froze as his gaze fell on the squad of men now at the bottom of the stairs, each with an M16 rifle aimed at his chest.

Quinn walked over, careful not to get in the line of fire. He smiled. “So, Mr. Griffin. As you can see, when everyone works together, dealing with people like you is just like swatting flies. If you're ready to talk, we might be willing to let you live a bit longer."

CHAPTER
THIRTY SIX

IT WAS NEARLY one a.m. by the time Quinn and the others finished taping Griffin's interview. There would undoubtedly be more interrogations in the future. Details were still missing—some names, dates, where the bodies could be found. But what Griffin gave them painted a picture even darker than they had presumed.

A career not going as expected? A competitor more problematic than desired? A negotiation not going the intended way? That's where Darvot Consulting came in. Using resources such as the flawed O & O, Morten and Griffin had been able to obtain information clients could use to cripple their adversaries. And where information alone wouldn't work, Darvot provided a heavier hand. Say there was an intelligent, ambitious diplomat whose star shone a bit brighter than yours, and would always be in your way to the career *you* wanted. No scandals to bring that person down? No problem. How about a nice, tidy car crash in a foreign country? And here you were now, ten years down the road, the assistant secretary of state, a position everyone knows you would have never attained if Miranda Keyes had lived. A horrible loss? A tragedy? Not to you. Though you could never say it out loud, you had always thought of it as a *happy* accident.

When everything was ready for the next phase, Quinn looked at the laptop from which Helen Cho had been monitoring the situation. "We're all set," he said.

"You're cleared to make the call," she told him.

Quinn turned to Dima. Except for his attempted escape after the lights went out, Dima had done well. "No screwups," Quinn said.

"I won't," Dima said.

They had rehearsed what he was supposed to do half a dozen times.

Quinn nodded at Witten, who then escorted Dima into the den, so the others could listen to the call on the laptop in the living room without their presence being picked up over the line.

For a few seconds, they all stood there waiting—Quinn, Nate, Daeng, Misty, Howard, Lanier, Berkeley, Curson, Witten's team, and, remotely, Helen. When the sound of the ringing phone suddenly blared from the speaker, Misty jumped. Quinn turned the volume down a few clicks, and looked around to make sure everyone could still hear. He received nods all around so he moved to the side.

There were three rings before the line was finally answered.

"Yes?"

"MR. MORTEN? THIS is Central at O & O."

Morten looked at the clock on his desk. "Do you realize what time it is?"

"Yes, sir, I apologize, but Mr. Griffin asked that I call you."

Morten paused. "Why would he do that?"

"I'm told by our team on the scene with him that he's interrogating a suspect at the moment."

"He's using one of your teams?" Morten asked.

"Yes, sir. We received a call from him a few hours ago requesting emergency backup. Thankfully, we had a team available and were able to dispatch it right away."

That actually made some sense, Morten had to admit. If Griffin found himself in need of manpower right away, O & O would have been the quick solution, despite the organization's recent failures.

"So why are you calling?"

"Mr. Griffin thought that you might want to talk to the suspect. He said to tell you that…" Central paused. "I want to make sure I get this right. He said, 'Tell Mr. Morten suspect knows all, and insists on talking to him before giving up network.'"

Holy God. The mention of network meant there were more than just a couple other people who knew. He and Griffin needed those names, but Morten was reluctant to involve himself at this level. He dealt with the client end of things. Griffin handled the dirty work. Of course, this wouldn't be the first time Morten would have to cross the line.

"Mr. Griffin can't handle this himself?" he asked.

"I don't have the answer to that, sir. I only got the impression this was time sensitive."

Indeed it was. Griffin undoubtedly could get the names on his own, but, from the sounds of it, it would take too long. If Morten making an appearance sped up the process, then so be it.

"Where is he?"

MORTEN LOOKED OUT the window as his driver turned the car onto the cul-de-sac. Though this was not his first time visiting one of the houses he owned there, it had been a while. They were used more for Griffin's work.

As expected, the street was quiet, all the houses dark. The one Griffin was using was straight back in the middle. No car was in the driveway, but Morten assumed Griffin and the O & O team had parked in the attached two-car garage to avoid being seen when they transferred the prisoner into the house.

Morten instructed his driver to pull into the driveway.

"I shouldn't be long," he told the driver, hoping he was right. He had several phone conferences planned for not long after sunrise, so whatever the prisoner had to say, he'd better say it quickly.

Morten exited the car and walked over to the darkened

porch. As he neared, the door opened.

"Mr. Morten." The man who greeted him was in the dark-suit uniform preferred by O & O.

"Where is he?" Morten said.

"Downstairs, sir. I'll show you the way."

Two other O & O men were in the basement, one sitting in front of a computer station set up next to a closed door, the other standing in front of the door itself. The monitor showed a box clearly intended to display a video feed, but at the moment it was black. Below it was a second rectangular box, housing an undulating series of vertical bars.

The man at the computer stood up the moment he saw Morten. "Good morning, sir."

"What's going on? Where's Mr. Griffin?"

"He's in the interrogation room, sir." The man nodded toward the closed door, and then turned to the computer. "We're recording the session. There's a problem with the video at the moment, but the audio is working."

"You've been listening?" Morten asked, concerned.

"No, sir. Our instructions were to monitor the signal only. See?" He pointed at the rising and falling bars. "It's strong and clear. If *you'd* like to listen, I can plug in the headphones."

"Please."

The man plugged a set of headphones into the computer, and handed it to Morten. "You control the volume there on the side," he said.

Morten donned the headphones. He could hear a voice, but it was too low to understand, so he turned up the dial.

"…took the shot through the window and hit him in the head," a male voice said. The audio wasn't as clear as Morten would have liked. It was full of digital distortion that he assumed was connected to the visual problem with the camera. "The car went off the side and tumbled all the way down. They were all dead. Morten showed up right after the police got there and identified the bodies."

Morten tensed. The prisoner was clearly talking about the incident in Turkey. He knew precisely how it had occurred.

This was what Morten had feared. Peter had obviously talked before he was killed, and whomever he told had picked up the investigation.

Morten started to pull off the headphones, wanting to go inside right away and find out how many more people know, but the voice stopped him.

There was a loud digital hit, then, "…who made sure the original report disappeared. Only the doctor who performed the autopsy and the lead investigator knew. The doctor had to go, but the police officer was more open to an arrangement."

How the hell could the man know that much detail? Griffin had handled those matters personally. As far as Morten was aware, his enforcer was the only other person who knew.

He ripped off the phones and marched over to the door.

"Out of my way," he barked at the man standing in front of it, but the command was unnecessary. The agent was already stepping aside.

Morten yanked the door open and stormed inside. In his anger, all he could see was the man strapped to the chair in the middle of the floor. It didn't even register with him that the rest of the room was empty.

"Enough! Tell us who else…" The words died in his mouth as he neared the man.

The prisoner hadn't been sitting up, talking. His head was lolled forward. But it was more than that. He looked…familiar.

Morten froze two steps away.

"Oh, shit," he mumbled.

This wasn't the prisoner. It was Griffin.

MORTEN WHIPPED AROUND as if about to run from the room.

"You must be Kyle," Quinn said.

He was standing just inside the doorway, Nate and Daeng on one side of him, Misty and Howard on the other. Behind him were Lanier, Berkeley, and Curson, and behind them, right outside the room, were Witten and his men.

Morten jerked his head left and right, his gaze in constant motion.

"Perhaps I should make some introductions," Quinn said. "These three men behind me and my colleague here"—he nodded toward Nate—"were on the list with Peter. You know which one I'm talking about, of course."

Morten blinked several times as his right hand began to shake.

"The lady is Misty Blake," Quinn went on. "She's Peter's former assistant. So not only did you kill her boss, and her boss's wife, you almost had our new O & O friends in the back there kill her the other day. As you can see, we've forgiven them, but I'm afraid I can't extend that same amnesty to you."

Both of Morten's hands were shaking now. He moved unsteadily backward, not stopping until he bumped into Griffin.

"I'm Quinn, by the way. I was supposed to be on Duran Island, too, but Romero screwed up. Good for me, not so good for my friend here." He patted Nate on the shoulder, careful to avoid the whip welts. "What you did to me, though, was nearly take away the woman I love." He paused. "You screwed with the wrong people this time."

Morten's lips parted. "I…I want my lawyer." Looking past Quinn toward Witten and in a louder voice, he repeated, "I want my lawyer!"

No one moved.

"I want my lawyer!"

Quinn looked back at Witten and nodded. Witten worked his way through the others until he was standing next to Misty. In his hands was the laptop computer. On the screen, a video link to Helen Cho.

"Mr. Morten," she said. "Do you know who I am?"

A hesitation, then a nod.

"Then you know I speak for the US government. Here's what's going to happen. You are going to stay right there until you have given a full and complete accounting of everything you've done. After which, you will be locked away for the rest of your life. Don't even think that you'll get out someday. That will not happen. If, on the other hand, you do not make a full and complete accounting, you will be put to death in a manner decided upon by the people gathered in this room with you. I can't imagine whatever they come up with will be pleasant, but the choice is yours to make. You have ten seconds."

"No. You can't do that," Morten protested. "I'll tell you everything, but not before we negotiate terms."

"Negotiate terms?" Helen sneered. "Here are the terms. Your friend Mr. Griffin, though he's currently taking an induced nap, has already agreed to share everything he knows and, in fact, has already started to do so. You were listening to part of his confession a few minutes ago."

Morten's eyes widened.

"See, the thing is," Helen went on, "we only need one of you. I'm letting you make the decision who it's going to be. You have four seconds."

"No! I have rights! I'm an American citizen! I want my lawyer!"

"Your time is up, Mr. Morten," Helen said. "I leave you to these fine people here."

As Witten closed the computer, Morten said, "No! You can't do that! You can't!"

No one said anything.

"I'll talk! I'll tell you everything! Whatever you want."

"I'm sorry," Misty said, "but you're too late."

Quinn stepped forward, raised the gun he'd been holding at his side, and put a bullet through the center of Morten's head.

Once it was clear no second shot was needed, they exited the room one by one. Quinn and Misty were the last. As he turned to leave, he put his arm around her shoulder. She leaned into him, exhausted.

"I think I could sleep for a week," she said as he escorted her out.

"You should," he told her.

"Thank you," she whispered. "For Peter. For everything."

ONE MORE PIECE of business needed to be taken care of, but there was no need for everyone to come along. The party consisted of only Quinn, Witten, and two of Witten's agents.

The two agents remained in the car while Quinn and Witten walked up to the front door of the townhouse. Despite the hour, their knock was answered immediately, an earlier phone call from Helen having alerted the resident that a car was coming to take her to a meeting, one where the president might be in attendance.

The woman, dressed in a dark gray business suit, and looking as fresh and awake as if it were ten in the morning, stepped outside and closed her door behind her.

"Good morning, gentlemen," she said.

"Assistant Secretary," Witten said.

Quinn merely nodded.

They escorted the woman—Assistant Secretary of State Diane Sutton—to the waiting Suburban. While Witten took his seat up front, Quinn climbed in next to Sutton.

The assistant secretary of state remained quiet as they drove through town, undoubtedly thinking there was nothing worth talking about with the security detail sent for her. It wasn't until she realized they were heading into Virginia that she seemed to register something was wrong. She looked at Witten.

"Is the president not at the White House?" she asked.

"As far as I know, he is," Witten said.

"Then is he going to meet us somewhere?"

"Not that I'm aware of."

She looked from him to Quinn to the fourth man sitting in the row behind her. "I was led to believe I was meeting with him."

Quinn responded this time. "I believe, ma'am, you were told no such thing. While it might have been unclear, no one actually said who you would be meeting with."

"How would you know? You weren't the one I talked

to."

"No, ma'am, but I was listening in on the conversation."

"You were *what*?" she said.

Quinn turned in his seat to face her. "I don't appreciate the tone, ma'am."

"Excuse me? I am the assistant secretary of state. You are aware of that, aren't you?"

"I'm very aware of who you are. We all are."

Her eyes narrowed. "What the hell is that supposed to mean?"

"Miranda Keyes."

"Stop the car," she ordered.

There was no change in their speed.

"Stop the car! Did you hear me? Stop it!"

"That's not going to happen, ma'am," Quinn said.

"You all have no idea the trouble you're in."

Quinn pulled his phone out of his pocket, and started the recording that was waiting to be played.

Out of the speaker came Griffin's voice. "She hired us."

Quinn: "Who hired you?"

"Diane Sutton."

"The assistant secretary of state?"

"Now, but not then."

"What did she hire you to do?"

"Clear things out of her way."

"What exactly did that mean?"

"Eliminate Miranda Keyes."

"By eliminate—"

"Kill her. She hired us to kill Miranda."

Quinn switched off the recording.

"Lies," Sutton said. "Whoever that is is simply trying to undermine me."

"Except that it isn't a lie. You know it. I know it. The secretary of Homeland Security knows it."

"The secretary?"

"Darvot Consulting is no longer in business. Mr. Morten and Mr. Griffin are now in the custody of the US government."

Her eyes lost focus momentarily as she processed what it all meant. "I want to speak to the secretary…no, to the president. I want to speak to him now."

"I'm sorry, but that's not an option."

"It damn well is if he wants to avoid a scandal!" she retorted. "Can you imagine the kind of circus there's going to be if you put an assistant secretary of state on trial for this?"

"You mean for conspiracy to commit murder?"

"That's exactly what I mean."

Quinn smiled. "I see where the miscommunication is coming in here. You see, Ms. Sutton, there will be no circus because there will be no trial."

"So what? I'm supposed to resign? Is that it? No way in hell I'm going down without a fight."

"No, ma'am. No one's asking for your resignation."

"Then what? Why this power play?"

"I'm sorry to be the one to tell you this, but in about an hour's time, there's going to be a horrible, tragic car accident."

CHAPTER
THIRTY SEVEN

7 DAYS LATER
WASHINGTON, DC

MISTY CHECKED HERSELF in her mirror once more. Everything looked as it should—her hair, her makeup, her conservative black dress. She'd thought about wearing a hat, but that wasn't really her style. Satisfied, she headed out into the living room.

On the table near the door was the urn Helen Cho had sent her the day before. Inside were Peter's ashes.

She had offered to wait until Quinn could come out, but he had said, "I don't know when I'll be free. And I kind of think this is something you should do yourself."

It was actually a relief.

This *was* something she wanted to do on her own.

The drive to the cemetery went surprisingly fast, and before she knew it, she was standing in the lobby of the facility's main building.

"Miss Blake," William Samuels said as he crossed the room. "Would you like me to carry that?"

Misty pulled the urn tight to her chest. "No, I'm fine."

"Very well. This way, then."

He led her back outside to the mausoleum, and down several rows before stopping in front of a small, open crypt.

"Thank you," she said.

He gave her a sedate smile. "I'll be in my office when

you're done." With that, he walked back the way they'd come.

Misty stood in front of the open door, unmoving. After several minutes, she whispered, "I wish I knew what to say. I wish I didn't have to say anything, and you were still here." She could feel the tears starting to build, but she pushed them back. She'd cried enough already. Now was the time to move on. "There's so much I need to thank you for. Everything, really." She raised the urn. "Rest in peace, Peter."

She moved the vessel into the crypt, setting it next to the one that was already there, the one containing Miranda's ashes.

"Rest in peace."

IN FLIGHT OVER TEXAS

QUINN SAT NEXT to Orlando, not once leaving her side since the private jet had taken off from Isla de Cervantes. She'd been drifting in and out of sleep. Sometimes she'd wake long enough to talk for a few minutes, sometimes only long enough to give him a smile. Through it all, she kept her fingers entwined in his, gripping as if she would never let go again.

"How long now?" she asked, her eyes barely open.

"Still a few hours."

"Ugh. It's like the longest flight ever."

"Not even close," he said. "Don't worry. We'll be home soon."

She squeezed his hand and smiled. "Home. That sounds good."

"It does, doesn't it?"

For a second he thought she was going to say something else, but her eyelids slipped shut again as the pain medicine she was on pulled her back under.

A few quiet minutes passed before his phone rang. Not wanting to wake Orlando, he waited until it stopped before he pulled out his cell. He could see the call had come from Helen Cho. As with the last five times she'd called, she'd left no message. There was no need, of course. He knew what she wanted, because the first time she'd called, four days earlier, she *had* left a message. It was still sitting in his inbox. He played it again.

"Quinn, Helen Cho. I know you're kind of tied up at the moment, but when you get back to San Francisco, I'd like you to stop in and see me." She paused. "I'm starting up a new agency. Something small and specialized, and I'm looking for someone to set it up and run things. After seeing how you handled the Morten situation, I think you'd be the perfect candidate. Anyway, whether you're interested or not, come see me."

He laughed to himself as he hung up.

"What?" Orlando asked, riding a short wave into consciousness.

"Nothing."

"You sure?"

His hesitation lasted but a split second. "Absolutely."

7933563R00163

Printed in Great Britain
by Amazon.co.uk, Ltd.,
Marston Gate.